THE WRONG ENEMY

THE WRONG ENEMY

Jane Lebak

Philangelus Press
Boston, MA USA

Other Philangelus Press titles:

Seven Archangels: Annihilation
Seven Archangels: An Arrow In Flight (Fall, 2014)
Seven Archangels: Sacred Cups (Spring, 2015)

Other Jane Lebak titles:

The Boys Upstairs

ISBN: 978-1-942133-01-8
eBook ISBN: 978-1-77127-173-8
Library of Congress Control Number: 2014951256

Cover Art © 2012 by Charlotte Volnek
Edited by Lea Schizas of MuseItUp Publishing

For Jameson Brewer:

Thank you for answering a little girl's fan mail.
May perpetual light shine upon you.

One

Raguel waited at the back of the Judgment Hall to hear the verdict passed on the boy's soul: Heaven. He nodded as he registered the word, but without rejoicing as he should have. Based on the expressions of the other witnesses, neither was anyone else. Half the angels in the room watched the boy as he leaped in delight and hugged the angel at his side, but the larger number studied the angel who stood at the back of the hall, Tabris.

Tabris had not reacted to the echoing verdict. Staring only at the chains binding his wrists and securing him to the floor, he stood like a horse at a hitching post. Only once did Raguel see him look up, struggling to get a glimpse of the boy before the other angels crowded into his line of sight, but then they'd taken him away, and Tabris said not a word.

Two Archangel guards flanked Tabris, one wearing a thousand-mile stare and the other struggling against grief. Everything about their posture read *duty* to Raguel, broadcast without words in their alert stance, the readiness of their weapons, their raised chins. Between them, Tabris seemed smaller, slumped, his two-toned wings touching the floor. With a shudder, Raguel realized at least one of the guards had probably been his friend.

They had no idea how to act. And rightly so. Angels didn't usually take one of their own into custody.

In the wake of the boy's removal, motion animated the hall. Some celestials left, but many more took seats on the benches in front of and to the right of the judgment throne. The intensity of the Father's light heightened to a brilliance that made Raguel gasp, but Tabris brought up his wings as a shield.

God, have mercy. He looked again at Tabris, and the words cycled in his mind, a prayer tinged with dread when he considered what would happen next.

One of the Archangels glanced at the other, and Raguel felt them exchange an unspoken question.

He flashed to the trio, reappearing there the same instant he vanished from the previous spot. He had the highest rank of any present—one of the Seven Elite as well as the officer in charge of all guardian angels—and at his appearance, both Archangels saluted. Tabris recoiled and wouldn't meet his eyes.

With a gesture, Raguel made the chains disappear. The Archangel with the thousand-mile-stare snapped to and looked at Raguel with relief, but the other guard protested.

Raguel said, "He can't run anywhere. And unless God damns him, he's still one of us. Don't forget that."

Tabris shivered. Even with the chains gone, he didn't move.

Raguel reached out with his emotions to reassure Tabris, a communication process angels use more efficiently than words, but Tabris retreated from his soul's projection.

Uneasy, Raguel advanced to the long table at the front of the room and leaned his muscular form on the edge to await the next phase of the trial. With raised wings, he inspected the broken angel. Then, sighing, Raguel turned toward God's throne.

One of the angels sounded a Shofar, and the room came to attention. The pair of guards escorted Tabris to the fore.

For the last millennia, only humans had stood this kind of trial, the sorting of those who should enter Heaven from those who belonged in Hell. This time, the subject was Tabris, an angel, and until an hour ago, a guardian angel. Until an hour ago, just as sinless as the rest of them.

Without any presentation of evidence or arguments from either side, God presented to all the witnesses what Tabris had done, and what he deserved for the crime.

Raguel could feel the guards recoil, but Tabris remained still. His hands: he kept staring at his hands.

Swallowing against nausea, Raguel stepped toward Tabris. "Do you have a statement in your own defense?"

Tabris didn't look up. "No."

"Then I do." Raguel turned to the throne of the Lord, his face bathed in the radiance that had dispelled chaos in the first moments of creation and acted as his beacon ever since. His heart trilled as he glimpsed infinity, but he focused himself. "I would beg you for mercy." He ignored the tendrils of hope and outrage that swirled from the other angels. "Tabris panicked. I don't think his crime was premeditated. If he'd thought about it at all, I'm sure he would have stopped."

"The boy's dead!" shouted a voice from across the room.

Raguel forced himself to look only at God rather than toward the voice. "Tabris's intentions—"

"I said—" the voice continued, closer, "the boy is dead. Regardless of Tabris's intentions, Sebastian died. Tabris short-circuited God's plan in the worst way possible, a plan that—if you recall—one-third of the angels were thrown into Hell for failing to fulfill. And now you want—"

Raguel said to God, "One more angel in Hell won't resurrect the child."

The accuser took form immediately beside Raguel. "That would be justice."

Raguel still wouldn't turn. "Tabris is sorry. It was a rash action, not a rejection of You."

The accuser said, "The boy is dead. That's all the rejection possible."

At that moment, the light of God took form at the head of the room as Jesus Christ. The angels bowed, but Tabris prostrated himself.

Jesus advanced to the accuser, who looked him dead in the eye.

Jesus said, "Your point is understandable."

Raguel turned for the first time to look at the accuser, who wore an icy glare and had every feather on every wing standing out, typical for a demon.

"*Understandable?*" said the demon. "Everything here is perfectly understandable. Angels have only one written law, am I correct? And that law is shown to every single guardian angel before beginning his assignment, am I still correct? Including Tabris? No one forgot to show it to him because they were too busy polishing their harps and reciting your cute scripted praises?"

Jesus waited him out. Raguel had less patience; his sword had manifested at his side, and his palms itched.

Jesus glanced at Raguel, acknowledgment in his eyes.

The demon cocked his head and folded his arms. "And would I still be correct if I were to recall that the law says, explicitly, *Do not kill your charge?*"

Jesus said, "You have a thorough grasp of the facts."

The demon said, "Shocking that you even need such a written law. But your playthings want so badly to brainwash their toy monkeys and

3

get them here, so it makes sense. Polish them to a high shine and then kill them. Ta-dah, instant sainthood."

Jesus said, "Again, you have a good grasp on the guardians' desire to get their charges into Heaven."

"The only thing I can't grasp is this," the accuser said, his voice flat. "If I'm in Hell for far less a crime than he committed, I fail to see why he should receive the mercy you denied the rest of us."

Jesus said, "Tabris still loves me."

"You have to admit," the demon said, stepping closer and lowering his voice, "that his demonstration of that love falls short of ideal."

Jesus turned to Raguel, who forced himself to look away from the demon. "Why are you pleading for Tabris? He hasn't pleaded for himself."

Raguel folded his arms over his chest, but Jesus touched his shoulder, and Raguel looked up. "My Lord, he's in shock. I'm convinced he had no intention of doing what he did, and given the chance, he'd change it. He's condemning himself. I think you want better than that for one of your own."

Looking at Tabris, Jesus said, "How much do you believe in him?"

"I wouldn't challenge your judgment," Raguel said.

"But you want that judgment to be favorable?"

Oh, God, Raguel thought, *thank you for an opening here.* He ignored the demon's outraged huff. "Please have mercy on him."

He looked again at Tabris, still prostrated, still not projecting any of his emotions. Raguel wondered if maybe he'd stopped himself from reacting to his own Creator debating whether to discard him.

"He does still love you." Raguel's voice turned urgent. "For that alone, you might be able to show him mercy."

Jesus stepped toward Tabris, who pulled his wings tighter over his head, a brown and green shield of feathers. Raguel noted both the brightness and softness in his Lord's eyes as he studied the prostrated angel, the contemplation that stretched into a question-mark, and for a moment Raguel feared it was God lingering over a last look. Tabris himself had gone motionless, and Raguel fought panic as Tabris's fear filled the room.

As if voicing Tabris's own thoughts, the demon said, "There isn't a choice. He deserves to burn."

Jesus kept his gaze on Tabris. "Raguel, answer me, how much do you believe in him?"

"Completely."

"Then I release him into your custody. Do with him as you wish."

4

The demon let off a flare of rage. The rest of the angels in the room reacted with simultaneous surprise and relief, tainted by confusion and anger.

Raguel bowed. "My Lord."

"Tabris?" Jesus's voice sharpened, but Tabris still didn't raise his head. "You're on probation. One more act of disobedience means damnation. You are clear on that."

Tabris projected his emotions so all could hear him: understanding, and thanks.

Jesus looked Raguel in the eyes. "Accompany him to his next assignment."

Jesus vanished even as Raguel felt himself filled with that assignment's details.

The demon pushed past Raguel to Tabris. "They've only delayed it. You're still mine."

Raguel put his hand on his sword, and the demon vanished.

Tabris raised his head, then got to his feet, his eyes wide but otherwise expressionless. The other angels watched as he looked at the spot the demon had stood, then to the last place he'd seen the boy.

Raguel touched his hand. "Come with me." And they departed.

Tabris still trembled with fear, with hopelessness, with desperation. He followed Raguel by doing automatically what would confuse any creature with a body, *going* somewhere without a destination. Angels traveled by thinking about where they wanted to be, and they arrived without passing through the intermediate space, whether the thought was "corner of 83rd and Park" or "wherever he's taking me" or even "wherever Gabriel is right now." This time Tabris's intention had been the second, so he felt surprised when he found himself surrounded by the paperish scent of Raguel's study, a familiar room in one of Heaven's "many mansions." Familiar because he'd gotten his previous assignment here. Being brought back at the end felt like a mockery of closure, the breaking of that long-ago promise.

Raguel had Tabris sit. "Take a few minutes to get yourself together. I'm going to leave you here, and I think it would help if you prayed."

"Please—" Tabris's voice sounded uncertain even to himself. "I'd rather you didn't."

Raguel hesitated, and Tabris waited for the inevitable recoil, but instead Raguel settled on the couch beside him. Tabris inclined his body away but found himself searching out Raguel's eyes. What he wanted wasn't there, of course. He couldn't find what wouldn't be found.

Raguel said, "I wasn't going to lock you up here. I wanted to go ahead of you to your next assignment."

"To warn everyone? That way they can resign before they have to work with a—"

Tabris's voice refused to complete the sentence, but the final word rang in his head like an echo in an underground cave.

Sebastian had gotten into Heaven. Hold onto that thought. Because that was good, the only good to come from this whole disaster. It wasn't Sebastian's fault that Tabris had taken his life. Tabris, however, was guilty of murder, and murder cried out for nothing less than damnation, sharp and swift. If only to keep the other guardians faithful, Tabris had seen no other way things could unfold.

He'd felt the other angels' agitation about God sparing him, and really, Tabris himself wasn't sure how he felt. Even here, sitting on Raguel's couch and feeling like a homesteader after the tornado has blown past, he knew he was by no means out of danger.

"I—" He quelled the instinctual projection and forced himself to translate into words. "I wanted to say thank you. For pleading for me. I..."

He couldn't continue. He wanted to push the words, but they wouldn't come. *I didn't deserve that.* Deserve. Didn't deserve anything.

Raguel reached for Tabris's hand, and the reassurance flowed from him, unrestrained emotions from an unsullied heart: Raguel would have done it for anyone.

"You did it for me." Tabris's voice deserted him again. He strangled down his feelings until he could figure out how to keep speaking.

Raguel said, "I won't be gone long. But I want to go ahead of you."

"I know what's going to happen." The inner darkness surged, and Tabris stared again at his hands. "Wherever you stick me for this next assignment—if it's a small city, a corporation, an apple tree out in the middle of the Great Plains—no one's going to want me there."

Raguel said, "I'm going to intercept their objections," and beneath the words, Tabris sensed a tease: he hadn't guessed it.

Tabris looked up. "A star? I could handle that. Make it about a thousand light years from anything else." His voice dropped. "And make sure there aren't any black holes near by. Just in case."

Raguel squeezed his hand. "You're being hard on yourself, and it's not all about you. Stay here and get your equilibrium. I'll be a few minutes."

"The reality couldn't possibly exceed imagination." Tabris's eyes narrowed. "What am I assigned to?"

"Not what," Raguel said. "Who."

"What?" Tabris leaped from the couch, his wings flaring as he backed across the room, eyes round as full moons. "I hope you mean an animal!"

Raguel shook his head.

"No!" Tabris exclaimed. "Absolutely not! I—you can't! The one-person rule!"

Raguel stood. "It's been suspended so you can guard a second human being. And you won't be the primary caregiver. It's a secondary guardianship."

"But—"

"You can't refuse." Raguel's voice turned insistent. "You *cannot* refuse. You're under obedience to take it."

Tabris covered his face with his hands. His thoughts ricocheted like atoms in a nuclear reactor, and every attempt to get them under control only sped them up. Another person? A human being? Someone else whose life he could screw up—could *end*? Why would God do that—unless God wanted him in Hell all along and wanted to prove it wouldn't have helped to be merciful. No one would plead for Tabris again. No one.

Eventually he whispered, "What about the other guardian?"

"He'll have no choice. He's under the same directive you are."

Directive. Oh, God, please, no. He'd *had* a directive! The word *Sebastian* was strong enough to break through every barrier Tabris had thrown up against it, and he knew when it hit Raguel like an arrow in the heart. *Sebastian.* Little one. Brown-eyed, clever, assertive, curious, responsible, generous, impulsive—and *his*. His charge. Not his charge anymore.

Tabris groped for a chair, and then, huddled with his arms wrapped around his waist, he did everything in his power to push it down. Stop thinking. Just stop thinking. Everything had changed. He couldn't go back.

Raguel neared him, and Tabris shook his head. "If you're going to do it, we should do it now."

Raguel hesitated.

"Waiting won't make it easier."

Tabris took a few deep breaths to steady himself, his color darkening, his wings enriching to a deep jade and an even deeper mahogany.

He regarded himself momentarily, then looked back at Raguel, and in the next moment, Raguel took him away.

Two

"No!" the guardian angel shouted. "I won't allow it!"

"Rock!" Raguel tried to block him from Tabris. "Rachmiel, stand down. Tabris—"

"—murdered the last one, and I'm not letting him get near mine!"

Tabris backed through a pile of resin horses until his back hit the wall, and he took every verbal lash without protest. Rachmiel had drawn his sword and positioned himself between Tabris and the tiny form who slept beneath the tousled covers. In the grainy midnight, Rachmiel's eyes and weapon shed a glow like moonlight. So far the noise and the emotions had left the child undisturbed.

Raguel began exerting emotional pressure on Rachmiel to get control of himself even as Rachmiel tightened his grip on his sword. "If you think," Rachmiel said, "even once, that I'm going to let him touch—"

Raguel got between them and disarmed Rachmiel by strength of will, but even without his sword, Rachmiel had his wings spread in a battle-stance. Tabris pressed against the scant security of the bedroom wall, knowing he could have passed through it and left at any moment. He and Rachmiel wanted the same thing.

Other angels flooded the room, a torrent of high alert and horror that swirled through the air. One of the other angels hovered alongside Rachmiel to urge calm, but he persisted. *No, he wouldn't let* him *near her, and this was obscene, and how could he be expected to guard her when they were bringing an enemy right into the home?*

Tabris focused on the messy room rather than the whiplash of the angel's anger. Posters of fluffy animals, ballet slippers and piano keyboards. Beside a heap of clothing lay a teddy bear, pushed out of bed by a sleeping arm. Tabris leaned toward it, then jerked back against the wall. Not his child to guard. Not really.

Rachmiel folded his arms. "And that's final." His pallor had given way to a flush, and he breathed heavily.

Raguel said, "They're Divine orders."

Rachmiel locked his teeth and blew out a long breath. His eyes glittered, sharp sparks Tabris could read as a demand for the exact specificity of how those orders were worded.

Then Rachmiel closed his eyes and flexed his head just a fraction, and Tabris could tell he was listening to God. Rachmiel's light turned to gold, and Tabris sensed the other angels clustering nearer to Rachmiel as the Spirit wrapped around him. Like snowflakes in the sun, his objections melted. Tabris leaned away from his corner, his eyes round as he watched their Creator's hand working on Rachmiel's spirit.

He stepped forward, closer to Rachmiel—but also closer to the child. She stirred, and Rachmiel glared at him. "You," and it was a whisper. "Out."

Tabris blazed from the room like a comet, but he knew—he couldn't outrun this, couldn't evade, couldn't leave it behind. He couldn't shed himself. Like a laser he streaked across the clear sky, parallel to the ground for two miles before realizing in panic that he'd been bound to the child by a spiritual tether. It snapped taut, crashing him to the ground in agony.

He couldn't move any further. His eyes stung and fingers clenched. He needed to move closer to his new spiritual homebase.

Guardian.

Tabris inched backward through the brown grass until sensation returned and he no longer trembled with cold. As the whistling subsided, he rubbed his temples to clear his mind. Stupid, stupid. A newbie mistake, forgetting the tether.

When semicorporeal, as they are most of the time, angels have subtle bodies, and those bodies have limits. In their purest form they exist as unalloyed intelligences, knowing and loving God in His most profound aspects. In order to act, however, they become more solid, opting for the shapes humans recognize as winged men and women. Tabris knew if he'd persisted in widening the distance between himself and the child, he wouldn't have died, since angels are immortal, but he'd have lost consciousness until someone pulled him closer.

He lurched to his feet and scanned the area. Raguel had brought him to the countryside, far enough from any city that the sky looked deep, the stars distant, and the universe heartless. Fighting a gnawing sense of abandonment, he turned his gaze to the stars, remembering how a sky unpolluted by city lights looks like a dome that gets more distant toward its apex. He couldn't recall the last time he'd seen one.

He walked. The cricket song reminded him that not all in the world had changed. His last assignment had been in one of the modern city walls people called *suburbs*, the rows of identical houses with identical lawns and an identical tree and driveway, each with a picture window and a potted plant beside the kitchen sink.

Guardian.

That child, two miles away, he thought—and then paused. He wanted to think of it as unlucky, but he couldn't. Its heart was pure. Her heart, he corrected himself. He knew her to be innocent. Young. The best way to help would be to jettison her and never touch her. If God wanted him to guard her he could very well do it from two miles away and, over time three, four, five, infinity. He could pray for her just as well from Jupiter as from her bedroom.

But another part of him, the part he had to call instinct, felt compelled to fight anyone who might harm her. It wasn't like being told to guard a bank or a country. There you wanted to do it because you wanted to do a good job. But guarding a human—it wouldn't let you not do it. Your soul vibrated in time to the human's soul. You fit together. It felt wrong to be apart. Be there, be near, be her defense. Guard that purity and innocence.

Rachmiel and I are a lot alike.

Except, of course, Rachmiel hadn't raised his hand against the girl. Tabris should never forget that. When danger had appeared, Rachmiel had driven off the threat, and Tabris had turned against the victim.

He spread his wings and flew the perimeter of his tether. When what bound him to the girl was love and not force, he'd be able to travel anywhere in creation and still feel her heart beating within his own. Now he wouldn't have recognized her existence at all except for the chain pinning him to one spot, making him a radius that strained ever outward.

No, that's wrong, he thought. *Do that and she'll grow up feeling abandoned.*

As he glided, he thought how different this was from his first guardianship. It had been textbook-normal until the disaster. Nine months curled up beside a developing embryo, snuggling the child and shielding it as it grew, semiconscious days of dreaming protection, loving what as yet had four cells and an immortal soul and had rooted itself in the body of another living thing. Then birth, the laughter, the admiration when he first saw the tiny body, the pride as he stood over the bassinette in a hospital room—Sebastian! His vows still rang in his ears.

11

He sailed over the remnants of a rock wall and cupped his wings, angled upright, and dropped to a stand. The long grass licked his calves, tickling him where it could, but he had no energy to play with the plants, to tell them to think about God while they stretched their blades toward the sky. The grass settled back, disappointed after he passed, then forgot him and returned to playing tag with the moonbeams.

Tabris embraced the cold as he walked, draining all the warmth from his body for an instant to crystallize the evanescence that was him. He loved God's world. It was good to be here.

A trickle caught his attention, and he angled toward it. His favorite season was fall... *Autumn*, he corrected himself. Within a few weeks the piles of snow and blistering wind would settle on the land, and he could lie on the rooftops at night, warming up the ice dams and talking to his Father.

He stopped in his tracks.

Wait a minute—could he even...?

No, not that. He wanted to know, but he didn't, couldn't. He shut his eyes and struggled to force down the fear, then told himself to delay, don't ask that question right now because you shouldn't ask questions whose answers would destroy you.

He'd arrived at the stream, but for now he ignored it.

The black shape of trees and the subtle farmland gave the gift of silence Tabris both needed and feared. He hadn't prayed since it happened. He'd been too stunned at the time, too numb afterward, too afraid now. Just as Sebastian's parents hadn't spoken to each other when they'd learned of the accident, gripping each other's hands in wretched silence, so too had Tabris gripped God's hand without words, not wanting to let go until the moment God would rip him off like brittle duct-tape. He'd only released his grip when Raguel took him home.

No, actually. It was a few moments earlier. Tabris thought back through time to the echoing judgment hall and realized his sense of God's presence, what humans call the Beatific Vision, had been strangled down at the same moment he'd been placed on probation. What he had now wasn't a Vision. More like a Glimpse. He could still make contact, but as if through layers of glass, and that change had shocked him into releasing his grip.

Tabris shuddered. *Can I pray?*

Asking God would be a destructive test: reach for God with his whole heart and either God would fill him, or more likely, God would say nothing, which would be its own answer. So Tabris answered himself:

he wouldn't try anything more than reciting words, not yet anyhow, not real prayer. He'd avoid the purer forms: contemplation or meditation or unification...he'd wait. Maybe it would become clear. Maybe it wouldn't have to.

Finally he stepped into the stream and walked against the flow of the water to the furthest point of the tether. Numb, he lay full-length in the center, allowing the wet cold to rip right through him. He couldn't fly any further, but if he lay still and let the water rush past, it was almost the same. He could let the stream scour his soul, untangle his hair, and saturate the two-toned feathers, and maybe when it was done, maybe there wouldn't be that blot of ugliness after all.

He dug his hands into the tiny stones at the bottom until he found the softer sediment, and he closed his eyes.

Guardian.

I'll do it, God.

The moon shone its round glory on the sleeping hills, casting a haze on the inhabitants of the night. Tabris, his eyes and ears closed by water, realized the glow was vanishing when he felt another angel's spirit brush against his own.

Rachmiel.

"Come back," said the other guardian. "It's not right to leave you out here."

Tabris followed, dry the instant he left the water, and was brought directly to the girl's bedroom. Full sensation returned as the tether slackened. The room was empty of all the other angels that had filled it earlier, even Raguel.

The other guardian made it clear he should sit on the bed. Tabris complied mutely. Rachmiel too had remained wordless, his heart rather than his voice conveying the instructions.

Rachmiel settled in the chair by the corner window, the moon illuminating him like a spotlight, revealing that the other angel's previously-strained features were sensitive, his blond hair had a gentle curl, and his wings were orange. The moonlight accentuated the color of his eyes, sunset-toned so they would range the full spectrum of a night sky, most likely orange when he was calm but deepening to purple when he was upset. Now they were purple. He'd drawn his knees against his chest, and while Tabris studied him, he studied Tabris.

For a while they remained in this still-life, Tabris longing for a way to cover up his soul, but he braced himself and let his new supervisor inspect him.

13

Finally Rachmiel turned his gaze to the sleeping girl. Images appeared in Tabris's mind, accompanied by Rachmiel's gestures, his carriage, his emotions: thoughts of time, of compelled acceptance, and of the child. He unclenched his hands, and then looked at the girl and smiled.

Tabris said, "Elizabeth?"

Rachmiel's confirmation filled Tabris with sadness, enough at odds with everything else that it had to be Tabris's own. Facts blossomed in his mind like a tree erupting in springtime: Elizabeth Hayes was ten years old; she had three brothers; she liked pounding on the piano; she was smart but shy. Her personality unfolded for Tabris, her history and her skills, and underlying all this was Rachmiel's love that started cracks spreading along Tabris's already-striated heart.

The love changed then to ferocity: if Tabris hurt her, Rachmiel would defend her with his life.

Tabris whispered, "I wouldn't."

The other guardian's eyes flared.

Tabris averted his gaze, at first pretending to look over the girl and then actually doing it. He reached out to touch the red hair that covered her shoulders, then stopped himself. "May I?"

Sullen for only a moment, Rachmiel nodded.

Tabris extended a hand to her cheek, freckled and soft, in the process of losing the tan earned bit by bit every day of the summer. With two fingers he traced the curve of her cheek, the information now coming to him as readily as if he were a doctor reading a patient's chart. She had good health except for a scab on one knee. Her eyes, he learned, were blue. Her face hadn't lost its baby-roundness yet. Trivial information: her shoe size, the length of her hair, her blood pressure, her lung capacity, what she'd eaten for dinner. Her pulse and her temperature. And he could feel her dreams.

Tabris said, "She'll wake in an hour?"

Rachmiel shrugged, meaning a little longer.

Tabris winced, looking again at Elizabeth because it was better than letting Rachmiel look into his eyes. As if he'd sensed this, Rachmiel reappeared in front of him, on the other side of the child. A question: would he like to meet the other angels in the household?

He had no choice, so why phrase it as a question? But Rachmiel wanted a response, so he agreed.

Rachmiel flashed them downstairs to a living room. Two angels sat talking on the thick carpet, and a third perched on the carved mantelpiece. Rachmiel projected to the others, who faced Tabris and extended a greeting by smiling and opening their hands. It felt staged.

Rachmiel gestured to a female angel with straight brown hair that rippled over her shoulders. "Josai'el guards Elizabeth's grandmother, Bridget." His voice sounded much gentler than his initial protests. Josai'el bowed, and Tabris made a deferential gesture toward her as the head of the household.

Rachmiel continued, "This is Hadriel. He guards Elizabeth's mother, Connie."

Hadriel greeted him, but Tabris could feel the tension, the objection. Rachmiel said, "And lastly—"

"I've met Mithra." Tabris didn't look him in the eyes. "Hello."

The smaller angel said, "I guard Andrew, her father."

Tabris's mouth tightened. "I remember."

Josai'el projected a call, and three more angels appeared, the guardians of Elizabeth's brothers. Tabris felt the names and identities slipping past him, too much to absorb. But over time, he'd be able to match the personalities and the pairings. Katra'il, a female angel with blond hair in tight curls. A blue-and-white eyed angel named Voriah. An archangel named Miriael. The names came and went, and Tabris would just have to figure them all out again later.

The introductions made, Tabris felt the others anticipating something. Only what could he say to allay their fears when he wasn't sure he could do that for himself? He looked at his hands. Rachmiel had known his crime the instant he'd arrived, so there was no reason to assume the rest of them didn't know. But conscious that he rode the fringes of being tolerated at all, he forced the words. "Thank you. I'll probably be asking a lot of questions about how things run here."

"You'll get into the routine quickly." Rachmiel's eyes had gone softer. "I'll talk you through at first, but I'm sure you won't need much help." The emotions projecting from him had changed, less sharp and more warm, and Tabris shifted backward: he'd expected protectiveness from Raguel, but not from Rachmiel. "The days can get pretty hectic, but at night you'll get a chance to recharge."

"I know—" Tabris began and then stopped when he thought about the past. The past? Yesterday? Yesterday, when he and the guardians of Sebastian's parents had sat on the rooftop to pray the evening offering together, and then curled beside their charges in their warm beds, an angelic wing thrown protectively over human shoulders.

Miriael's voice drew him back to the present. "The demons around here tend to attack in groups. This household is large enough to ward off most strikes, and sometimes we'll go out on loan to the neighbors if they need us."

Mithra said, "An old woman lives alone at the top of the hill. I help her guardian a lot."

Tabris took in the seven of them with a glance and registered how they fit together, their familiarity with each other's motions and habits, how they anticipated which one would speak next and made space for one another. In a living room that had long since sacrificed elegance for practicality, this team resonated with unity and flexibility. With mutual trust. But him? Would they ever trust him? More than that, would he ever feel as comfortable again with anyone?

Even a human could have deciphered the tension ghosting their eyes: *Why are you here?* Raguel must have taken advantage of the time he'd spent outside, sitting them together on the worn sofas and explaining that damnation had been as close as the dotting of an *i*. He'd probably teased out their concerns, persuaded them to confide their worries, and then urged them to call if they had any doubts. Like a session for friends of a teen suicide: get them all in one place and talk.

And once that meeting had ended, Rachmiel had been sent to fetch him, the boys' guardians had dispersed, and the guardians of the three elders had remained to discuss how you handle a threat God orders you not to send away. Apparently you bring it into the living room and introduce it to everyone, and then wait for a speech.

Tabris shivered. "Thanks for taking me in." His voice sounded thin, but he thought it was expected, and he could never let his guard down, never let himself forget this community of angels was doing him a favor.

Josai'el embraced him, and he allowed her. "Welcome, Tabris. We're glad to have you."

Three

Josai'el's first impulse had been that one more angel meant that much more strength against demonic attacks. Her second thought came right on the heels of the first, and that was the one she held onto: Tabris needed them. A heady thought, that one. Of all the families on Earth, God chose hers as the best stronghold for a wounded angel.

The whole story felt like a disaster. The instant Tabris had arrived beside Raguel, his pain had overwhelmed her. Worse, when Rachmiel had towed their new member back from the outside, she'd sensed that despite his best resolutions, Rachmiel had been harsh. A wingspan before her, Tabris had stood with the hollowest expression she'd ever seen on an angel, and the impulse to embrace him had been so strong. The damage of the past twenty-four hours was etched onto his face, especially his eyes, and Josai'el wondered how many other signs she hadn't recognized.

With the family due to awaken soon, she invited Mithra and Tabris to accompany her on a survey of the house. "You have to know the place since you'll be working here."

The others remained silent while she led them from room to room, introducing the human inhabitants (but allowing Mithra to introduce his charge.) Tabris couldn't possibly be retaining all the names and relationships, but he'd piece it together during daily interactions. She brought them outside, showing him the limits of the property, then detailing the places she loved and the spots most likely to hide demons.

Outdoors again, Tabris stood a bit freer. "It's a far cry from suburbia." His voice was low, restrained. He flexed his wings and craned his neck toward the cold expanse of the predawn sky.

Josai'el said, "The Hayes family has lived here over two centuries. Bridget was born in the master bedroom of this house."

Mithra did a perfect imitation of her voice. "Andrew was born in room 302 of the city hospital."

She made a face at him, and he laughed.

"How far is the city?" Tabris asked.

Mithra pointed south. "About fifteen miles, but we don't go often. Elizabeth's school is in town."

Tabris began to speak, then stopped. They continued walking while Josai'el wondered whether she ought to press him or give him breathing room. Mithra remained quiet, and because he'd known Tabris longer, she followed his lead.

At the woodshed, a hiss stopped all three. "*Tab-riss!*"

Tabris and Mithra whirled instantly, manifesting their swords from their own soul-material. Even brighter than the light of their weapons, Josai'el rose into the air, illuminating the field with a spiritual glow.

"No need." An angelic form appeared sitting on the wood pile, his sharp shadow jolting where it passed over split logs. "I'll show myself. Tabris and I go way back. You're my pal. Tell them."

Tabris said, "Zeffar."

"I go by another name now. You can call me Accuser."

As Tabris trembled, Josai'el moved closer. "You're not wanted. Leave."

"Tabris missed his destiny." Accuser drew up his knees and spread his wings. "I tried to help him along, but your Jesus sinks in his claws and never lets go, even though Tabris couldn't have made his intentions clearer. I told Tabris to fight for his freedom, but he was too weak."

"Quiet," Josai'el said. "Go."

The demon vanished. Mithra put away his sword, but Tabris kept his raised.

Mithra sounded upset. "He asked for your damnation?"

Tabris nodded.

Mithra projected disgust, adding that Satan always sent someone to a trial. Tabris sighed, then extinguished his sword.

Mithra turned to Josai'el. "Maybe we should go back inside." She realized with a jolt that because of the demon, Mithra had swung to Tabris's side. "Demons will have a harder time getting to us there."

Tabris shook his head. "I'd rather stay outside."

Josai'el said, "Then let me show you my favorite place. There's a pond."

The pond turned out to be the source of the stream Tabris had discovered earlier, and she hung back while he drew nearer the water. Surrounded by trees decorated with prayers like streamers, Tabris relaxed even more, and for the first time Josai'el caught wisps of his thoughts. Brown eyes, brown hair, a boy's laughter. Hunger for prayer. And emptiness.

Pines and oaks mingled with willows around the water, sharing the neighborhood with shrubbery and wild strawberry plants that had lost their fruits to birds and children. Insects came in search of the angels only to pass right through them, and then, confused, resumed their feeding. A muskrat swam on the surface of the pond, then ducked under.

Tabris's soul vibrated as though he were very close to projecting something, but then he only spoke. "This is wonderful."

"Bridget likes to come here on sunny days to read or sit," Josai'el said. "I come whenever I can to pray."

Mithra had approached a sleeping finch on a tree branch, so Josai'el said more softly, "Come here yourself whenever you want. Feel free to make use of everything we do."

"I'm still tethered."

"You're not at your limit, are you?"

"Close. My hands are numb."

Tabris stopped, his eyes widening as he regarded his fingers, his open palms. Josai'el caught from him a fragment of the thought—not even a day before, these hands had robbed the world of a life.

She rested her hands on his, and Tabris's head jerked up. She squeezed his fingers, projecting with her heart wide open, *All is forgiven.*

Tabris slipped his hands from hers. "When will Elizabeth wake up?"

Josai'el's mouth twitched. "Soon."

"I should return." Tabris glanced toward Mithra, then back to her, then off toward the house as if he couldn't find a safe place to look. "I want to get to know her better. You understand." And he vanished.

Josai'el closed her eyes and clenched her hands. Because she thought she did understand.

When Tabris appeared, Rachmiel offered a smile he didn't return. Instead, the two-toned angel sat on the floor, near the teddy bear, and refused to look at him.

Rachmiel burned with irritation. *Good morning to you too.*

Regardless, they had to work together, so Rachmiel forged on. "I was going to call you anyway because she'll be up in a minute." He curled over her body and whispered, "Sleepyhead, it's time to get up."

19

Elizabeth stretched, then rolled over beneath the blanket, and Rachmiel waited for that first waking sigh to coax a smile from Tabris. "Come on, Sleepy. It's morning."

Elizabeth sat at the edge of her bed, unfocused.

Rachmiel continued watching her, acutely aware of Tabris leaning forward, his eyes devouring her, and he hoped Tabris approved of how well he'd guarded her these last ten years.

"She's very sweet." Tabris sounded hoarse.

Rachmiel let the emotions flow from him toward Tabris, little teasers: was that all he had to say? Didn't he have a right to be proud of her? What did he think?

She went to the dresser to get the day's clothes. Tabris said, "Is she small for her age?"

Rachmiel acknowledged this, but with the caveat that her mother was slight as well. He stayed close, fussing over her as she readied for the day, and momentarily he found Tabris at his elbow, very close now to the child but keeping Rachmiel between them.

Elizabeth's brush caught on a snarl, and Rachmiel adjusted it so the hair parted. "She's the only redhead. The rest of the children are blond."

Tabris watched over Rachmiel's shoulder as though bewitched. It was *that look,* the look Rachmiel had seen on guardians of newborns, as if they could barely comprehend why one awkward human in a world filled with millions would enthrall them so much. But in binding an angel to a human, God manifested some of His own brightness in the child's soul, and any angel would become intoxicated by the craftsmanship of the Most High. Those intriguing interlocking pieces existed in their full form in every part of her...poised to become something. Ten years ago, the first words Rachmiel had murmured to Elizabeth had been, "Who are you going to be?" and the adventure of every day was watching the changes that would transform her. Even unperfected, her soul was glorious. Naturally Tabris would love her, maybe as much as he did. He'd figured Tabris would gush with amazement and hunger to know more about her.

Instead, Tabris stopped himself from speaking.

Rachmiel looked up with concern. Was something wrong?

Tabris's attention shifted around the room, back to the girl and then away again. He wasn't communicating anything, but Rachmiel could feel him vibrating with tension. Finally Tabris said, "I can't."

Watching Tabris was like watching sailors batten down a ship, reefing the sails that should have filled with the wind and taken them wherever

God wanted. A momentary anger swelled inside, but then Rachmiel realized Tabris wasn't being coy. In the face of a storm, you had to reef the sails or the ship got torn apart.

Rachmiel said, "How old was Sebastian?"

"Twelve."

Questions, so many questions. But how to ask them without shutting down Tabris completely? *Did you love him?* would be painful and redundant—or worse, what if he hadn't? *What did he look like?* would have been pointless. And in the face of Rachmiel's silence, Tabris himself stayed silent by the window.

Tabris had trouble deciding which was worse: the day at school, surrounded by hundreds of angels whom he didn't know but who knew about him, or the time spent with seven angels whom he expected to get to know well and who in turn would try to become close to him.

He had no reason not to want them for friends. On principle, it would be a good idea. But these angels had accepted him as a service, and gratitude required distance. He should preserve formality at all times and say nothing unless asked. If he did that for a week or two, maybe they would stop condescending and treat him the way he deserved.

On the drive home from school, the household angels shared notes about the day: what the children had learned, what their friends were doing, which students were absent and might be in need of health-related prayers. They took places in and atop the car, playing as only angels can, perfectly reckless with their hearts trained on God's. The five angels who had enjoyed this routine for years bantered with one another, calling to angels they passed in the pickup lines and saluting (in unison) the green-eyed guardian of the school. When Tabris shot Rachmiel a questioning look, he laughed: "About two years ago, Zohar tried to pull rank. We're never going to let him forget it."

The guardians watched for demons on the road, of course, and alerted Connie to one distracted driver who might have t-boned the car, but for the most part they relaxed—all but Tabris, who still trembled at the thought of having so recently brushed shoulders with damnation.

He sat behind Connie, arms locked around her seat and wings tucked forward, eyes mesmerized by the road being sucked under the tires.

Hell. Not the concept of Hell, but the reality. The way you know it when you watch your best friend abandon God and in turn be aban-

21

doned by Him. Tabris didn't think about the flames and the pain—those seemed less real than the way he'd have lost his personality. The demons had rejected God in favor of independence, of course, but from his perspective, he'd seen angels switch from loving God one moment to cursing Him the next, hating the things that resembled their Creator, and then striking at them. First among those things would be His image and likeness in their hearts.

Tabris had no reason to believe he'd be any different. If anything, he'd have more reason to tear himself apart.

Or maybe not. Zeffar didn't blame himself for his own decision. Maybe like him, Tabris would have convinced himself he was right. Maybe he would have dug deep enough, cut hard enough, and pulled free that wriggling, living thing that was the breath God had breathed to create him all those eons ago, the moment he'd looked up and felt his soul thrumming with a name, his own name...

Rachmiel touched him, and Tabris felt the concern. He tensed. "Don't worry about me."

Rachmiel chuckled, and Tabris got the sense that it was too late. He pulled his thoughts deeper inside so they wouldn't filter out of his heart into the chatter filling the car.

Or maybe he'd have blamed Sebastian. That would be twisted. *I'm in Hell because that ridiculous brat made me kill him.*

As the nausea built, Rachmiel's wingtip touched his again. Tabris pulled his wings closer.

Don't think about that. Think about something else. But how could he possibly not love God any longer? He did. He always had. Thinking about how he'd betrayed God's trust hurt worse than considering what he'd done to Sebastian. It wasn't like God had asked him to do something six billion angels weren't already doing. "Here, look out for this human." How hard could that be? And his accuser's words rang back at him, that his expression of love "fell short of the ideal," leaving Tabris always more certain: he should have been damned. A just God could do nothing else.

A merciful God had.

Tabris hadn't been facetious when he'd reflected that he'd been only the dot of an *i* away from damnation. The *t* had already been crossed, and by his own hand.

A third time, Rachmiel touched him, swirling with concern.

Tabris leaped onto the hood of the car. He stared into the wind, letting it sting tears into his eyes, and then cupped his wings to catch as much of it as he could.

Voriah sat with his heels against the bumper. "Glad you could come onboard, Tab."

Tabris let his ears ring with the sound of the motor under his knees and the children at his back. "I like the wind," was all he said.

Voriah smiled. "Then this is the place to be."

Having satisfied Voriah's curiosity, Tabris tried to return to his thoughts, but abruptly he felt the other five angels begin praying. Alan's teacher had gone on maternity leave; they were praying for a safe delivery.

Rachmiel reached for him, projecting an invitation, so Tabris slipped back onto the roof. He listened to their prayer but cringed at the thought of adding his own and discovering here, in the middle of everyone, that God didn't want to hear from him. With his eyes downcast, he wrapped his fingers around one another in a tight weave and felt all too glad when they pulled into the driveway so he could stop what had become, for him, a charade.

Just a little longer. He just had to get home.

As he'd hoped, the children dispersed to separate rooms for homework. Tabris followed Elizabeth to the messiest bedroom on the second floor, and as she unpacked her bag, it hit him: he'd been banking on time alone, but as long as he was with Elizabeth, he'd also be with Rachmiel.

Rachmiel turned with surprise and a question.

Tabris clamped down again. "She needs to do her math."

Rachmiel said, "I know." And then, "She does math last because she hates it."

Tabris folded his arms and leaned against the wall. "All the more reason for her to do it first."

"We're angels," Rachmiel said with a chuckle, "not miracle workers."

They quieted down, and Tabris kept himself to himself through a spelling list, vocabulary sentences, a paragraph about the American Revolution, and a sheet of multiplication problems (which, to be fair, were interspersed with two snacks, a drink of water, a fifteen-minute pause in front of the TV, a phone call from a classmate, dinner, and four experimental outfits on a fashion doll.) The bedtime routine left him edgy, and as soon as she fell asleep, he asked permission to go outside. With a shrug, Rachmiel indicated he didn't object. Before he'd even finished, Tabris flashed to the pond.

It wasn't yet full dark as Tabris settled at the edge, plopping pebbles into the water one after the next while avoiding the gaze of the waning moon. A musical world greeted his ears, a song no human had ever heard.

The tones had been formed long ago by the stars, sent on notes of light aimlessly through the empty distances until somehow they all collided on Earth around Tabris in a serenade. He could hear the rhythmic foundation provided by the water lapping the pond's edge, harmony contributed by the breaths of sleeping birds and the crinkle of rodents searching for food in fallen leaves. A descant of promised snow hovered in the air, and all for Tabris because he was the only one out that night.

"Raguel," he said as though dictating a letter, "I think I'm doing all right. So is Elizabeth Hayes. There's nothing challenging enough here to require two guardians, so it's not very stressful. She's very sweet, by the way. I think I— She's ten." He fingered a brown seed head. "The other angels have been very accommodating. Please let me know if I'm in danger of violating probation. Thanks. Tabris."

Surrounded by dying cattails, he tossed another pebble into the pond. It skipped before plunging under.

"Tabris," drawled a voice.

"Accuser," he replied, his features unchanged although his voice had deepened. He didn't turn. The demon was behind him.

"I've gotten tired of that name. Call me Unbridled."

Tabris smirked. "Are you the wind?"

The demon inched forward from the shade of a pine tree to within arm's reach of the two-toned angel. "I am. I'm free to go wherever I want rather than chained within a circle with a two-mile radius."

"There's plenty of beauty in my circle."

Tabris forced a tight and symmetrical smile that grew easier to maintain the longer he did it. In response to the demon's nearness, he pulled his wings close to his body, fingering the green outer feathers.

Unbridled said, "Are you going to kill Elizabeth?"

"Are you going to go before God and beg for forgiveness?"

Unbridled laughed. "How can *you* ask me that question? You're hardly qualified."

Tabris maintained his nonsmile.

Unbridled rested back on his hands. "I've been watching you all day, and I'm fascinated by your new companions. Could the other angels possibly want you around any less? They might as well imprint their names on a petition."

"Should that surprise me?"

"I want you." The demon sidled closer. "Come with me."

"Can't." Tabris tilted his head as though gesturing. "Tether."

"Shed it! Let go of the girl and come with me. Let's dance together in the Alps or dive under the Arctic ice or explore galaxies so far from Earth that their light will never reach it. Please. It's been so long."

The smile had frozen on Tabris's face. "Thank you, but no."

The demon sighed. "Can I just stay with you? We don't even have to talk. I just want to be with you again."

"You're not my friend anymore." Tabris shifted further away. "As long as it doesn't involve me, do as you want, *Unbridled*."

"Oh, irony!" The demon's head picked up. "It's so hard to find someone with your sense of humor!"

"Place a Craigslist ad."

"You see!" Unbridled sat upright, wings flared. "That's the Tabris I've missed so much."

Tabris closed his eyes.

"Let's go North and ride a cold front."

"No."

"If I could get you to say yes to any one question, what would that question be?"

"It would be, *Tabris, would you like me to go away and leave you in peace?*"

Silence.

After a long moment, Tabris extended his senses and confirmed the demon had gone.

He didn't move from his spot. The trees lost leaves one by one to the childlike hands of gravity, their descending tones adding to the midnight music. He lay back to linger in the symphony when Raguel arrived.

Tabris flashed to a stand and bowed, his two-toned wings scissoring.

"Please relax," said Raguel. "I'm sorry I couldn't arrive sooner."

"I didn't think you needed to come at all." Tabris squinted until he could look up without any spark in his eyes. "I figured I needed to send an update. Am I doing something wrong?"

"Not at all." Raguel sat on a rock. "At ease, soldier." He laughed, and Tabris self-consciously shifted his weight, then perched on a fallen tree that would have slid down the pond bank if he'd had any more substance than moonlight. He smiled the same nonsmile he'd worn for Unbridled.

"Are the other angels treating you well?"

Tabris nodded.

"And Elizabeth is what you expected?"

How to answer that question, when he hadn't expected Elizabeth at all? When on meeting her, he hadn't dared think of her as anything more than a potential victim, or maybe the nasty side effect of a medication you take to disinfect a wounded soul. He hadn't thought to wonder what she'd be like, but moving through the day, parts of her had felt familiar and others deadly wrong. The schoolwork was far too easy for her—except it was just right for her and would have been too simple for Sebastian.

Maybe his silence was an answer to Raguel, who studied him in the moonlight. "Remember, you're in my custody. I'm directly involved in everything that happens to you, so if for any reason you want me, call. I'll do what I can."

"I think I'm managing as well as you'd expect." Tabris shook his head. "I'm still getting used to this."

Tabris wondered if Raguel would call him out on the half-truths, having seen it all before. Except nothing like this had ever happened before, so he hadn't seen it all. Raguel said, "And you'll call me if you need help?"

"I would." For whatever good it would do. "Don't you trust me?"

Raguel paused a long time. Then, "I took your side at the trial, didn't I?"

"Then trust me once more." Tabris looked at the ground. "I'll call if I think I should."

Raguel took his leave. Tabris pivoted on the rotting log and stared back over the pond.

Four

After lunch the next day, Elizabeth and her friends played "wall-ball" against the brick sides of the school. Their guardians played alongside the girls, having just as good a time.

Rachmiel said, "I'm going to sit on the roof. You'll watch her?"

"I will." Tabris settled himself against an unused space on the wall and regarded her with dark eyes.

Rachmiel flashed to the rooftop where he joined Voriah and a few others.

"Rock!" Voriah said, laughing. "I didn't expect you to join us."

Rachmiel sat on the short wall designed to keep the maintenance workers from falling, but which also trapped any balls thrown injudiciously high. It served as an excellent perch for guardians. In addition to Rachmiel and Voriah were a smoky silent guardian who cared for one of the teachers, and Zohar, the green-eyed guardian angel of the school.

"What, no salute?" said Zohar.

Rachmiel only leaned over the edge to watch Elizabeth.

Zohar whistled. "You're not giving yourself any time off."

Rachmiel huffed. Then his mouth twitched. "I need to see how he operates, but I'm not leaving him alone with her. At least with a demon I'd know where I stood, but with him... No, it would be irresponsible."

Voriah rested on the roof beside Rachmiel, glancing down at Tabris two stories beneath. "Has he spoken to you?"

"You mean more than to anyone else?" Rachmiel sighed. "Not really."

Zohar said, "The strong silent type?"

Rachmiel projected negation. "That came out wrong. Look, Sebastian died...when?...on Wednesday, four PM Pacific time? It's now Friday, twelve Eastern time. That's not long. I'm surprised he can talk at all."

Voriah grinned. "That's so sweet of you."

Rachmiel's wings flared. "You saw him! The shock was still on his face when Raguel brought him to us! He needed some time to recover. I have no idea why he was sent directly to us."

Despite sounding more understanding than the other two, Rachmiel hadn't taken his gaze from Elizabeth and Tabris.

Voriah and the green-eyed angel projected back and forth to each other so quickly that Rachmiel couldn't catch their conversation. Finally, Zohar said, "I'd like to know his thoughts too. He really doesn't speak?"

"Oh, he'll answer if you ask a question," said Voriah. "He just won't talk on his own."

"Probably shock," added Rachmiel.

"Mithra used to know him," Voriah added, "and he says the changes are obvious, whatever that means, and that Tabris used to speak and laugh just like the rest of us."

"You mean he projects everything?" said Zohar.

"Well—no."

Voriah stopped. Rachmiel reached forward as Elizabeth jumped for a ball and lost her balance, but Tabris steadied the girl. Voriah continued, "Now that you mention it, I don't think he's projected anything."

Rachmiel said, "He hasn't to me."

Beneath them, Tabris moved nearer to Elizabeth. The closest angels stopped bantering and got right up next to their charges.

Voriah waited a beat. Then, "He's the life of the party."

"Well, naturally," said Zohar. "He's a murderer."

Rachmiel shook his head and half-closed his eyes—but not enough that he let Tabris out of his sight.

Zohar said, "It's the truth."

"Watch it," Voriah said. "Rachmiel had no choice in the matter. They have to work together for the next few decades. We hope."

"I don't know the whole story," Rachmiel said. "I can't judge him."

The green eyes flashed. "God judged. He put Tabris on probation."

"Not damnation."

Zohar folded his arms. "I just wonder what horrible thing the kid did to deserve it."

Both Voriah and Rachmiel started. "What?"

Zohar shook his head. "There can't be any other reason he didn't get put in Hell. I've seen a lot of kids come through here, and I talk to the guardians of other schools. Without getting into specifics, yes, I've seen very young humans do things that deserve death. Would I mete it out on my own? No. But I could understand why Tabris might have been pardoned if there were extenuating circumstances."

Rachmiel wrapped his arms around himself. "Wow. That would make it both better and worse."

Voriah whistled low. "Elizabeth would be safe as long as she was innocent. Afterward, well, you call in backup."

Rachmiel's wings slumped. "I can't believe that. Tabris hasn't spoken about Sebastian at all, but he'd have mentioned if the kid had done something that evil."

Zohar chuckled. "You couldn't believe ill of anyone. Your name means *Compassion*."

Rachmiel rolled his eyes. "Ask Voriah what Raguel had to do to get me to accept him."

Looking disturbed, Voriah nodded.

The complicated projection settled on Zohar for several seconds before he absorbed all the information. Then he shrugged. "You'd see his good side anyhow. Last year you were trying to explain how Lucifer must have felt before he fell."

"I never said he was justified, just that he might have thought he had a case." Rachmiel bit his lip. "I don't think Tabris is justified either. He's in trouble. But that's why he needs our help."

"Because you certainly don't need his."

Rachmiel pivoted, glaring. Zohar recoiled, offered an apology, and left.

Voriah moved closer. His heartbeat steadied Rachmiel, who folded his arms. Rachmiel said, "Am I Tabris's guardian too?"

Voriah smirked, as though to say, *You've become his defender.*

"I'm sure he has a reason, if only he'd tell us." Rachmiel studied Elizabeth, then shuddered as if cold.

Voriah said, "Don't think about it."

"I can't help it."

"Well, then tell me."

Rachmiel leaned further over the building's edge and extended his heart to touch Elizabeth, and then, calmer, said, "I can't imagine—but I guess I *can* imagine it—him sitting on the edge of that child's bed one night and plotting to kill him. I can't conceive of him premeditating the act, saying, *this is how I'll do it.* God would have removed him once he decided."

For the first time, the fourth angel spread his wings and moved closer. "Wouldn't that compromise his free will?"

"Only if God removed him before the decision. The free will is in the decision, the way attempted murder and actual murder are the same." Rachmiel squinted. "If he'd decided in advance, God might have removed him from the situation until he had a better grip."

The dusky angel came very close and pitched his voice so they couldn't be overheard. "Raguel came to my household also."

Curiosity flooded him. Rachmiel leaned forward. Voriah moved nearer too.

The other angel said, "I don't believe for a second the kid did something evil. Raguel's having meetings with all the local guardians, he and the rest of the Seven. They're talking about what happened and how we can take steps to prevent a repeat of Tabris. From what they said, my guess is Tabris had no plan."

Voriah projected what a human would express as a gasp. "Thought and action were simultaneous? No time for second thoughts?"

"That's what I understood. That's why Raguel got involved." The other angel glanced at Tabris. "I'm betting he acted on impulse, but he never stopped loving God. No one contests that he was wrong. He looks to me like he was ready to throw himself into Hell."

Rachmiel took his gaze off Elizabeth and glanced at Tabris instead, who raised his head and returned the look. Rachmiel squinted and pointed at the girl. Tabris turned back to her.

Voriah laughed out loud. "That'll show him!"

"I didn't mean to be funny. He should be watching her."

The dusk-colored angel frowned. "He doesn't project anything, does he? I'd have expected him to radiate laughter or hurt, but I didn't read a thing."

"He just doesn't," said Voriah.

"I haven't seen him laugh," added Rachmiel.

The other angel settled on the edge, his feet hanging free against the wall. "But he knew the instant you focused on him. He must be one raw nerve."

"He spent last night outside alone." Rachmiel shook his head. "I'd have gone to him, but I wasn't sure if he wanted it. He's got to be reeling."

Tabris's power surrounded Elizabeth as she jumped for the ball and came inches away from crashing into another player. He sent Tabris his approval, then hesitated and glanced at the dusk-colored angel.

The other angel said, "Raguel advised us not to let pressure build up. That we needed to rely on each other."

Rachmiel hummed. "Maybe I should try talking to him, then, rather than waiting." He looked into the schoolyard at the only angel whose wings were two colors. "If I start by talking about Elizabeth, I might get him warmed up."

Voriah sent a negation. "Remember that look he gave us the night he arrived, when he realized we'd been talking about him?"

Rachmiel winced.

The other angel said, "It must sting to be the object of that much attention. How would you feel?"

Rachmiel kept his heart trained on Elizabeth but closed his eyes, and he tried to imagine the shame of having committed a capital crime, then the unease of knowing everyone else knew exactly what he'd done. It felt like heat, like a spotlight. For a moment, he cringed with the same feeling that drove Adam to find cover in the garden.

"Whoa, Rock," Voriah whispered. "Tone it down."

The dusky angel said, "Pray for him. I think that's all any of us can do right now."

Rachmiel bit his lip. "I want to talk to him."

The other angel shook his head. "Just let him know you're available. When he's ready, he'll talk."

Voriah snickered.

Rachmiel huffed, but the other angel projected confusion. Voriah said, "We'll be waiting a long time if we wait for him to open up on his own."

In the yard beneath, Tabris leaned against a fence, his eyes downcast, his attention centered on Elizabeth and not on the discussion of him that occupied an entire schoolyard full of angels after lunch.

Five

After two weeks, Josai'el appeared in Elizabeth's bedroom as Rachmiel settled her dreams. "Come downstairs. We're having a night off."

Rachmiel pulled Tabris with him so Tabris wouldn't take off the instant he could, by now a nightly ritual. A night off meant—well, a night off. After over a dozen days of mutual tension, they each needed it.

Once all eight of the household angels arrived, Josai'el asked Tabris, "Has Rachmiel explained?" Rachmiel flushed, and she laughed. "Don't worry, I'll do it. Once every few weeks, we'll leave the house and have a break. All but one of us will go outside and we'll have some activity for the night, like a picnic. The last one remains here on duty."

Tabris looked uneasy, and Rachmiel remembered the first time he'd heard of this: he hadn't wanted to leave Elizabeth either. But Tabris only said, "Is that safe?"

Rachmiel tensed. As if they'd do something that wasn't?

Josia'el nodded. "Whomever stays behind places a Guard on the structure of the house. We can be recalled instantly."

Tabris frowned. "A Guard that size wouldn't be able to repel demons acting in force. Whoever stays behind could be overwhelmed."

"It hasn't happened yet." Katra'il sat on an end-table, her gold eyes sharp. "Didn't your other household do this?"

Tabris flinched. "No."

"I thought it strange too, when I arrived," said Hadriel. "The other guardians in Connie's family never left their charges, but it really does help to get out of the house as a group."

Rachmiel wished he could read the feelings behind Tabris's expressionless eyes.

Katra'il said, "Whose turn is it to stay behind?"

Oh, no. Of all the lousy timing. Rachmiel sighed. "It's—"

"I'm staying," said Miriael.

Before Rachmiel could protest, Miriael stood, his eyes glinting like silver. Forceful pressure from the other angel's heart: not a compulsion, but assurance. "You go. Have a good time. You'll have a turn soon enough."

"Wait." Tabris sounded uncertain, and Rachmiel wondered if he realized what Miriael had just done. "I can't exceed two miles."

Josai'el shrugged. "We'll stay close. Whenever Connie or Bridget was pregnant we had this difficulty, but it's easy enough to handle."

When Tabris didn't object again, Josai'el flashed seven of them a mile away, to a slope bordered by trees. Katra'il called a guitar to her hands and strummed the opening of Fleetwood Mac's "Big Love," but when Voriah tossed a fistful of leaves at her, she laughed and altered the strings so she could play Spanish guitar. Hadriel settled beneath a tree with a book.

Voriah sat beside Rachmiel. "Hey, we've got seven players! Who wants to play Settlers of the Cosmic Civilization?"

Mithra said, "Only if we can use all thirty-eight expansion sets."

Voriah gave him a thumbs up. "I'm in! I'll start setting it up, and by the time we get it all laid out, we'll have to box it up again."

Tabris was staring. Rachmiel said, "Don't worry. They're joking." He flung his arms behind his head and lay looking into the sky. "Guess how long it's been since my last nap?"

"At least eleven years?" said Josai'el.

Voriah gasped. "You'd use a night off to sleep? That's nuts!"

"And a board game with thirty-eight expansion sets—that's perfectly sane."

Tabris walked away from them, settling at the top of the hill to stare into the darkness of the trees on the next. Rachmiel shifted onto his side to focus on the isolated copse, its darkness standing apart from the star-bright night they'd chosen for their leisure time.

Tabris tucked his knees to his chest, his wings up. Quiet like the trees. Rachmiel said, "Tabris? What do you think of Elizabeth?"

"She's very cute. You've done a good job."

Rachmiel waited for more, but nothing came, and he lay still in the hope that everyone else would pretend that exchange hadn't just happened. Voriah went back to teasing Mithra about board games, and Rachmiel waited for his racing heart to calm.

You tried, said God to Rachmiel.

It was a dumb move, Rachmiel prayed back. *Is he offended?*

God indicated no.

So much for creating an opening. He'd be better off waiting for one.

Josai'el called, "Tabris, you can come back. They're not really going to rope you into a seven-player game of whatever it is."

Forcing a smile, Tabris returned. Although he'd seemed thoughtful from a distance, he once again wore that alertness which characterized his expression, his mahogany eyes blending with the night.

Mithra looked up. "Has that demon bothered you again?"

"Once. I sent him away."

Mithra's mouth twitched. "I hate meeting ex-friends. It's such a senseless loss, like you know they were smarter than that."

Tabris looked back at the cluster of trees. "Yeah. I think that a lot."

Rachmiel said, "He was your friend?"

"Before the Winnowing."

Said with no inflection. Cold.

Voriah said, "I was lucky. None of my close friends fell."

"It's awful," said Mithra. "Their whole personality changed. They hate themselves, hate each other, hate that dandelion, hate everything. They change their names and eventually they're unrecognizable except when remnants of their old personalities come back up, and then it's just nauseating because you remember how they were created."

The whole time Mithra spoke, Rachmiel sensed a shadow overstealing his heart, and he shifted to relieve the pressure until he realized the feeling wasn't his own. He glanced at Tabris to find him utterly still, as though he'd looked into a mirror and seen only a skull.

Rachmiel said, "Is that what it's like for you?"

Tabris's wings flared. "What?"

"About your former friend."

"Oh." Tabris looked aside. "Um—I guess."

Rachmiel leaned forward. "What was he like? Does he follow you a lot?" His heart thrummed—what if God had given him an opening here? "What's his name?"

Tabris clutched the dead grass. "I— It's not like I have that much contact with him. I'm not—"

"Rachmiel!" Josai'el's voice was as stern as a rap with a ruler. "Ease up on him. This isn't an interrogation."

"I'm sorry." Rachmiel felt himself radiate awkwardness. There had to be something identifiable in Tabris, some emotion he could latch onto and maybe begin understanding him. They'd been together two weeks and his emotions were still locked down. "I didn't mean to pry."

Tabris tucked up his knees, and his eyes went cold. "No, go right ahead."

As Rachmiel watched, Tabris exerted control like iron, and in the next moment it was just like talking to a suit of armor long after the knight that had worn it had gone home. No emotions, no depth—just Tabris.

"He changed his name from Zeffar," Tabris said, "but for now he calls himself Unbridled. He left me alone before now, but recently he's made it clear he wants my damnation. He insisted that God do exactly that at my trial."

Like a shadow, Tabris absorbed the starlight and let escape only faint points. "Have I answered your questions sufficiently?"

Katra'il's fingers had slowed on her guitar, and Hadriel had looked up from his book. Trembling, Rachmiel shook his head.

The shell of a spirit where Tabris sat gave off a resonance almost demonic in its emptiness. "You can ask anything you want."

He gave Rachmiel a smile, but Rachmiel could feel nothing behind it. Not anger, but certainly not friendship.

Mithra sounded unconcerned. "Well, we won't let him have you. If he keeps hassling you, I've got your back."

Voriah said, "He's got your back *and* thirty-eight expansion sets."

The conversation went forward, but Tabris stayed silent, and Rachmiel just felt mortified. Eventually, he walked away from the group and fingered a stripped tree branch. Tabris still sat as if he didn't belong to such a frivolous gathering, and all together they looked like a double exposure, a family picnic superimposed over a war memorial.

Rachmiel climbed the tree, following his hands as they grasped higher, filling his fingers with the branches and leaves until he'd reached the crown. There he looked at the stars as they showered old light onto the planet, light shed hundreds of years ago and unrefracted until this moment; and now that it had struck, the Earth would never be exactly the same.

The breeze caressed the withered leaves, and Rachmiel let it rock him as well, like a kitten stroked by the fingers of an old, old woman. He closed his eyes, drew up his wings, and let the hands of God draw the tension from his tired spirit. His worries eased as he settled along a branch.

When the battle cry sounded, he started: Miriael's soul, summoning help. He'd hardly moved before he realized Tabris had shot toward the house, Mithra in his wake.

Tabris flashed into the living room with his sword drawn. His wings spread, displaying both the jade outer feathers and the inner mahogany ones.

Mithra joined him. "Where to?"

Miriael said, "Check the family."

Tabris coursed over the walls, then checked Elizabeth's bedroom. Mithra checked the others. They both returned to Miriael.

"We're uncompromised," said Tabris.

Miriael's voice trembled with strain. "I can't keep the Guard together."

Mithra said to Tabris, "Let's take it outside."

The pair flashed outside the Guard, slicing into the throng gnawing at the spiritual shell. Tabris changed his weapon to a broadsword and unleashed a mad energy into the demons. Beside him, Mithra used a sword and shield, and together they carved apart the demonic hoard that clung like cockroaches to a bag of sugar.

Josai'el and Katra'il joined them, and the tide turned. The demons fled, and Josai'el shot through the property to flush out any stragglers. She caught two.

Mithra high-fived Tabris. "We're done. Let's go."

Katra'il and Mithra vanished. Josai'el had already gone. Tabris looked at the sky instead. It wasn't a hard decision, when he thought about it. Either go back to a group of angels that didn't want him, or go inside so there would be only one.

Miriael projected relief when Tabris returned. "I told Josai'el the Guard held. You can go back."

"I'd rather not," said Tabris.

Miriael's gratitude changed to concern.

Tabris smiled, a successful venture.

Miriael took a seat. "I was shaken before, but Hadriel shot me full of energy, and I'm okay again. I know you didn't think it safe, but we're secure."

Tabris studied Miriael, unable to detect sarcasm or revulsion. Yes, Miriael was trying to get rid of him, but not for the obvious reason. He could deal with that.

Miriael's aura turned curious.

Tabris said, "It should have been Rachmiel's turn to stand guard."

Miriael shrugged. "He needed the time off more than I did."

"But it was his turn?"

Miriael opened his hands. "I thought he might want to spend time with you to get to know you better."

Now why would Miriael think that? Perhaps because Rachmiel's curiosity at times became a flavor you could drink out of the air, and that was with Rachmiel attempting to hide it. Small wonder he'd blurted out a hundred questions about Zeffar.

"I watched you fighting. You're powerful."

Tabris inclined his head. "Thanks."

Miriael said, "I was wondering...would you mind if we sparred?"

Tabris studied him. While he guessed a few million angels wouldn't mind running him through with a sword, Miriael didn't appear angry as much as eager.

"No one else enjoys a good fight." Miriael looked up, blue eyes bright. "Mithra spars, but he keeps himself in check. I want to go all out, as if I'm defending Kyle's life." Tabris caught Miriael's flinch, but before he could feel hurt, Miriael had already corrected with, "Or God's throne. It's been years. Demons in these parts flash in and out and they're gone. Two angels draw swords and they run away."

Tabris tried not to sound stung. "They fought me."

Miriael's eyes glinted. "You're new. They wanted to test you."

They wouldn't be the only ones. "Did I pass?"

"I'm going to hazard a yes." Miriael laughed. "You gave a few of them blows they're going to remember for weeks."

Tabris looked at his hands.

"Well?" Miriael came closer. "Would you spar with me?"

"Now?"

Miriael brightened.

Tabris produced a sword, lighter and shorter than what he'd used outside.

"No." Miriael folded his arms. "Absolutely not. All out. As if you're battling Satan himself."

Tabris frowned "And when we knock one another uncon-scious—?"

"Josai'el will return the instant she feels the Guard go down, and after a display like that, the local demons won't want anything to do with either of us."

Miriael grinned as Tabris's sword changed, and he summoned his own. They spread their wings. Miriael crouched.

"Ready?" said Tabris.

Miriael sprang, and they clashed a few times before Tabris pulled back. "You weren't kidding!"

"To the death!" said Miriael.

This time Tabris was prepared. They struck and parried, flashing around the living room and using the structure of the house to defend against each other. Tabris had the greater strength, so Miriael adjusted his technique to rely on his agility. Even as they fought, Tabris and Miriael manipulated their armor and weapons to compensate for one another's skills. For fifteen minutes, neither scored a hit.

When Tabris drove Miriael to flash aside, he flashed a fraction of a second before the other angel moved, arriving in the same place at the same time, knocking Miriael to the ground. He brought up his sword to slash at his neck, then hesitated. Miriael twisted face-up and thrust his sword into Tabris's stomach.

"Game," Tabris called. Miriael pulled out the sword, glowing enough to see where he'd struck, and whistled.

While the wound closed, Tabris stretched. "You're good. You've trained a lot."

"I spent five hundred years under Michael before transferring to a special ops team." Miriael examined his sword, then dispersed it back into his soul. "You get good in a hurry. But you're no pushover either. A couple of times I thought you had me."

The spiritual blood evaporated off Tabris's clothes, and the fabric mended beneath his fingers. Angels heal from the inside out, and the wound had been painless because Miriael had wanted to cause only temporary damage, not to inflict suffering.

His wound gone, Tabris dropped to the couch, spreading his wings with a sigh. "It was a long time for me too, since the last hard workout. I'd forgotten the fun."

Miriael's armor changed back to workout pants and a t-shirt. "You'll be a great guardian for Elizabeth."

"Thanks."

"Don't be sarcastic," Miriael said, and Tabris clamped back the emotions he hadn't realized he was emanating. "You've got reflexes, vigilance, energy, all the things that make a good soldier *and* a good guardian. Rachmiel does an amazing job keeping her soul in order, but he doesn't always fight. I've seen him draw his sword once in ten years."

Once? Oh, of course. Tabris shuddered. In that case, he'd seen it too.

Miriael continued, "His line of defense is in her psyche, but I'm guessing you won't even let the bad guys near."

Tabris closed his eyes and nodded.

He felt Miriael test and strengthen the Guard around the house, then reach for Kyle's soul. Across the room, the angel relaxed. All was well.

By reflex he extended his soul toward Elizabeth to do the same, but then he flashed to her instead. Asleep. Dreaming of swords. He fought a smile and returned to Miriael.

Rather than tired, Miriael looked invigorated. He was running his fingers through his feathers, straightening them.

Tabris said, "Are you a flier?"

Miriael flexed his wings. "Someone told me that's what these are for."

"You know what I mean. There are fliers and there are non-fliers. Are you a flier?"

Miriael grinned. "I suppose I'm not, then."

"Oh." Now that would have been fun: combine flying and combat and he'd be all set for entertainment until Elizabeth or Kyle left home.

Miriael said, "You're a flier?"

Tabris nodded. "On cold nights, when the stars are out and the wind is brutal? Now that's fun."

Miriael gestured to the outside. "Go!" When Tabris hesitated, he said, "It's a night off, and you're supposed to have fun."

Tabris didn't need another invitation. Away he flashed.

He'd have shot straight up to the mesosphere if only he weren't bound to Elizabeth. Instead, he did his best to soar within the limits, closing his eyes in an attempt to pretend he was somewhere else.

Skies feel as different to angels as landscapes feel to humans. Some skies are turbulent, some placid, some smooth and others grainy, and angelic spirits are fine enough to detect the most subtle changes. Here the sky felt as smooth as Jell-O, silken against Tabris's face and cold like water to a slow swimmer. Yuck. This type of air would be great for gliding and reflecting, but it served only poorly for what Tabris craved: rugged, almost painful. The richness of this air would drag a speeding angel.

During his time in the suburbs, Tabris had taken advantage of any rare occasion when he could leave Sebastian to stretch his wings in the polluted air of Los Angeles, so cluttered and foreign he rejoiced not to breathe. But that tainted haze had been a delight for diving since an angel can slide along threads of carbon monoxide as they rise into the higher levels of the atmosphere.

Three time zones distant from Los Angeles, much further than two miles from a polluted city, Tabris found himself trapped in thick air like a world-champion skier dealing with granular wet snow.

He cupped his wings and landed by the pond, resigned to boring flight until Elizabeth's bond to him had aged enough to leave here.

Here. Where was *here*, anyway? In so many respects it didn't matter, but he might as well find out. Tabris pressed his palms to the ground and asked the Earth where he was. The fallen planet gave Tabris a reluctant answer, but even that flooded Tabris with information knowing neither name nor border, but rather what neighbored what and relative distances. It functioned better than a push-pin on a map. Tabris was in the northwestern part of Chittenden County, Vermont, north of Burlington and south of St. Albans.

The land continued talking to him as though it could read his soul in return and had found a peer. He learned of the animals readying for hibernation belowground, the dead things decomposing in the brush, the multicolored leaves already beginning to rot.

Tabris leaped off the ground, feeling like a grandmother who asked what her granddaughter learned at school that day and got treated to a dirty joke. His mind reeled from the broken contact, but he knew nature had turned perverse, and the next information would have been about how bacteria decompose a body, and the direction and condition of the newly-dead.

No. Little fragile bodies, gone still with the life snuffed out. No. He fled back to Rachmiel.

Rachmiel saw rather than felt Tabris's return. He drew back behind Hadriel, who was reading aloud.

Josai'el waited for a pause, then said, "I was wondering where you'd gone."

"I stayed with Miriael." Tabris settled himself. "The demons didn't return."

Rachmiel watched over Hadriel's shoulder, fixated on the angel as though he had a camera and an almost-focused view of a rare bird.

"I'm sorry we made you uncomfortable before," said Mithra.

That was braver than Rachmiel would have been, but Tabris only said, "Don't worry about it. I'm sure you didn't intend any harm."

The edge on those words could have split a hair. Rachmiel opened wide to catch any echoes of emotion, to test whether tension had transformed into anger.

Tabris looked at him, so Rachmiel said, "How's Elizabeth?"

"Sleeping."

Rachmiel wondered if his own discomfort could cast Tabris's words in a different light than Tabris intended. If that was true, would it be wrong to take note of which things Tabris tried to hide? And then...what were those things?

Katra'il grabbed Rachmiel by the hand and forcibly flashed him to a stand of trees that had begun picking up dawn on their crowns. She glared into his eyes. "You're radiating curiosity."

Rachmiel shook his head.

"Keep it under control," she whispered, her golden hair framing her round face.

She returned without him, and he stayed on the hill without looking again at Tabris. He pulled his wings closer and knelt on the ground, then extended his heart to God.

The returning hold engulfed Rachmiel. He fell forward, his body curled, hands flat on the ground beneath his shoulders, wings spread over his head: the angelic worship posture. He quieted immediately, and the awe of being touched by God melted under reassurance of a love stronger than time.

God prompted Rachmiel to speak. Sitting up, Rachmiel opened his heart so the love poured out, an oblation of spiritual wine on an altar that was the whole of creation. He revealed his soul to God like a child showing his mother a shoebox of his priceless treasures: a dragonfly body and baseball cards and small red trucks and plastic jewelry that glittered. Rachmiel opened all the boxes in his soul, gave God every thought and rededicated his every deed.

God thanked him, and Rachmiel thrilled. The presence receded, but Rachmiel didn't scramble to keep hold of the ungraspable. The world burst with glory, and he could view it with eyes like diamonds. He hungered in that moment to take the diamonds from his sight and hold them for Elizabeth to gaze through, then to hold her hand while she got her first glimpses of everything God had done for them.

He flashed to Elizabeth's bedside and beamed just like the sun edging into her room.

"Wake up, Sleepyhead," he whispered as the other angels returned. "Wake up. See what God's done for you today!"

Six

Tabris found inspiration in camaraderie, but not the type he would have bet Josai'el wanted him to. The best inspiration had been Rachmiel's soul like a radar dish scanning for any emotion he allowed to escape.

Every morning, they gathered to say a prayer Tabris had said every morning of Sebastian's life, something he'd learned only as *the guardian prayer*, the prayer of an angel over his charge. He'd said the words with them. Words were easy, but afterward he wondered which of the two he'd prayed for.

The hardest part was the small talk; he etched the smile onto his face, nodded at the end of every phrase, and in turn watched each angel who spoke. They responded well to this. See? He'd just needed to relax.

It worked. The more he acted what they considered "normal," the more they acted normal themselves. In time, they might even forget they were associating with a near-demon.

Empowered by success, Tabris concentrated his efforts on Rachmiel, whose curiosity was stifling. So in an effort to get Rachmiel to back off, he asked for help getting to know the family members.

Rachmiel nearly exploded: of course Tabris needed more than the most basic introductions, and his eagerness flooded Tabris like a tide.

Tabris had needed to get around to that anyway. In his mind, the family was little more than names: two parents, a grandmother, and three brothers in orbit around Elizabeth. But to be honest, in order to help her, he needed to know what resources he had on hand, and the best resources were her family.

With Rachmiel looking just like Sebastian had on Christmas morning, Tabris said, "Let's talk to Miriael first."

Two seconds later, they were in front of Miriael. He was the only Archangel of the household guardians, but despite that, Tabris felt most comfortable around him.

When Miriael described his charge Kyle, he glowed. At fourteen years old, Kyle loved sports and competitive gaming. He enjoyed logical challenges that could engage his mind's engines until he pronounced the problem solved. He could become so intent on these challenges that, Miriael said with a laugh, he'd become just as absorbed and work together with Kyle to piece together an answer. With one hand on the boy the entire time, he seemed to be marking his heart's property. Tabris tried to avoid seeing the hand or the pride, instead focusing on whatever Miriael mentioned: the quick eyes or the strong arms, the hunger for mastery that imbued his spirit.

Kyle's roommate was the oldest son Martin, guarded by Katra'il. She spoke with deliberate restraint about Martin as a responsible boy who liked to read and who loved the sciences and computers. At sixteen, the boy was already thinking about college, and Katra'il could have talked for hours about locations and majors without ever touching on what really mattered: the sharpness of Kyle's mind or the way he focused his efforts.

Voriah's charge Alan was thirteen, and that was uncomfortable because Alan was only a year older than Sebastian. Tabris did his best to look impassive and ask about details. Details would distinguish the boys, and then he wouldn't have to think "Sebastian should be doing this next year" or "Now Sebastian won't ever get to experience that." Full of his usual energy, Voriah helped Tabris without realizing it, bounding from topic to topic as if trying to cover the entirety of a person in ten minutes. Alan had become a household mediator, always on everyone's side, well-respected by adults, not prominent in any one area but efficient in all. Of the three boys, Alan was quietest, an unlikely complement to such an angel as Voriah.

But Alan was hard to look at, so hard when he seemed so much like another boy, and Tabris asked Rachmiel to postpone the adults' introductions. Although disappointed, Rachmiel agreed.

Tabris had forced a few expected polite remarks and questions about each of the boys. During the introductions, they'd transformed from brothers with identical haircuts to three individuals with strengths, faults, and quirks. But then Tabris considered their guardians...Miriael in particular, with fire in his eyes as he equated protecting Kyle to defending God's throne. If angels could die, these angels would be willing

43

to give their lives in the service. All three of the boys' angels emanated love and pride that left Tabris breathless. Rachmiel felt the same about Elizabeth, a warmth that surrounded every movement as he followed her days. When Tabris talked to Josai'el, Hadriel and Mithra, no doubt they'd feel the same.

And then there was himself. A month ago, had he looked and sounded just like them?

Unanswerable questions. Except for the fact that of course they could be answered: he'd interacted with other guardians every single day of Sebastian's life, particularly the guardians of Sebastian's parents. He could have sought them out and asked them. No doubt they'd been interrogated in the aftermath of the death, either by Raguel or a team of Archangels asking over and over again: what was Tabris like with Sebastian? Did he even like the kid? Was he any good as a guardian?

And what on earth would they have answered?

He would defend Elizabeth with all his strength: absolutely. But Sebastian...

Rachmiel always moved nearer to him when his thoughts went down those paths, and that spawned another phase of action: small talk. The more he asked Rachmiel about inane things, the less Rachmiel felt curious. The fits of needing-to-know still overtook him, but not as often, and not to the same degree. The curiosity eased even though Tabris never supplied the answers to the questions Rachmiel might have asked on his own—questions that would have required a look through the pages of his soul. Instead, with the angelic equivalent of discussing the weather, Tabris discovered his own version of "supply and demand." If he spoke at all, Rachmiel felt satisfied with the little information he had, and that made living together a lot easier.

The schoolyard scene was more uncomfortable than home, even though only a few weeks ago he and Sebastian had been very much a part of the play and the socializing. Elizabeth was still part of the social-izing. Therein lay the problem.

A hundred children of assorted ages ran about, shouting to one another, pushing the limits of the schoolyard rules. Older girls clustered in groups near the fence; younger girls played jump rope by the building or played tag with the boys. Every section of the wall had been claimed for wall-ball, neatly divided by the classroom windows. Park benches sliced the yard into two sections, the larger one for running games and the smaller for hopscotch, marbles, or just talking.

Tabris found his place in the melee, his consciousness trained on Elizabeth at all times so that it might have been only him and her in the playground. Wearing a deep silence, he walked past other angels. He had nothing to say to them. Like angry suns the other angels radiated—most of them. Indignation boiled in their hearts, and he guessed half of them wanted him gone. Gone back to Heaven to sit out the rest of eternity, or if he absolutely must be on Earth, assigned to an inventory of dandelions at a garbage dump. Not near their kids. Not near anyone's.

But maybe anger was just the loudest emotion. Maybe sometimes he was right when in an unguarded moment he caught an angel studying him with sadness.

Elizabeth stumbled while she played hopscotch, and Rachmiel steadied her. Tabris reached out too but then hesitated, and several angels pivoted at his movement. He forced himself to stand still, as if he hadn't moved and hadn't noticed their reaction.

This is eerie, he thought, knowing even as he did so that *eerie* wasn't the right word, but unwilling to find the exact one because he knew what it was.

Rachmiel turned to him, refracting the sunlight through his orange eyes. It was a projection that didn't involve his emotions at all. "This will be one of the last warm days before winter sets in for good."

Winter had set in for Tabris six weeks ago. "I like the snow," was all he said.

Rachmiel inhaled, stretching his feathers. "Cold is invigorating, but I like it this way. Actually, so does she." He smiled at Elizabeth, waiting for her turn at the hopscotch grid. "The Earth is alive now. I mean," he added with a laugh, "it'll be alive then too, but so much will be in hibernation. Hibernation is amazing. God is amazing." He grinned. "But the creatures that are up and about interest me more than sleeping ones."

Tabris clamped down on the parts of his heart that wanted to argue. He'd always loved the lifeless cold, most of all the near-nothing of deep space. He'd flown through that eternal night between stars, isolated except for his soul's constant touch with God, and in those times he'd been happy. Months spent near absolute zero until the numbness made his wings ache, and then he'd flashed back to his home in Heaven—a log cabin in the mountains—and wrapped himself in his wings before the fire until the love of God and the warmth of his native country restored feeling to his wings and fingers.

45

Prying himself back from his thoughts, Tabris studied Elizabeth. There was no cold aspect to her, nothing isolated, nothing in need of space's distances. She needed people—as did Rachmiel. Rachmiel instinctively reflected and expressed the feelings of his companions. He comforted by sharing the problem. No doubt Elizabeth could do the same.

Tabris rose into the air and scanned the schoolyard until he found what he knew had to be nearby: every schoolyard had one. After a moment he nodded, saying, "Elizabeth?" and focused on his target.

Elizabeth looked up from hopscotch to scan the yard until her eyes fell on the same thing: a girl alone on a park bench, watching the other kids. To Tabris, the girl radiated loneliness.

Elizabeth turned back to the grid chalked on the ground, and Tabris again brought up that girl in her mind.

Tabris could tell when Rachmiel saw her too when he felt him project how it would feel to be a misfit.

Tabris brought Rachmiel's feelings to the forefront of Elizabeth's mind. Not everyone would respond without a good push, but Elizabeth was innocent and the reaction innate; the knowledge of the need might be all the motivation she required.

Elizabeth took her turn, and Tabris again put pressure on her heart: a lone figure on a park bench. Isolation. Need.

Fidgeting, Elizabeth looked at the girl. Rachmiel had flown behind Tabris and gripped his shoulders, but Tabris only looked between Elizabeth and the other girl. And when he looked at the bench this time, he saw that girl's guardian staring back: protective. Mistrustful.

An arrow of hurt shot through him, and it went from his heart into Elizabeth, who in an untutored imitation of her first guardian was just imagining how it felt to be all alone in a schoolyard full of people. She winced, then left her friends. While Rachmiel followed, she crossed the ground to the benches and introduced herself to the other girl.

Rachmiel glowed. Tabris flashed to the corner of the rooftop while Elizabeth made a lonely soul a little happier.

"I was surprised," Rachmiel said later.

"Why?" Voriah sat on the ridgepole of the Hayes house while the family slept. "He's still an angel."

"It was just so *nice*, that's all." Rachmiel sent a small stone skittering down the roof and summoned it back before it dropped off the edge. Beneath him, he could feel the rhythm of Elizabeth's breaths, the warmth of the blankets keeping her fully relaxed. When his heart reached for her, he relaxed too. "There wasn't any ceremony about it. He started looking and then sent Elizabeth to her. I was shocked. I still am."

Voriah's smile glimmered like stardust. "You must be. You're verbalizing everything just like him. Where is he now, by the way?"

"By the pond, like every night." Rachmiel shrugged. "Maybe he finds peace there, or maybe he's praying."

Voriah huffed, and Rachmiel felt his irritation as keenly as if he'd voiced it: Tabris certainly didn't pray with them.

"That's not funny," Rachmiel said. "He's been hurt by all that happened."

"Get your priorities straight," Voriah snapped. "He killed a boy. If he's hurt, then it's not undeserved."

Stung, Rachmiel tucked up his knees and stared at his feet.

"You can't turn it around like he's a victim." Voriah glared over the rooftop, jaw tight. Rachmiel didn't need to look at him, though: anger emanated from his heart like a pulse. "I would never kill Alan. Maybe not even if ordered by God—I can't imagine doing it. What kind of disordered mind would it take to kill your own charge?"

Rachmiel put his hands over his face. "That's why there have to be extenuating circumstances."

"So extenuating that he didn't speak a word in his own defense? This had all the elements of a soul-killing sin."

Rachmiel tensed.

"Want to run down the requirements?" Voriah's face had flushed. "A serious matter—check! Consent of the will—check! Sufficient reflection—"

Rachmiel straightened.

"No," said Voriah. "He must have planned it. Something can't have turned the world on its head and been accidental. I don't care what Raguel said. I can't fathom why God didn't drop him straight into Hell."

"Voriah!"

"You aren't angry?" Voriah said, eyes flaring.

At the moment, actually, Rachmiel was absorbing and amplifying Voriah's anger, but he choked it down and forced himself to focus on that feeling of Tabris standing beside him like a hollow space, the emotional vacuum of an angel in denial. That haunted feeling had never quite left his soul since then.

Rachmiel said, "I can't wish him damned."

"I don't wish it either," said Voriah, "but for the life of me, I can't understand why he's not."

There had to be something beyond this, more than the surface of the actions. "Tabris still loves Him."

"Loves him so much he doesn't pray anymore. Some love."

Rachmiel said, "He does pray. The morning offering—"

"Oh, my mistake. He says all the words. He's locked tighter than a drum, but he's saying everything he ought to in the script." Voriah huffed. "Well, if Tabris struck down his charge in 'love,' then God could well have returned the favor and dropped him into the pit."

Rachmiel shuddered. "And you're on his side?"

"No, Rock. Not once did I say he was right."

Rachmiel huddled over himself. This was wrong, all wrong. Angels in the same household shouldn't be taking sides or wishing each other gone. They already had an enemy.

His voice was low. "Tabris never said he was right, either."

"He'd be in Hell for certain if he had." Voriah paused. "Okay, so I'm on his side. I'm not in front of God's throne every night asking for his removal, and I'm not urging Alan to run away from home." Rachmiel chuckled, but Voriah said, "I'm not going to countermand God, so I'll give Tabris a chance."

Rachmiel let out a long breath. "That's all he asked."

"No, that's all *you're* asking. He never asked for anything." Voriah looked right at Rachmiel. "But I don't want you wandering around blind, assuming everything's peachy. What are you going to do if he tries the same thing with Elizabeth?"

"I doubt he would. He's tentative around her, as if she frightens him." Rachmiel closed his eyes. "That argues for it having been accidental."

"Not good enough." Voriah leaned closer. "You've got to find out exactly how it happened. No matter how much it hurts him, you can't just shove it to the back of the closet and hope things take care of themselves. For Elizabeth's sake, you've got to find out all the circumstances around Sebastian's death."

Rachmiel had gone cold, and he shook his head. "I can't do that! He could barely tell me Sebastian's age, let alone—"

"As her guardian, it's your right to know the details of any possible source of harm."

48

Rachmiel got to his feet and walked to the edge of the roof.

Voriah was standing too. "Do you want him to murder her? Are you sure you'd be able to stop him?"

"It's not one or the other, either I interrogate him or he pulls out the sword. I can't force him to open up."

"You most certainly can."

"You know I wouldn't." Rachmiel wrapped his arms around his stomach and looked down. Twenty feet below was the empty garden where Bridget had grown a thousand pounds of zucchini and a hundred tomatoes. "I don't want to know."

There. Right there, out in the open for Voriah to dissect.

When Voriah spoke again, he sounded gentler. "Hearing how it happened can't cause it."

"No, but if I learn why and how he did it, I might find myself in the same situation and do the same thing."

"I'd think the same would be truer for him." Voriah extended his wings, and Rachmiel flexed his back so they touched at the tips.

The breeze troubled the dead leaves still clinging to a few trees, and in their rustle Rachmiel heard Tabris: cut off from the Life-Giver and in the last stages of spiritual starvation before letting go and falling through the sky.

Voriah moved close. "Don't do that."

"I can't help it." Rachmiel closed his eyes. "I'm scared."

At his back, Voriah started praying, and Rachmiel opened his heart to join him. It was Voriah who compacted the whole situation into one thought, one need, and presented it before God. The response came like light through both angels, illuminating every corner of the translucent material that made their souls. The response wasn't a solution, but reassurance: God was near; God was helping; God loved them.

Voriah stepped aside so Rachmiel could spend the time with God, heart open and soul engaged.

Seven

About a week later after bedtime, Josai'el followed Bridget into her granddaughter's room to drop off her laundry. Tabris looked away from the window and said to Josai'el, "Would it be all right to do introductions tonight with the parents?"

Josai'el felt Rachmiel's heart jump from across the room, and she grinned, projecting to Tabris that of course it would be fine. Rachmiel kissed Elizabeth on the head and followed them into the hallway.

First they stopped by Andrew Hayes, Mithra's charge. He had a job in St. Albans that kept him busy even when he was at home, often working late in his basement office. Mithra added, a little grim, that much of this work served as an escape from his family. He had a presence that could quell conversation just by being in the room, but at other times he was surprisingly friendly. He'd cultivated for himself the idea that a good father was a stoic man and a reliable provider, and he'd achieved both, an accomplishment he sometimes regretted.

Josai'el watched the interaction between Mithra and Tabris, taking place over Andrew's desk, and remembered Mithra's arrival almost fifty years earlier: his exuberance, his energy. His delight with the potentiality of the new human he'd vowed to guard. Now as they spoke, she noted the dimness of his eyes, a certain character she had to call "careworn" because although Mithra had seen the heights of which his charge was capable, he'd also seen the depths. And for his part, Tabris avoided Mithra's gaze while he talked. Later, he avoided Hadriel's.

Hadriel guarded Connie, Elizabeth's mother, who had recently returned to work in order to defray college costs. Her part-time job allowed her to drive the children to and from school and to an assortment of after-school activities.

Tabris said, "She always seems tired."

"Most days, I'm pumping energy into her just to get her through to the evening," Hadriel said. Josai'el had already known this: Connie's job was boring, her children demanding, and her husband non-demonstrative. For that reason, Bridget shouldered much of the housework.

Tabris said, "That must be difficult."

Hadriel offered a dry chuckle. "At least she's too tired to sin."

Small consolation, Josai'el knew. Bridget had lived through years like that as well.

By then Bridget had gotten ready for bed, so Josai'el joined her in evening prayers and then turned to Tabris. "What do you want to know?"

Tabris looked Josai'el in the eyes, blank, and for a moment she wondered if he really wanted to learn about the people, or if he was feigning interest to get Rachmiel off his back. A glance at Rachmiel revealed nothing. She said, "Well, for starters, Bridget is seventy-two." Which also meant that as the most-experienced guardian in the family, Josai'el was the nominal head of household. "The house and property have been in her family ever since they came to the United States. She inherited it from her father."

"And it goes to Andrew next?"

"There will have to be some kind of split in the inheritance," Josai'el said. "Andrew has brothers, but Bridget will take care of it in the will. She sometimes resents having to share the house with Andrew's family, but she understands it's too big for her to maintain alone, and she couldn't bear to sell it."

Tabris frowned. "It's unusual to live your whole life in one place nowadays. Didn't she want to get away?"

"She's a homebody." Josai'el chuckled. "It's exotic enough to take long walks and appreciate that the air she's breathing has emigrated over the Canadian border."

Rachmiel laughed. Tabris wore a disbelieving look. "If you say so."

"That wouldn't work for you," she said, "but it works for her."

Tabris turned to Rachmiel. "Elizabeth needs to travel. A lot."

Rachmiel grinned at him, projecting that it was hardly decided. Tabris replied, "We'll see."

He'd relaxed, sitting on the foot of Bridget's bed. When Rachmiel shot Tabris a look, he returned a mischievous smile, and for a moment Josai'el wondered what Tabris had been like long ago, before God had given him a child to guard and Tabris had given it back.

Josai'el sat by Bridget's side. "I didn't know what Bridget's life would be like either. It's impossible to predict. But she's done quite a lot with it, and she's at peace."

Tabris said, "Given what you said about sharing the home, and how she's helping Connie, she must feel resentful sometimes."

"Yes, but when she tells me that, I pray with her to channel that energy toward growing more holy." She touched the woman's shoulder. "Sometimes the greatest holiness is doing the work right in front of you."

Rachmiel's wings raised. "Excuse me—she talks to you?"

Josai'el nodded.

"You never said she talks to you!"

Josai'el flushed. "It doesn't happen often."

Tabris said, "But ever? How does she know?"

"She doesn't know my name." Josai'el laughed. "But yes, when she was a child, someone told her to talk to me when she needed help, and sometimes she does. Then I pray with her, and I also know a little better what she wants or needs."

Rachmiel whistled. "Could you encourage her to tell the grandkids to do the same? Because I'd like Elizabeth to talk to me. And Tabris," he added. "How well can she hear you?"

"Probably no better than Elizabeth hears you." Josai'el sighed. "She did tell Andrew to talk to Mithra, but Andrew forgot all about it. Connie blew her off. She's never talked to the children about angels because she doesn't want to interfere with what their parents are teaching."

Rachmiel looked awed. "All the same— I'd be overwhelmed."

"I was, too, the first time." Josai'el ran her fingers over Bridget's hair. The woman had fallen asleep. "But that's all beside the point. Tabris wanted to get to know her."

"This is fine," said Tabris. "She sounds a lot like— Well, I know her better now. Thank you."

Now there was an opening large enough to drive a truck through. Josai'el said, "Did you have any questions?"

"Well—" Tabris checked Rachmiel, still enraptured by the idea of Elizabeth talking to them. "I guess. Does she ever— Did Bridget—" Josai'el caught the image of a brown-eyed boy, a sense of rising guilt. "Does it bother you when she sins?"

Behind Tabris, Rachmiel pulsed with curiosity. Josai'el felt it surge and worried that Tabris might lock down.

"Of course it does. I encourage her to look at her actions for what they are, and when she's no longer defensive, she will feel remorse, and I help her ask forgiveness."

Tabris was staring at his hands. "And— the first time— how did you handle it?"

"She was just a child." Josai'el looked Tabris in the eyes and tried to keep him from noticing Rachmiel's curiosity or sudden self-conscious-ness. Leaning closer, she dropped her voice to match Tabris's tone. "It was a shock, and I wasn't sure what to do. I worked with her until she felt remorse for what she'd done, and fortunately it was something she could un-do on her own."

Tabris studied his hands, staring hard. Josai'el caught it again: an image of the boy, a yearning.

Tabris said, "Theft?"

Josai'el chilled. The flatness of his words, but also the way he was fishing—and why would he want to know that except to think badly of an old woman? Or of her as a guardian, maybe trying to level the playing field? But on the other hand, the image of that boy kept presenting itself. That wasn't condemnation. It was a drowning man flailing for a handhold.

Josai'el said, "Yes."

"I think maybe the first one is theft for most of them."

Rachmiel excused himself from the room with, "I'm going to check on Elizabeth." And abruptly he left.

Tabris hadn't noticed (or if he had, he wasn't reacting to) what Rachmiel had just sacrificed. He'd given Tabris space. It was the biggest gift he could offer.

Tabris hadn't looked up. "It's difficult. That first serious sin."

Josai'el took his hand. "I remember. They recover from that, though. Far worse are the sins they love, when you try to talk to their conscience and it refuses to hear. Those are the sins that kill."

Tabris blinked hard, and Josai'el took his hand. "Sebastian never got to that point?"

He frowned. "No. But I'll have that to look forward to with Elizabeth, won't I? They say it happens to even the best guardians."

"Who says it?"

"The guardians at my old household." He looked around and noticed for the first time that Rachmiel had left. He stood. "Thank you for talking to me. I know Bridget better now."

53

And like that, he snapped shut. No projections, no stray emotions. Josai'el only said, "I look for excuses to talk about Bridget. Thank you for providing one."

Tabris attempted a smile, then left for the pond.

Reputation. Rachmiel had never thought about it before, but since Tabris's arrival, he'd noticed it constantly. Noticed it every time Elizabeth walked into a room and every guardian turned toward Tabris, wings flared and with their hands on their charges' shoulders.

Information spreads among angels like fire through dry brush. It's not that they gossip, but anything dominating the thoughts of a spirit can escape, projected without effort and concealed only with hard work. Work Rachmiel had begun doing more often nowadays, and which Tabris did as a matter of course.

In the seconds after Sebastian's death, every angel on Earth knew as much as the angels on the scene. The witnessing angels had fled for help: to Raguel, to Michael, to the archangels, to one another. One of Miriael's friends had appeared at the dinner table, grief streaming from him like water from a colander. He'd begged, "Please pray—now—" and with a sickening finality, the story had burst from him. Josai'el had shot out of the house to pass along the request even as Bridget passed the potatoes. Before the end of the trial, more angels had been praying for Tabris and Sebastian than either could have guessed.

But now, without immediate need for prayers, the other angels still remembered, and Rachmiel found himself the second ring around the bull's-eye, with Tabris in the red circle.

It wasn't just reputation, though. Tabris had something else, something Rachmiel had to call "presence." Because if everyone knew about Tabris then they also knew about Rachmiel, yet Rachmiel didn't find entire rooms of angels organizing their positions based on him. And when he wondered how that felt, he found himself burning inside, seeking out corners, either in the room or in his own mind.

Many had recognized Tabris even before his assignment to Sebastian. Mithra, who had known him since before the Winnowing, guessed Tabris had to be in the top percentile of his choir, in the top five hundred if not higher. His two-toned wings and dark, dark eyes gave him a peculiar presence, an appearance many angels found disconcerting. Most angels have wings of one solid color, so an angel with two-toned wings is like a human with one eye green and the other brown.

They knew him. But they didn't know him, didn't know the things Rachmiel knew. The few stray emotions that Tabris let slip, or the way Tabris looked sometimes at Elizabeth with a frustration he couldn't quite pin on her but didn't fit anywhere else. Or the way every morning, after the household guardians gathered to say the daily guardian angel prayer, Tabris slipped aside to recite it a second time.

As the family entered church one Sunday, Rachmiel picked up the emanations of the other guardians, and his stomach twisted: confusion, anger, questions about how Tabris dared show his face. Without thinking about it, Rachmiel found himself in front of the "loudest" of the protestors, the force of his will exerting pressure on the angel to get a handle on his own feelings.

The angel looked startled, and this time, Rachmiel got to experience the attention. But whether Tabris appreciated or resented it, he said nothing.

After getting home from church, Elizabeth and Alan stayed outside to play in the first snowfall; Andrew, Kyle and Martin shoveled the driveway. While Tabris lay in the snow with every feather spread, Rachmiel craned back his neck to watch the naïve sunlight get snared in the ice dotting the pine trees.

Voriah perched over the front door. "Tab? Are you making snow angels?"

"Kind of."

Rachmiel stayed beside Elizabeth while she dug lines in the ice crust atop the snow, shifting so her shadow didn't cover the designs. Shadows were funny. An angel's subtle body never throws a shadow, so it had startled Rachmiel when Elizabeth's did. A spirit that pure shouldn't block the light, and yet wherever she went, this dark Elizabeth followed, joined at the heels, sometimes longer or maybe in a pool beneath, easily ignored and not a part of her, but a part of her regardless.

Rachmiel looked at Tabris on the snow, and for a moment he imagined him as another being joined to a shadow, always at his heels on the side opposite the light, an image in reverse. A shadow with a name. A dead boy.

Elizabeth crunched her feet through the snow, punching out perfect prints, and instead of following her, Rachmiel leaned forward to look at Tabris's wings, then flashed up close. The outer feathers were jade, putting Rachmiel in mind of the forest during a wet summer. The inner feathers were more like redwood bark. He leaned in, noting the sudden change of brown feathers to green.

Tabris sat up, pulling in his wings.

"I'm sorry." Rachmiel's heart hammered. "I wanted to see the pattern."

Tabris tightened around himself. "Why?"

The curiosity flowed from Rachmiel. "I— You had them spread out. I wanted a closer look."

The two angels locked gazes for a long moment, and Rachmiel drew back. Brilliant move. Stop the church angels from making Tabris feel uncomfortable and then go ahead and do it himself.

Tabris finally tucked his knees up and relaxed his wings. "Fine. Inspect me." Then he called, "You too, Voriah!"

Voriah flashed down, shaken, and projected thanks.

Rachmiel moved to Tabris's back and touched the feathers, then preened where the barbs on several feather shafts had gotten detached. Relaxing, Rachmiel worked his fingers over the barbs and relocked them to remove the splits, rubbing some of the pinfeathers until the feathers became glossy. Each was a single color, but although the primary, secondary and tertiary feathers were green, the brown contour feathers at the top of his wings were packed tight enough to hide the flight feathers at their bases.

"You're color-coded," Voriah said.

Another angel's laughter stole over the trio, and all three jumped to their feet.

"You're a carnival freak to them!" called the demon who recently had called himself Unbridled, standing on the walkway. "They're inspecting you to gratify their lust for curiosity."

Rachmiel flushed, pulling his wings tighter.

"Get out," said Tabris. "In the name of the Holy—"

"But you can't say His name, can you?" Unbridled folded his arms and raised his chin. "You can invoke it, but He'd never allow His name to come out of your filthy mouth."

Rachmiel went cold.

And then Tabris said it.

Rachmiel thrilled even as Unbridled flinched, but then the demon turned to Voriah. "Weren't you the one who told everyone Tabris couldn't pray anymore because he couldn't say God's name?"

Rachmiel exclaimed "What?" even as Voriah said, "No, and you're a liar," and Tabris said, "Shut up. I told you to leave."

Unbridled strode toward Tabris. "You're going to be mine. By virtue of one flick of the wrist, you're mine." Tabris took a step backward, and Unbridled laughed. "Do you know it still hurts Sebastian? Every night, he gets shooting pains where you grabbed him. Where you broke him in pieces."

Rachmiel called his sword to his hand even as Voriah pushed Tabris behind him.

Amber eyes blazing, the demon snorted. "You can't fight all his battles."

"You're not all his battles." Rachmiel's sword burned brighter than the demon's eyes. "Leave."

Unbridled sneered for all of a second before Miriael hurtled down from the roof, shooting through the heart of the demon and blasting him apart. The instant Miriael charged, Voriah flashed Tabris into the house, but Rachmiel witnessed the whole thing. Horror and disgust burst out of his heart without being channeled in any direction, and he covered his face with his hands, struggling not to cry out.

Mithra cocooned Rachmiel in his wings and arms, and Miriael dropped his sword before rushing to join them.

"You just—"

"We needed to shut him up. I didn't want him baiting Tabris." Miriael's eyes were round, pouring concern into Rachmiel. "Don't let the demons talk. Don't ever let them talk or they'll wrap you around."

Mithra released his hold on Rachmiel. "Are you all right?"

Rachmiel turned to the snowy yard, covered with demon residue. And yet even now, it began to reconstitute. At some point it would all draw together in one place and retreat of its own accord. Maybe back to Hell. Maybe somewhere else.

"Could you—remove him?"

"I will." Mithra helped Rachmiel stand on his own, and Rachmiel wrapped his wings about himself. They'd gone butter-yellow. "Let's get you inside first."

Elizabeth went inside too, and Rachmiel wondered how much of his fear she'd picked up. She turned on the TV and dropped to the floor to watch, and Rachmiel leaned against her. Tabris had curled around himself on the couch.

When Tabris still hadn't moved after a few minutes, Rachmiel's heart ached. About to speak, his resolve broke, and he flashed over to the limp angel, wrapping his arms around him and projecting reassurance.

And from Tabris, a raw burning: the image of Sebastian hurting. Alone. Crying.

"He's a liar," Rachmiel whispered. "It's just a lie."

Miriael and Mithra returned, their hands and clothes stained with residue from both the demon and Rachmiel's emotional outburst. Miriael said, "Are you two okay?"

Smoothing the brown feathers, Rachmiel projected affirmative.

Mithra flashed outside, but Rachmiel thought he'd detected surprise about to pulse off him. Miriael checked on Elizabeth and then sat across the room.

"Thank you for getting rid of him."

Miriael huffed. "He's going to return. Pain never daunts those things."

Rachmiel kept preening Tabris. "But thank you. He didn't hurt you, did he?"

"No, but *you* nearly did!" Miriael laughed. "You exploded. Are you all right now?"

Rachmiel projected he was fine, realizing as he did so that he had pulled himself together for Tabris.

Tabris sat away from him. "He hurt you? I didn't realize that!"

Rachmiel demurred. "It was shock." And he reached for Tabris again.

Tabris withdrew, leaving Rachmiel unsteady. "You don't have to. I'm okay."

Rachmiel projected his emotions before he realized—a mixture of need, care, asking, and self-consciousness. He swallowed. "I just want you to feel better."

Tabris's eyes tightened. "I feel fine now. But you look rattled. Why don't you get a break?"

Rachmiel had just flooded over with emotion twice, and his control was shaken. He looked at Tabris's eyes to find him frigid.

He said, "You can leave Elizabeth with me."

Rachmiel shrank back from eyes fierce as ice picks.

Miriael touched Tabris's arm. "Hey, back off."

It would be the first time Rachmiel had left Elizabeth alone with Tabris. He looked over at her, watching the television.

Tabris said, "You're going to distress her if you stay. She picks up your feelings. You know that."

He might have been a demon himself, and Rachmiel couldn't get his balance: everything Tabris said was correct, but maybe his conclusions were faulty. Maybe he should leave. Maybe it would be better if he stayed. Confusion swirled around him like a dust cloud, and he grabbed for God's presence with his heart.

Tabris said, "What's the big deal? I can handle her."

Rachmiel waited until God prompted him that it was okay to leave. And then he flashed away.

Tabris dropped back onto the couch, glowering.

Miriael folded his arms. "You don't play fair."

"I wasn't aware this was a game."

Miriael shook his head. "Then don't play Rachmiel like it is."

Tabris watched Elizabeth. "He's trying too hard. I think he'd breathe for me if he could."

"He's got a vested interest in you." Miriael chuckled. "See that child? That's his pearl of great price. He'd give up everything for her."

Tabris murmured, "Yeah. I know the feeling."

A mindless series of colors paraded across the television, serving only to dispel spiritual peace. Tabris pulled his wings closer to his body, still straightened and glossy from Rachmiel's touch. "Do you hate me?"

"No."

Tabris flashed to the floor beside Elizabeth.

"Let me ask you, then," Miriael said. "Do you hate Rachmiel?"

"How could I?" Tabris followed the rug's pattern with his eyes, a swirling design where the inside of a curve suddenly became the outside if you traveled far enough. "He's a child of God in every sense you can imagine." He didn't need to look at Miriael to feel the projected challenge. "I can ask if you hate me because I'm not. I'm capable of being hated."

Miriael huffed. "God loves you too."

"Not like you. Not like Rachmiel."

"Would you want Him to? He loves us all differently."

"You know what I mean."

Tabris could feel Miriael studying him, but he kept tracing the pattern on the carpet with his eyes. Inside of the loop, curl, pivot, turn, and suddenly you're on the outside.

He projected a question, pushing it toward Miriael with force, a combined dare and concept all in one unvoiced nugget: *Trust?*

Miriael bowed and vanished.

59

Tabris scanned the living room, empty now except for Elizabeth and the flatscreen god of electrodes and plastic. Mithra was with Andrew, shoveling. Katra'il and Miriael were with Martin and Kyle, helping. Alan played outside with Voriah. Josai'el and Hadriel were in the kitchen with Connie and Bridget. And Rachmiel, of course, was gone.

He towered over Elizabeth, spreading his bi-color wings in a wide arc. She giggled at a funny commercial, and he knelt behind her, then put his hands around her neck.

And waited.

No one came.

Tabris closed his eyes. *God,* he thought, *"they do trust me.*

He flashed back to the couch, frowning. He'd expected the entire household would have been there, pulling him off her, screaming for Rachmiel.

His hands tightened on the arm of the sofa. His sword appeared at his side.

Elizabeth laughed again, the giggle of a soul untouched by serious sin, and Tabris looked into her heart where the light of God gleamed unrefracted. God and His creation, and His delight in her.

A good guardian would be vigilant. What else would a good guardian do? Well, a good guardian would stand watch, always examine the charge's soul for the first signs of demonic penetration. A perfect guardian wouldn't get distracted by the first snowfall. He wouldn't test the tether every night, rejoicing in every extra inch, because he'd dread to leave her. Her needs had to come first.

You deserve the best, Elizabeth, he thought. *And you've got me instead. Me and Rachmiel, but he's good for you. Me, though—since God put me here, shouldn't I do for you what I couldn't do for Sebastian? I can't promise perfection, but I'll try to do better.*

He concentrated until his clothing changed into armor, darker and tighter, complete with boots and gloves. Standing, he rested his hand on his sword, glittering in the afternoon sunlight of Chittenden County, Vermont.

Eight

After an hour's meditation, Rachmiel returned at peace. That peace splintered apart when he met Tabris armed for battle.

"Welcome back." Tabris even stood at attention. "It's my impression she's watching too much television. With your permission, I'd like to encourage her to play outside in the snow."

"Ah—sure." Rachmiel looked at the girl and then back at Tabris. "You don't need my okay."

Rachmiel felt Tabris surrounding Elizabeth's mind with thoughts of snowballs and snowmen. When she ignored that, Rachmiel put an image of his own into her mind: icicles hanging from the corners of the house. She began staring out the window, and Rachmiel could feel the power of Tabris's suggestion clinging to her.

"Was she attacked?" Rachmiel asked.

Tabris's eyes widened. "Do you think she was?"

"No, but—" Confusion churned inside, and he shook his head. "You're armed. Battle-ready. That demon couldn't possibly be ready to return by now."

"I've decided," Tabris said without moving his gaze off Elizabeth, "that I need to take this guardianship seriously."

"I wasn't under the impression that you didn't."

Elizabeth walked to the window, where Tabris pointed out the berm kicked up by the snowblower on either side of the driveway, and what a great snow fort it would make. Rachmiel still studied Tabris. "Were you given a warning about your probation?"

"No." Rachmiel thought Tabris sounded a little panicked there. "I made a decision. You don't need to question it. There's nothing wrong."

For a long instant, Rachmiel teetered on the brink of saying this level of formality had to be wrong, but he couldn't formulate why, only that it felt off. Elizabeth shut the television and ran to get her coat, Tabris following.

Once outside, Tabris didn't relax in the snow the way Rachmiel expected. He shadowed her as she made a snowball and hurled it at Alan, then deflected the snowball Alan hurled back.

Voriah drifted toward Rachmiel, silently projecting, *He's gotten serious?*

Rachmiel sent a hesitant affirmative, followed by a question: wasn't this odd?

"A bit," murmured Voriah.

So while Tabris watched Elizabeth, Rachmiel watched them both, surveying Tabris's technique and looking for any clue as to what Tabris meant by 'taking it seriously.' "He's guarding her physically," he murmured to Voriah. "I think intellectually, too, but I'm not as sure."

Voriah said, "Your forte is the spiritual?"

Rachmiel nodded. "They're all important, but if she had to lose a leg or her soul, I'd choose the leg, you know?" A snowball shot toward Alan's head, and Rachmiel swatted it off course so it grazed his shoulder.

"Thanks," said Voriah. "Yeah, I agree with you. But Satan would maul every one of them if he got the chance, and that's not a fair fight."

"I never said it was." Rachmiel frowned. "But if you think about it, a lot of temptations are mental, not physical. Even lust is largely mental."

"Don't over-analyze," Voriah said. "He's been like this for what, an hour? Anything he does is extra help anyhow. You managed perfectly well for a decade."

Rachmiel felt Katra'il catch his attention, and when he glanced at her, he felt her question: Should Tabris be doing that?

Instead of looking at Tabris, Rachmiel looked at Elizabeth. Two sprays on her coat showed where she'd been hit by snowballs, but she was unharmed. He winced as Martin hurled a snowball at her and it exploded into powder, and then realized Tabris had broken the snowball apart only a micrometer away from her. She'd felt the blow because the air and snow were moving, but no pain.

"Tabris," Rachmiel called across the yard, "you can't do that."

"Of course I can." He didn't look away from Elizabeth. "I just did."

Rachmiel flashed near to him. "If you do that, she's not going to learn to dodge them, only that snowballs don't hurt."

"Why should they have to hurt?" Tabris frowned. "I can keep them from hitting her."

"Because actions have consequences, and she should be protecting herself. It's a healthy fear. The one time Martin throws an ice ball at her head and we miss, she can save her own life."

Rachmiel punctuated this by changing the flight path of a snowball so it only glanced by her shoulder, and Tabris broke it apart.

"Working together, we won't miss," Tabris said. "We can keep her perfectly sheltered."

Frustration frothed inside, and the next minute Rachmiel realized Voriah had flashed over to them.

"The object of the assignment," said Rachmiel, struggling to keep from raising his voice, "is not to shield her from every opportunity of pain, but to shape her into a child of God. Pain isn't pleasant, but that's part of how God deepens their ability to love Him. That's how He changes them."

Tabris swung around to face Rachmiel. "What would you know about pain?"

Rachmiel recoiled.

Tabris flashed to the nearest tree and watched Elizabeth from there, and Voriah pulled Rachmiel back toward the house.

From Martin's side, Katra'il sent Rachmiel an apology.

Rachmiel stood smoldering, his eyes on Elizabeth alone, counting the snowballs and avoiding any look toward Tabris. *God, please send a message. I want Raguel to visit tonight. We need an arbiter.*

As soon as Elizabeth fell asleep, Raguel summoned Tabris and Rachmiel onto the driveway (spattered with snowball detritus) and then, on second thought, invited Josai'el to join them.

"I've reviewed the incident," Raguel said when all three had gathered, "and first, I'm glad you're negotiating this now rather than waiting until you have more serious problems." Although Rachmiel was looking him straight in the eye, Tabris seemed unimpressed. Arms folded, he leaned back on one leg and watched the pavement in silence. Not a good sign. "I also don't think either of you is entirely wrong, and I know you both want what's best for Elizabeth."

Rachmiel glanced at Tabris, then tightened up.

"Rachmiel," said Raguel, and Rachmiel turned to him, "Tabris has a few more years experience than you, and his previous charge was a boy. The average boy does require more physical protection than the average girl, and no doubt he's acting on his own experiences. He's still settling into his new role, so I would ask you to please be more understanding."

Rachmiel deflated. "I will."

He hadn't wanted to do that, but Tabris needed to feel he'd been even-handed. Raguel said to him, "Since Rachmiel has been Elizabeth's guardian from the start, he's got the expertise on her specific needs. As her primary guardian, he has the right to make all decisions about her care, and in this case, I also believe he's correct. You exceeded the scope of your duties. You have to shield her without being overprotective."

Tabris acknowledged, blank-faced.

"They have to be allowed to grow on their own into the creatures God intended, and that means that while we're minimizing the demons' intrusions into their lives, we also need to minimize our own."

The pair stayed silent. Between them Josai'el projected her understanding.

Either this was the easiest mediation in history, or else someone was repressing a whole lot of anger. "Do either of you have any questions?"

Tabris glared at the ground. "Why am I here?"

And there it was. "You're the secondary guardian," said Raguel. "You're subordinated to Rachmiel but still responsible for the care of Elizabeth's soul and body. You'll be following the course of a regular guardianship, and over time your insight into her heart will be equal to Rachmiel's."

"But if I have all the responsibilities of a full guardian then how can you justify—"

Tabris cut off both the words and the burgeoning sense of anger. As if he'd slammed a door, his soul reverted to emotional silence.

"Excuse me?" Rachmiel sounded tentative. "I asked you to arbitrate because I shouldn't rank over Tabris. We're *co*-guardians, and our power with respect to her will be equal in a very short time."

Raguel looked him in the eyes, projecting surprise.

Rachmiel trembled. "Since Tabris's arrival, I've tried not to pull rank, and for the next eighty to a hundred years, I intend to do the same. I didn't want to give him orders. But we were deadlocked, so I needed you to negotiate a consensus."

Raguel looked at Josai'el to find her just as surprised as he felt. Raguel projected a question, and Rachmiel returned an affirmation.

"You have to be committed if that's what you want," Raguel said. "You can't be a team until the first serious disagreement and then override him."

Rachmiel hesitated, then said, "I'm committed."

Raguel turned to Tabris, expecting to find the mahogany eyes ice-hard and his mouth tight. Instead, Tabris was trembling, and tendrils of confusion kept escaping. His feathers were flared.

Josai'el reached for him. "Tabris?"

He sidled out of her reach. "I'm all right." His voice sounded too thin.

Raguel said, "Why are you upset that he trusts you?"

Tabris shook his head. "I was doing my best this afternoon. And you said that wasn't good enough." He looked at Rachmiel. "But you want me coequal to you?"

Raguel said, "Are *you* willing to commit to that?"

And for a moment, Raguel had the impression that Tabris wasn't, a sensation of vertigo and freedom he shouldn't have. But then Tabris avoided their eyes again and the feeling vanished. "I am."

Raguel let it go. "The two of you should work out the details of your partnership, since you have a better understanding of how you work together than I do. But for now, it's inadvisable to keep Elizabeth wrapped in a cocoon. Deflect obvious threats to her well-being, but avoid being overprotective."

Rachmiel opened his hands. "He didn't think he was being overprotective. That's the problem."

Tabris folded his arms. "Well, we need to work out a base level of acceptable risk because the next time a projectile hurtles toward her skull, I don't want to have to schedule a committee meeting on whether deflecting it constitutes overprotectiveness."

Josai'el snickered, and Rachmiel's jaw dropped. Tabris's eyes glittered, and Rachmiel, fighting a grin, said, "Of course not! I expect you to carry around the minutes of the last twenty committee meetings and look it up yourself."

At that moment, Raguel knew they'd be able to work it out. Laughing, he clapped a hand on Rachmiel's shoulder. "You're very brave."

Taken aback, Rachmiel said, "It's not brave. I can't subordinate him just because he came second."

Raguel nodded. "As you wish. Do the two of you think you can work this out on your own now?"

Rachmiel projected assent. Tabris said, "We will."

They sat on the roof afterward, Rachmiel watching the constellations while Tabris focused on the gutters and tried to prevent ice dams.

Rachmiel glanced at Tabris, wondering why the concept of trust had caused him fear, except that maybe Tabris didn't trust himself. It made sense, but then it didn't. If Tabris mistrusted himself, that might mean he wasn't fully responsible for what happened to Sebastian, and maybe God had forgiven him because Tabris hadn't done anything not to forgive. But that first angel who fled to them, begging for prayers... Raguel and his early explanations...the angels from other households who had been told not to let the pressure build up... All those pointed to a deliberate action.

In short, it made no sense. Maybe Rachmiel shouldn't have insisted on them being a team. Well, not now, anyway. If he ranked over Tabris, and Tabris had to carry out his orders, then he could have ordered Tabris to talk. *You are under orders to tell me the entire story of how Sebastian died.*

No. He'd have gotten the information, maybe. But he'd have lost far more than he gained. Tabris having his heart at Rachmiel's mercy would forever preclude trust and guarantee resentment.

All of which left him with the same set of questions and no way of getting answers.

Tabris looked at him. "What?"

Rachmiel frowned.

"You want to ask something."

Rachmiel nodded. "But I don't want to make you angry."

"Try me."

"What happened with Sebastian?"

Tabris went back to work on the ice dams. "What would knowing that do for you?"

Rachmiel struggled momentarily because *I'll know how to protect Elizabeth from you* didn't sound very trusting on the heels of having said he wanted Tabris coequal to him. He opted for the more tangential, "I thought if I knew, I could help you." Also true. It benefited both of them if Tabris didn't harm her.

"I don't want you to be self-conscious on account of me. This was your job first. You deserve to be comfortable."

"I'm comfortable with you. Most of the time." When Tabris turned, eyebrows raised, Rachmiel said, "Some of the time."

"You keep second-guessing yourself." Tabris shook his head. "You're fine."

Tabris focused again on the ice in the gutter, and Rachmiel looked into the sky, sorting the stars until he found the one he searched for. "Oh, there it is!" He waved while projecting long-distance. "A friend of mine guards it, and it makes her happy when I remember her."

Tabris laughed, and Rachmiel's head lifted. Had he heard Tabris laugh before?

The fingers of the wind lifted stray flakes of snow and blew them through the angelic pair. Tabris flexed his wings into the chill, inhaling sharply, then laughed again, a much richer sound than before.

Rachmiel realized right then that Tabris hadn't answered his question about Sebastian. Which in and of itself was a kind of answer.

Tabris was still smiling. "Have I told you how much I love the cold?"

Rachmiel projected that he'd guessed. "Where were you before?"

"A suburb of Los Angeles. Disgusting weather, always sixty-eight and sunny. Smog that could make an angel retch, although the people breathed it just fine. I wanted to comb out Sebastian's lungs every night." He shook his head. "Ten million people lived there, and I never understood how they could stand it. No space. No snow. No seasons to speak of."

"Some people would say that's the weather in Paradise."

"To me, it said ten million people *must* believe in Paradise because if they didn't, why spend their lives there?" Tabris shuddered. "Why wouldn't they be climbing mountains?"

"Were you in LA the whole time?"

"Thirteen years." Tabris sighed. "One New Year's Day the radio announcer said they'd exceeded federal smog regulations only one hundred seventy-one days the previous year. And it was an improvement."

Rachmiel flinched.

Tabris spread his wings and lay back in the snow, surrounded by the froth without marking its substance.

Rachmiel gathered himself, and although he radiated nervousness, he said, "So, about Sebastian. How did—"

"Snapped his neck."

Rachmiel withdrew into verbal and emotional silence. Tabris had closed his eyes, and beneath the snow, his hands were fists.

Rachmiel had more questions, so many more. But he'd never get a *why* now, and even the *how* was so sparing in information. But to push—Tabris might answer, but at the cost of any rapport.

Tabris finally said, "Rock, do me a favor. If they tell you I didn't love the kid, please—remember that I did. It wasn't what they think. You

67

don't have to defend me to them. In fact, don't say anything at all. Just you remember it."

Tabris arched his neck and looked behind him at the moon. Tension rolled off him, and Rachmiel knew he'd been right to hold back. They had time. They had plenty of time.

Extending a wing toward Tabris, Rachmiel touched him and projected nothing more than his presence. "I never doubted it."

They stayed quiet for a long time. The moon changed position. Rachmiel's friend waved back to him. Headlights passed on the state route. And after a long time, Tabris turned toward Rachmiel with an asymmetric smile. "Thank you."

Nine

While Tabris watched Rachmiel awaken Elizabeth the next morning, the guardian of the woman up the road called for help. Josai'el sent a question through the household: who wanted to take it?

Mithra started to volunteer, but Rachmiel called out, "I'll go. You stay with Andrew."

Josai'el appeared in Elizabeth's room, and Tabris thought she looked worried. "Are you sure?"

"Absolutely. It shouldn't take two angels to get Elizabeth to eat breakfast." Rachmiel shrugged. "Andrew's going to be heading to work in fifteen minutes anyhow." He bent low over Elizabeth, whispering, "Wake up, Sleepyhead. God loves you like crazy." He blessed her and then disappeared.

Josai'el returned to Bridget, and Tabris found himself alone with Elizabeth.

This was...odd. Odd because while no one had said so explicitly, they'd all pretended the house had "an extra guardian" and not that Elizabeth had two. When someone needed to pitch in elsewhere, the "someone" would go and the remaining guardians would scramble to cover the unguarded person, ignoring the obvious: that if one of Elizabeth's pair went, nobody needed to scramble at all.

No one in the household had said, "Obviously any guardian angel would rather struggle alone than have Tabris pitch in." And they'd been even more polite about not saying "Rachmiel would rather die than leave Elizabeth alone with him."

Hence Josai'el's concerned question. And Rachmiel's volunteering: because if he spoke with actions, he didn't need to say, "Okay, guys, panic's over. I guess we can trust him. Somewhat."

Tabris sighed: the politics of interaction. He'd never have dissected things like this last year. He was still considering this development when Unbridled appeared.

The demon said, "You need to know my name is no longer Unbridled. It's Irony."

"Thanks for the update." Tabris positioned himself between Elizabeth and the demon. "Keep your distance."

Irony stood on the window sill, and Tabris put a picture into Elizabeth's mind: people looking in the windows. She glanced at the window, even though on the second floor, then moved to the far side of the room to get dressed.

Irony tried to get a look at her. "She's going to be a beautiful woman. You need to pay attention to the shape of her body as she develops, though. Is it true what they say about redheads?"

"Her physical attributes concern me about as much as your opinion."

"You're too harsh." The demon crouched lower on the window, tucking his wings around him. "My opinions used to matter to you. We had the most amazing conversations."

Tabris divided his focus, partially on the demon but the majority of it on Elizabeth because it wouldn't be unheard of for others to attack while he was distracted. "Keep brushing your hair. You've got a knot in the back." She picked up her brush again. To Irony, he said, "But after all those conversations, the only one that mattered was when you said you hated God."

"I agree!" The demon leaned forward, eyes bright. "Conversations about the intricate construction of a flower petal become repulsive when it turns out you hate the designer and want to boycott everything He ever manufactured. Tyranny, though—that's worth a conversation or two. Do you still love this misbegotten world?"

Tabris focused on Elizabeth packing her school bag. "Remember your book for English this time."

She hesitated, then picked up her book from the desk.

"You should give it up before He breaks your heart again with His cold eyes."

Irony stood up, now on the inside of the room, but Tabris turned, and he retreated to the window.

Irony said, "Do you know where Rachmiel is?"

"Yes."

"Well, he's not there. He's before the Archangels asking to have you removed for Elizabeth's sake."

Tabris nodded. "He goes every day." The demon's lies would be easier to blow off if Tabris hadn't already imagined all these scenarios for himself: Sebastian in agony; Rachmiel begging Raguel to have him transferred. And now: Rachmiel pretending to help the old lady down the road because it made excellent cover for an appeal at the foot of God's throne. "By now he's decided to abandon proper channels and have a bunch of friends beat me up if I get too close to his girl."

"Be serious." The demon folded his arms. "I'm the Ironic one, not you. Rachmiel says he can't keep his eyes off your hands, and he imagines you'll snap her spine at any moment."

"And it naturally follows that he would confide his deepest fears to you." Tabris pointed to the demon. "Go."

Irony vanished. Tabris examined Elizabeth to make sure nothing had gotten past him, then touched her hair. Before heading down to breakfast, she inspected herself before the full-length mirror. She smiled, but Tabris couldn't.

Rachmiel followed Elizabeth into the school cafeteria, Tabris trailing. While the children stampeded either toward the long tables with their fixed benches or to the hot lunch line, their guardians took attendance and noted only whether Tabris was in the room. Elizabeth stood on a bench waving to Maura, the girl she'd rescued from social exile, and Maura saw her just before the lunch monitor ordered Elizabeth to sit.

Head to head, the girls chattered while forgetting to eat their sandwiches. Maura's guardian was trying to get her to finish her lunch even as the girl told Elizabeth all about her mother's fight with her sister.

Despite the attention focused on Tabris, Rachmiel detected a difference: today they were studying him, too. It took half a carton of milk and three bites of a sandwich for Rachmiel to realize word had gotten around that he trusted Tabris as a co-decision-maker, and as a result, there wasn't the same caution. A frisson of surprise shot through Rachmiel, the idea that so many angels based their opinions on his own, and for a moment he wondered what would have happened had he taken Raguel's authority and run with it.

Even worse, what if he was wrong? He couldn't see into Tabris's heart. Quite a number of angels had worked with Tabris before and never dreamed him capable of what he'd done, and with this many children at risk—he'd better be right.

Rachmiel spread out his attention to read the vibrations in the room, knowing Tabris kept watch over Elizabeth and now more than a little curious. The angels still reacted to the emotional void surrounding Tabris, the lack of an aura that was not only a cloud of emptiness but actually absorbed the emanations of other angels. They'd come to think of it as his trademark. But in addition to that, Rachmiel picked up an undertone: not that Tabris was sullen, but that he was focused; not that Tabris was withdrawn, but that he was vigilant.

All because Rachmiel had trusted him. Snapping back to himself, he wondered how his one opinion could tint the minds of so many.

He fussed a bit over Elizabeth and then glanced at Tabris, standing alone against the wall. His eyes had gone dark as he listened to the chatter, and Rachmiel wondered if Tabris could detect the difference too. Not likely: Tabris was so coiled in on himself to keep his emotions from getting out that nothing was getting inside either. Battered by noise, Rachmiel wanted to say to Tabris, *You can go. Find someplace quiet,* but he didn't. Only hours after opening up a little to Rachmiel, Tabris might take that as a proclamation of distrust.

And then there was Maura's guardian, radiating disapproval. He'd projected that and more ever since Elizabeth had first spoken to the girl, wanting Elizabeth and Rachmiel without Tabris. The angel flared with anger when Tabris got too close.

You'd rather she be alone? Rachmiel thought, making sure none of the emotions escaped. *There's value in solitude, but she wasn't choosing solitude.*

Three sixth grade boys had dialed up their volume at the next table. Maura turned to watch them while she finished her sandwich, and Elizabeth dug a yellow apple out of her lunch bag.

Tabris changed his focus, and Rachmiel felt his soul shift into high alert. Demon. And it had worked its way into the boys' conversation.

Without a wall between them, it would be impossible to Guard the demon away from Elizabeth, although the demon didn't appear to be interested in the girls. Instead, he was goading one of the boys, who started bragging about some websites he'd visited when his parents weren't home, and then describing the contents.

Not realizing they shouldn't be listening, Elizabeth and Maura paid attention. It wouldn't be very long before Elizabeth would ask her mother, or maybe one of her brothers, "What's a pole dance?" and then dwell on the answer for a while—or worse, take it inside and never ask.

Maybe she'd search for it online herself. In a couple of years she'd be able to handle that information—but she was still so young.

Rachmiel urged her to stop listening, but she was trying to figure out what they were talking about.

Tabris said, "Elizabeth! There's Alan!" and she looked to the other side of the cafeteria.

"Maura," said Rachmiel.

The other girl was still paying attention, and it wasn't a far cry that she'd ask Elizabeth about it.

Tabris glared at Maura's guardian. "Distract her! Get her to ask Elizabeth what's wrong!"

The other guardian resisted.

Rachmiel amplified Tabris's insistence, and only then did the other guardian wrench Maura's attention to Elizabeth, who was scanning the crowd.

Maura said, "What are you doing?"

Elizabeth said, "I thought I saw my brother, but he's supposed to be in the middle school."

They both looked, pointing and debating whether that blond kid was Alan, until the subject behind them changed, the incident forgotten.

Tabris spun toward Maura's guardian. "You can't just say no." His hands were fists. "You've got to give her something else to do, something good and interesting to take the place of something bad and interesting."

The other angel's eyes glittered. "I know how to do my job."

"Then do it." Tabris stepped toward him, lowering his voice. "You're standing between Maura and Hell. This isn't a spectator event."

Rachmiel moved in front of Tabris. "It's over. They're safe."

Tabris touched Elizabeth's hair and turned his back on Maura's guardian. Angels all over the cafeteria stared, and Rachmiel tried to relax his wings. At his side, Elizabeth dropped a piece of her apple, and Tabris made sure it landed in the napkin on her lap.

Ten

During the first week of March, Tabris read Elizabeth's English assignment over her shoulder while she sat on the couch, mixing the written words with the pictures in her mind. She alternated reading a paragraph of short story with writing a note she planned to pass to Maura before class tomorrow morning. Jottings about how mean their teacher was and how her mother hated a song on the radio but she thought the singer was cute.

Tabris said to Rachmiel, "Is it possible her teacher would be less 'mean' if Elizabeth worked a little harder on her homework?"

"Oh, just a bit." Rachmiel chuckled. "But that might take away time from listening to the guy on the radio."

Elizabeth's father brewed a cup of coffee, and Mithra stood in the kitchen entryway dividing his attention between Andrew and the other two angels. "Maybe the way Andrew's mother would be less 'mean' if he followed through on his offer to take her to the doctor rather than pawning it off on Connie?"

Rachmiel looked up. "I've been praying about that. Is he still angry?"

Mithra huffed. "Yes, and he has no right. No one forced him to make the offer, and his work could have waited."

"Connie was furious," Rachmiel said.

Mithra nodded. "And he's mad at his mother for feeling hurt, by some logic I'm not quite getting. I'm not looking forward to whatever happens when they come home."

Tabris concentrated until he could feel Hadriel and Josai'el: in the car, traveling toward them. They'd arrive in about fifteen minutes.

As Elizabeth went back to her assignment, another angel appeared and projected something privately to Mithra, who glanced at the two of them. Andrew had gotten his coffee and was heading toward the basement steps.

Mithra said, "Would one of you mind watching Andrew for a minute? I'm needed elsewhere."

Rachmiel said, "Tabris, you go. I want to see how the story ends."

"Sure. Just don't reveal the secret finale before I get a chance to finish it myself."

Tabris followed Andrew down the steps to his home office, taking a place near the narrow rectangular windows.

He'd never expected this development, and even after five months it still felt unreal. Rachmiel leaving him with Elizabeth was one thing, but the others leaving him alone with theirs—that bespoke a trust Tabris found incomprehensible. He'd have split himself in two rather than entrust Sebastian to an angel with his track record, and yet Mithra had left his charge without more than a goodbye. See ya, Andrew. Don't die or anything while I'm gone.

It wasn't just Andrew. Voriah had left him with Alan for half an hour. Josai'el entrusted him with Bridget, but not without warning him Bridget would require help with balance. Hadriel had taken off for six hours one night, asking Tabris to keep watch over Connie and maybe give her an energy boost. As if they trusted him. Which meant, inexplicably, that they did.

None of the neighbors had let him guard theirs, of course. They used the excuse that Tabris was still tethered, but the tether had almost doubled by now. So at least everyone hadn't lost their minds.

Different souls needed different sorts of care, and Tabris remembered that now as he had to switch between different people. Until now he'd let Rachmiel provide the nurturing attention Elizabeth required and which Rachmiel gave instinctively: he'd been made for her, after all, the two paired in the mind of God since before creation.

But now Tabris wondered if he should change his methods for her. He couldn't treat her like Sebastian, but then again, he wasn't truly aware of what he'd given to Sebastian that another angel would have found awkward or perplexing. He and Sebastian had interlocked like two gears in a machine, but he'd never analyzed how.

Mimicking Rachmiel's style would be ineffective at best, laughable at worst. But God had known that. With a billion Earthly households to choose from, surely God had accounted for Tabris's style to be complementary to the style of the primary guardian. Otherwise God would have found a soul similar enough to Sebastian's, with a primary guardian similar enough to Tabris, that the differences wouldn't register. So maybe Tabris had something to offer Elizabeth after all.

While Andrew worked, Tabris glanced out the window, noting how the sun glared off the snow. So bright. Clean light with no impurities. He felt a momentary jealousy.

The demon, whatever he was calling himself today, popped into the room, grinning and rubbing his palms together.

Tabris steeled himself. "You look pleased."

"Absolutely I'm pleased!" The demon chuckled. "You're getting sacked!"

Tabris made himself glow. "I was there when the Vandals sacked Rome—quite a day."

"Fired." The demon stepped closer. "Fired in the fieriest way possible. As soon as you got down here in the dungeons, Mithra and Rachmiel switched places, and Rachmiel went straight to Raguel with a formal complaint. You desert Elizabeth far too easily! And Raguel admitted you wouldn't be fit to guard the quarters inside a parking meter, but hey, God's orders are orders even when they're monumentally stupid. And they don't want to hurt your *feelings,* poor thing, poor little Tabris."

Tabris called to mind the image of Rachmiel standing between him and Elizabeth with his sword on fire. Sparing his feelings hadn't always been the order of the day. Probably lies.

"Do you even listen to yourself?" Tabris said. "I'm still tethered to about three and a half miles. How can I desert her?"

The demon dismissed him with a hand-wave. "So instead they're getting their documentation together. When they've got enough, they're going to head to God and say look, nice try, but it's over. They think they can do it this week." The demon's wings curved around himself, and he beamed. "And then you're mine! You won't have anything to stay for, so you can come with me!"

Tabris turned his back and made sure Andrew remained uncompromised. He was fine: working on a list of numbers rather than looking at his own anger toward his wife and mother.

The demon said, "Don't bother telling yourself Rachmiel isn't that deceitful. You're not special. You're not the only one who can fake friendship when you're really filled with fury."

Faking friendship. Interesting concept: he'd never decided if Rachmiel was his friend, or was just being friendly because God expected it. Familiarity would have been more comfortable than friendship. He'd expect less from a co-worker than a friend.

The demon said, "You should ask Rachmiel when he gets back. He can't lie yet. Not the way you can."

"Shut up."

"You believe me, don't you?" The demon chuckled. "You know the score."

Tabris whirled. "Get out! Go!"

The demon folded his arms. "I'll be quiet. I'll just stay in the corner until Rachmiel returns with Raguel, and when you get removed, you can curse God and come home with me."

Tabris's eyes stung as he watched Andrew pouring all his frustration into paperwork behind a locked door in a wood-paneled basement office.

The demon said, "If you haven't prayed in months, how can God still love you?"

Tabris went cold.

"He's got standards, and you're failing them. All of them. Ask yourself, jailbird, how long it's going to drag on until he says 'Poorly done, wretched servant'?"

Tabris forced himself to look bored, but he could feel his feathers standing out.

"Come with me now." The demon's voice turned pleading. "If you jump ship before He forces you to walk the plank, at least you'll keep your dignity."

Tabris summoned his sword to his hands.

"You really do belong with me, see? True angels aren't this short-tempered."

Tabris drove him off then, a combination of will-power and spiritual steel, then Guarded the room and stood with his arms crossed and eyes closed. He didn't dissolve the sword, but he did sheathe it.

A knock at the door: Connie. Tabris brought down the Guard so Hadriel could enter, but Andrew called through the door that he was too busy to talk.

Hadriel spoke through the door as though there were none. "Can you get Andrew to let her inside? She's very upset."

"I can tell." Tabris made his face a mask. "I'll try, but I won't have the same influence Mithra has. Can you go find him?"

"I'll mound a universe-wide search." Hadriel chuckled. "Or maybe I'll just call up the stairs. He's with Elizabeth."

Fear shot through Tabris like a lance. "With Rachmiel?"

His voice broke, but attending to Connie's troubled heart, Hadriel didn't notice. "Rachmiel went somewhere else, so Mithra's with Elizabeth and you're with Andrew." Hadriel shrugged. "I don't know. It seemed odd to me too."

Tabris glared at Andrew, and about to flash upstairs to Elizabeth's side, he wondered if that would mean he was deserting the person in his care. But they needed to switch places: surely someone had to go first? Tabris stuck his head through the door into the hallway. "Go get Mithra. Call back Rachmiel. And you know what?" His voice trembled again. "You're exhausted. I'll stay with Connie, and you get rested up."

Relief came to Hadriel's eyes. "Really?"

"Of course." Enough of this guardian-angel pachinko. "You're hemorrhaging energy into her, and you can't keep doing that. You'll help her better if you recover your strength."

A minute later, Tabris was following Connie back up the stairs to the sink, where she let her pent-up tears mingle with the steam from the dishwater. *I'm your battery right now, Connie. Take my spiritual energy. It's yours. I'm sorry it's tainted.*

Tabris plugged into her and let her draw strength from him, and in moments he felt her wear the sharp edges off his awareness. Good. Pull all his energy inside. Make everything go away.

Before the dishes were done, Tabris felt Josai'el appear at his back. "Tabris? Connie is—What's wrong?"

He pivoted to face her, and it was hard to concentrate. "Connie's distressed, and I gave Hadriel some time to recover. What about Connie?"

"Bridget's upset because she thinks Connie will break all the dishes if she keeps clattering them around. You're not all right."

Tabris managed a perfectly-executed smile. "Connie pulls the energy out of you. You told me Bridget used to do the same thing. Well, you've got an extra angel around here, so why should Hadriel collapse with exhaustion when I can help?"

Josai'el hesitated. "Do you want me to get Rachmiel?"

"I'm fine!" Tabris tightened his arms and glared at the no-wax floor while Connie stared out the window. "Hadriel does this every day. Surely I can manage a few hours."

Josai'el paused a long time, as if decoding the things Tabris wasn't saying, and Tabris buckled down hard on his heart. Connie could rub off the rough edges, but she couldn't numb the betrayed feeling. Mithra helping Rachmiel cull him away from Elizabeth. Rachmiel ratting him out to Raguel. And everyone going along with it. He might as well let Connie have his energy. It wasn't as if he'd be doing anything useful with it if Rachmiel succeeded.

Josai'el touched his arm. "Don't push too hard," was all she said before returning to Bridget.

Tabris stood, hands on Connie's shoulders, wondering whether Mithra would get Andrew to come upstairs and help Connie, or whether Mithra would fail and leave Tabris alone. As time passed and the dishes returned to their cabinets, it became apparent that Andrew would not leave the retreat of his basement office any time before dinner.

Connie sapped the remaining energy from Tabris, leaving little for dwelling on betrayal. By dinner time, he found himself listless behind her chair, wondering how he'd gotten there. Staring at the top of her head, he managed until bedtime without speaking to either Rachmiel or Mithra.

Hadriel returned, recovered, and then Miriael pulled Tabris aside. "Go spend time at the pond. You need it."

Enervated, Tabris went. *You desert Elizabeth far too easily.* He might as well go. They could talk in the open without him home.

Except that when he arrived at the pond, he found Rachmiel there ahead of him.

"What are you doing here?" Tabris went cold. "Who's with Elizabeth?"

"Miriael's watching her. You're the one I'm worried about."

Tabris wrapped up his heart with his will, a tourniquet around a gushing limb.

Rachmiel approached, but Tabris flared his wings and set his jaw.

Rachmiel stopped in his tracks. "Why are you so upset?"

"Could you leave me alone?" Tabris's voice was pitched too high, but he couldn't get it back where it should be. "It's not a crime to want some quiet."

Rachmiel's heart radiated hurt, and Tabris felt the emotion like fire. "I'll be quiet. I wanted to pray with you."

"You can pray for me from Elizabeth's room." His heart hammered. "Unless you think I'm *deserting* her. Does it really take two of us to keep her from kicking off the extra blanket?"

Rachmiel's eyes had gone purple, and his wings faded. Unflinching, Tabris folded his arms.

Rachmiel flashed back home.

Tabris faced the pond, a sheet of glass disturbed by the occasional ripple, struggling not to feel the pain in a distant house with a two-car garage and an office in the basement. He couldn't get Rachmiel's last look out of his mind, but then he thought about his partner lying to him and wondered how anyone could pretend to be hurt after all that. But he wasn't pretending. And yet he'd lied to Tabris. Who hadn't prayed in five months.

79

How long would God let that go on?

Keeping himself fully shielded, Tabris whispered, "God?"

They couldn't be doing this to him—God couldn't be allowing it to happen this way, could He? How was it fair to tell Tabris it was fine to leave Elizabeth and then punish him for leaving Elizabeth? Even human unemployment boards understood the concept of constructive dismissal.

He pulled his knees to his chest and rested his forehead on folded arms. His wings came up around himself like a cocoon as he clenched his teeth and closed his eyes. *God, I can't keep doing this. I need something from you. I need you to show me what to do.*

Only a wicked generation would ask for a sign, but that part had already been established, so he might as well. He needed more than just stubbornness to keep going, but opening up and trying to pray—what if God refused? Refused now, when he was already at the end of what he could do? He couldn't chance it. One open moment risked everything. But he needed a sign. Something to give hope.

God would want him to uncoil himself. It felt safer for now to keep tight, to make himself small, to try to disappear.

Rachmiel blazed back into the house like a comet, trailing a tail of confusion and rejection. He flung himself at Voriah, who wrapped around him and let him cry, releasing all his emotions without channeling them at all.

"Rock!" Voriah pulled him close. "What happened?"

He couldn't gather himself enough to talk. Tabris. Anger. Refusal. Anger. So much anger, and all focused on him.

The other household angels packed into the room, and they absorbed the emotions from Rachmiel even as they returned to him their own peace, their calm—their strength. He felt them praying for him, around him. After a while he was able to focus on the image of God in them, then from there the image of God stamped in himself, and then finally to look into God's heart directly. The tension melted, and the uncertainty firmed into strength. Rachmiel thanked God, and then he raised his head.

After all that spiritual contact, the other angels had learned everything that happened by the pond. The others wore an assortment of their own feelings: questions, irritation, and from Katra'il outright anger. She tried to flash out of the room—and didn't get anywhere.

Mithra was looking right at her. "You're going to attack him?"

"Someone needs to talk sense to Tabris!" She kept trying to flash away. "Let me go!"

Whatever Mithra was doing kept Katra'il pinned to the room, but Rachmiel had no idea what.

Josai'el shook her head, looking Katra'il in the eyes. "Don't go. Anger isn't the answer."

Katra'il folded her arms. "Fine, then call Raguel to us. Get Tabris transferred."

Rachmiel sent a negation. "I'm all right. Please don't."

Katra'il's eyes and hair glared with white light. "He's got to be part of the team. He can't just treat you like a nuisance."

"We're not a ready-made structure that each of us had to fit." Rachmiel rubbed his forehead. "The team changed for each of us as we arrived." He looked up, a little dizzy. "We're still adjusting to each other."

"He'd better do some adjusting for us, too." She huffed. "You're acting like a puppy that wants to please its master the more it gets beaten. Just because your name means Compassion doesn't mean you have to get walked on by everyone who wants to use you as his personal doormat!" She turned to Josai'el. "Why aren't you doing something?"

Josai'el said, "They're divine orders."

Katra'il said, "It's a divine order that he has to be here. It's not a divine order that we have to let him destroy our family."

Rachmiel had recoiled into Voriah's wings. Voriah said, "Calm down, Kat. You're not being fair."

"Fair to Tabris?" She opened her hands. "Tabris arrived five months ago and has done nothing but sulk, and if he doesn't change things in the next eighty years he's going to sulk his way through three households and any friendships he manages to pick up. He's nothing but dead weight, and he can't be trusted."

Josai'el whistled sharply. Miriael and Mithra were frowning.

Katra'il folded her arms. "See if I'm wrong. He'll move on Elizabeth soon, and then where will you be?"

She vanished. Rachmiel was shaking.

Josai'el turned to Hadriel. "Do go calm her." Hadriel left. Josai'el scanned the others before continuing, her long hair framing her face. "Do the rest of you feel the same?"

Mithra, Miriael and Voriah projected that they had their feelings under control.

Josai'el crouched before Rachmiel. "Do you want him removed?"

"No! I just want—" and as the emotions surged again, he leaned against Voriah. The touch calmed him. "I want to know why he was angry. I wanted to help."

Mithra said, "Do you think it had to do with empowering Connie?"

Rachmiel said, "Why would he be angry about that?"

Voriah touched Rachmiel's wings again and projected that with Tabris keeping everything to himself, all intuition was pure speculation.

Miriael said, "Then I'll go to him and ask."

"He told me he wanted to be alone."

Miriael's eyes narrowed. "He said he wanted to be alone. We have no idea what he actually wants." He turned to Josai'el. "Maybe Katra'il wasn't that far off in wanting to start a fight. I'll offer to spar with him. Afterward I'll ask him what in blazes he thought he was doing."

Mithra folded his arms. "I don't know if that's right either. When Andrew's sulking, it gives him a lot of power when they knock on the door and beg him to come out."

Voriah said, "Do you think Andrew's silent treatment is contagious?"

"Well, he was fine until I left them together." Mithra sighed. "Maybe it is."

Miriael said, "And that's about the time he started dampening conversation and just getting...darker. I don't think that's depression or a power play. I think something's really wrong. I'll get it out of him."

Josai'el folded her arms. "I think Mithra has a point. Tabris knows how to ask for what he wants or what he needs. We've been forthcoming about providing anything necessary. He told Rachmiel he wanted to be alone, and I'm going to say we need to honor that."

Miriael blew off a cloud of irritation, but stared at the floor, and Rachmiel knew he'd abide by Josai'el's decision.

Josai'el said, "He's also perfectly capable of apologizing for himself, so I'm going to suggest the rest of us stay out of it." She looked abruptly worried. "Rachmiel, can you handle that?"

Could he handle that? Interesting question. "I'll manage." Rachmiel's mouth trembled. "Even though I kind-of want to Guard the room against him."

They all fell silent, and then Mithra said, "You're at the end of your rope, aren't you?"

Rachmiel closed his eyes tight.

Voriah gripped his shoulder. "No, I didn't think you could go on this way."

Josai'el said, "Would you like some advice?"

Rachmiel took a deep breath. "Always."

She crouched in front of him and put her hand on his. "You've been very accommodating to Tabris, but that doesn't mean you can't have input into how you're treated. In the long run it benefits Elizabeth if you work as a team, and that means mutual respect."

"But—"

"Listen." She squeezed his hand. "Mutual respect begins with you respecting yourself. You have good instincts, but he's got a strong personality, and you've been passive about letting his moods dictate your interactions. God put you together because you have a lot to offer him, and you don't have to wait for his permission. You also don't have to abide by his refusal."

Rachmiel bit his lip. "I don't understand."

"What I'm saying," she said, "is that it's not uncompassionate for you to take control."

Hadriel sat on the opposite side of Martin's bedroom while Katra'il paced. Her eyes still glared with white light.

"I can't believe they're just letting him walk all over Rachmiel!" It was nothing she hadn't been saying for the past five minutes. "You couldn't find a nicer angel, and then God rewarded his hard work with Elizabeth by making it even tougher?"

Hadriel watched as her face hardened and softened whenever she passed before the starlit bedroom window. Then, mid-stride, she flashed to Martin and touched his hair. She smiled, breathed over him, and rested her hand on his shoulder.

She whispered, "He took a boy like this, and he *killed* him."

Hadriel projected understanding.

"Well, I don't understand. Martin has my whole heart. God told me to guard him, but I'd be here anyway. Even if He told me I could leave, I'd still stay." She pressed her head against his, then looked at Hadriel, wings arched over the boy. "I wish I could show you the interior of his soul. Every part of him calls to me. The things he thinks have his signature on them. I love watching his mind at work when he's playing a video game or getting the computer to do what he wants."

Hadriel leaned back against the wall. "Do you think Tabris didn't love Sebastian?"

"He must have hated him." Katra'il's voice was flat. "He probably resented the boy, wanting to be free but unable to leave when it was expected he'd stay. You see how much time he spends away from Elizabeth. Without a second guardian, he couldn't do that. He'd have been counting the minutes until Sebastian died. And then he decided to take care of it anyhow."

"That would be..." Hadriel couldn't think of a charitable way to say *unforgivable*, so he switched gears. "If you're right, then it might explain why he got assigned to another person. So he didn't benefit from what he did."

"Except that with Rachmiel around, he can get away for eight or nine hours a night anyhow."

Hadriel studied Katra'il. The light from her eyes mingled with the starlight and somehow reflected the light of time itself. He lowered the pitch of his voice. "Are you afraid of him?"

"Absolutely—I can't let him hurt Martin!" She sat up. "I can't imagine how Rachmiel deals with having him near all the time!"

"That's not what I asked." Hadriel noticed her light dimming. "I asked if you were afraid of him, not if you were afraid for Martin."

"What's Tabris going to do to me?"

"That's a good question."

Hadriel waited her out. She calmed as she thought, then shook her head. "There's nothing he could do to me. He could overpower me in a fight, since he can hold off Miriael. But then what?"

Hadriel said, "Then what? He could hurt you temporarily, but he's never raised a hand against any of us."

Katra'il smiled. "Except Miriael."

"Except Miriael. Who probably begged him to." Hadriel laughed, and Katra'il relaxed a bit more. "So why the fear?"

"I never said I was afraid of him." She frowned. "You're the one who said that."

"You're the one reacting violently to having him here." Hadriel nodded. "That's fear."

"Really?" She touched Martin's hair. "I think it's hatred of everything he did."

"No, because then all of us would be equally upset." Hadriel said, "Push on that thought."

"But—" And then Katra'il said, "Okay, so if he could do it before, and he looks pretty normal now, other than being sullen half the time, then he could do it again."

Hadriel opened his hands and projected for her to continue.

"And..." She chuckled. "You want me to say something, and I have no idea what."

Hadriel folded his arms. "If he seems normal and he could do that, then what's to say you couldn't do that too?"

She trembled. "I wouldn't."

Hadriel lowered his voice. "Maybe six months ago, he wouldn't have, either."

"But I love Martin."

"We don't know he didn't love Sebastian." Hadriel sighed. "We don't really know anything about him, but if he'd been giving off vibes of resentment, or anger, or malice—wouldn't someone have stepped in? It had to seem like he had everything under control."

Katra'il frowned. "And what if the kid did something so terrible that Tabris killed him in retaliation?"

Hadriel leaned forward. "Can you imagine anything so bad that you'd kill Martin for doing it?"

She thought a long time. And finally, "I know some sins cry out to God for vengeance, but what could a kid do? Sebastian was even younger." She looked up. "But there's something to that. There's no sin so awful that any of us wouldn't be capable of it without God's grace."

Hadriel nodded. "And the more aware you are of that, the harder it is to stand in judgment over someone."

"But why would God take that grace away from him?" She puzzled. "Or alternatively, why would Tabris deny the gift of that grace?"

"That's the conundrum," said Hadriel. "Only no one's asked Tabris. Rachmiel's the one with the best shot at getting an answer, and he doesn't want to press the issue."

Katra'il said, "Because if Tabris could do it, any of the rest of us might, too."

Hadriel projected agreement. "And that's what worries a lot of angels."

She tucked up her knees. "If you ever thought I'd kill Martin, you'd take me away from him, right?"

Hadriel nodded. "I would. You seem to be pretty good at venting your emotions before they get to that point, though."

She forced a laugh, although it sounded weak. "But I'm capable of angry outbursts, and I'm sarcastic. What if I was in a blind rage and I hurt Martin?"

Hadriel crossed the tips of his wings in front of his ankles. "What would make you that angry?"

"Sin."

"Right. But you wouldn't kill him if he were deep in sin because you wouldn't want him to go to Hell. You'd want him to repent, and by then you'd have had time to get calm, and you wouldn't be as impulsive. When he did repent, you'd be too glad to be violent."

She shrugged. "Okay, then. Tabris didn't do it in response to a sin."

"Or did he?" said Hadriel. "He's more pensive than you are. He's a watcher." Katra'il's eyes widened as he spoke. "He might mull over it long enough for the kid to repent out from under him, and then when he'd be ready to act, the child would be safe."

Katra'il whispered, "Is that what you think happened?"

Hadriel matched her tone. "It has the best chance of any theory I've heard."

At that moment Josai'el appeared, and Katra'il bowed her head. "I'm sorry I lost my temper."

"Are you calmer now?"

"Significantly."

Josai'el projected her thanks to Hadriel, who demurred.

Katra'il said, "Should I apologize to Tabris?"

"I can't imagine he picked up on your anger from that distance," said Josai'el, "so apologizing would create more confusion than it would resolve. But we're going to keep this between Rachmiel and Tabris. It's better for now if you're not involved at all."

Katra'il acknowledged, and Hadriel felt her for the first time calm about receiving Tabris back into their home.

Tabris returned to Rachmiel just after sunrise, his eyes gleaming and his motions stiff.

Rachmiel acknowledged him without any warmth. Tabris projected nothing at all, and Rachmiel deflated at the thought that he was stuck for the foreseeable future with an angel who didn't want him around—who didn't even like him.

"Is she well?" Tabris said.

"She slept fine."

"Good."

Tabris left the room. On the edge of the bed, Rachmiel found himself trembling as he reached for Elizabeth. "Wake up, Sleepyhead. It's time." He closed his eyes, then whispered, "Elizabeth, I need you awake now. Please, for me."

The girl stretched. As she yawned, her newly-awake sensations flooded Rachmiel, along with the head rush for the first second after she stood. Tabris said that wasn't normal, but it had always been normal for her. The slackness of sleep drained from her as she walked to the window to look outside, and Rachmiel smiled in imitation of the sunrise. The moments of most intense connection between her soul and his happened just after waking when she hadn't yet closed off her mind to possibility: to chance, to dreams, to God. Sometimes she prayed while waking up, and Rachmiel shivered when God touched her heart at that degree of closeness, and for the rest of the day he'd feel that fingerprint etched on both her and him.

Most mornings, of course, she simply awoke and got dressed. And that was all right too. He would still feel the swirl of her thoughts until she fully roused.

He'd focused on her so intently that he started when he heard her voice—and he bolted to a stand when he realized she hadn't spoken.

God, her prayer sounded in his heart, as strongly as if she'd projected it like an angel, *Grandma says I have an angel who watches me. Can you say 'hi' to her for me?*

Rachmiel shot toward her and embraced her so tightly, and he wished he could let her sense those arms around her shoulders, his hair against her cheek. *Hello yourself, sweetie. Did you know that angel loves you?*

At his back, he felt Tabris standing very close. "Did you just hear—?"

Turning, Rachmiel projected his joy. He reached into Elizabeth's imagination, but she wasn't thinking of angels any longer, only about whether her favorite shirt had come out of the wash. "I hope she does that again sometime."

Then he noticed the look on Tabris's face: stunned, but more than stunned. Rachmiel sent him a question.

Tabris said, "But I heard her too."

Rachmiel nodded, projecting, *Co-guardian.* Then he laughed out loud. "Ten years from now, when she's totally forgotten everything about us, remind me what just happened. I may need it then."

Tabris looked as if he'd needed it now. Rachmiel paused to regard him, even if curiosity might get his head bitten off one more time. Tabris didn't notice. He was staring through Elizabeth, but not as if fully concentrating on her either. His emotions slipped through: shock. Self-consciousness. And a bittersweetness Rachmiel wanted to call love but felt instead as a denial of being loved, a discomfort that left him wanting to squirm.

Elizabeth began brushing her hair. Tabris drew near to her, and Rachmiel wondered why Tabris couldn't meet his gaze.

"Were you going to go out again?"

"No." Tabris sounded stunned. "No. That's a sign, isn't it? A sign that I'm her co-guardian." He turned toward Rachmiel, eyes gleaming. "God doesn't want me to leave. I'm supposed to stay."

Eleven

After Tabris went to the pond one night the next week, Rachmiel visited Voriah in Alan's bedroom. With the moon obscured by clouds, the angels glowed so they could see one another. In their aura, the posters of airplanes and basketball players took on a half-alive appearance. The hamsters in the cage on the dresser struggled to get Voriah's attention, running on their wheel until Alan half-woke, and then Voriah blessed them so they'd quiet down.

Rachmiel sat on Alan's desk, strewn with paper and colored pencils. It was the only disarrayed part of the room, and he grinned as he told God he'd have felt uncomfortable sitting where it was neat.

Once Voriah settled the hamsters, Rachmiel said, "Tabris did something strange today."

Voriah shrugged, projecting that this was a normal state of affairs.

"Stranger than that." Rachmiel tucked up his knees. "While Elizabeth was at school. It was really quiet because the other guardians tend to get quieter when he's around."

Voriah rolled his eyes, projecting, *He's an emotional black hole.*

Rachmiel went still, and Voriah lowered his head. Rachmiel turned toward Alan, who had settled now that the hamsters had stopped rattling their wheel. "Is he dreaming?"

"Not yet. I'm sorry—you can tell me about today. I'll behave."

Rachmiel looked up, but still he didn't speak. Tabris couldn't defend himself as long as he wasn't here, but he probably wouldn't defend himself anyhow. And Voriah—half joking, but not fully—was a part of his household. His support team.

Rachmiel excused himself to check on Elizabeth.

Voriah followed. "I'm sorry. I shouldn't have said that."

Rachmiel projected his frustration. "No. You shouldn't have."

"But you do know it's true." Voriah folded his arms. "It's gotten to the point that whenever he comes into the room, you can tell it's him by what he *doesn't* project. No, don't protest. You're with him so much that you've gotten used to him, but think about how we feel."

"I'm thinking about how he feels."

"You'll have to trust me that everyone else is wondering how he feels too." Voriah's eyes gleamed. "And then we wonder how the rest of us feel, because he also dampens the other angels' emotional auras. That's why he stops conversation."

Rachmiel's eyes narrowed.

"You of all angels should know that, since you're the most sensitive to everyone's projections. Doesn't it feel like you're muffled whenever he's around?"

Rachmiel grudgingly agreed that an emotional black hole was an apt description.

Voriah projected laughter, and teasing. "Now unless I'm mistaken, you had a story to tell."

Voriah vanished. Rachmiel followed, and they were back in Alan's room. "You're terrible," Rachmiel said.

"But I can make you smile." Voriah chuckled. "Okay, so Tabris did something unusual today. Proceed."

"Elizabeth was learning fractions," Rachmiel said, "and she had a hard time figuring out what they were. Music is more up her alley, although I guess math plays an important part in that as well. She'll be an amazing piano player if she applies—" He caught himself. "Sorry."

Voriah leaned forward. "Don't be sorry! It's been too long since you just got on a roll about her. I'm not about to cast any stones at you in the mad-about-your-charge department."

Rachmiel met his eyes, and he relaxed. "My point was, she didn't understand fractions. So Tabris...taught her."

Voriah's eyes widened.

"He showed her, in her mind, what it meant to have a fraction. I can't explain it. But that's what he did."

Voriah spoke slowly. "I've helped Alan understand new concepts."

"Not like this. I'd tried helping her understand. He *taught* her. He conceptualized it for her and then said her name repeatedly, that he knew she knew it, and her head snapped up, and she did."

Rachmiel felt Voriah's surface thoughts spinning, while below that simmered amazement. Finally Voriah said, "He's new. She's not used to him yet, not enough to ignore him as totally as she can you."

"Maybe." Rachmiel shook his head. "But I think it was his technique. The other angels in the room looked like they were waiting for me to do something, as if he were killing her or trying to make her insane."

"I wonder which would be worse?"

Rachmiel's heart pounded. "I don't want to find out!"

"I didn't think you did. I also don't think he's going to drive her around the bend. At least not more than fractions would." Voriah rubbed his chin. "So what did you do?"

"I thanked him. What else could I do? He's taking Elizabeth very seriously."

Voriah puffed out a quick emotion, one that dispersed before Rachmiel caught his meaning. The earlier feeling crept back up on him: that Voriah was part of Tabris's household, and they shouldn't be fighting each other. He projected a question.

Voriah said, "He's like the British honor guard. Yeah, you could call that taking her seriously. Hardly taking unless you ask him to. Never defending himself to the other angels. That's intense."

Rachmiel's mouth twitched. "Is that what he was like before?"

Voriah shrugged. "You'd have to ask Mithra. I can't imagine it's something he could do for ten years at a shot."

The hamsters began moving around the cage again, and Rachmiel watched them nose through the bedding. "Do you think he'll burn out?"

Voriah projected concern.

"One of the symptoms of burnout is irrational anger at the person you're caring for." Rachmiel wove his fingers around one another. "Which might explain what happened."

Voriah projected agreement, then added, "And since prayer is one of the preventatives for burnout..."

Rachmiel shivered. "What can I do about that? He's not likely to accept a suggestion to back off."

"Didn't Josai'el tell you to start taking control? Maybe that's how to start. Do whatever it takes to make him decompress." Voriah shrugged. "I figure that's why he's going out at night. And you can ask leading questions without being critical. I don't need to tell you that. Empathy is your nature."

Rachmiel snapped, "How do you empathize with an emotional black hole?" before cringing at his own words.

Voriah flashed close to him. "I think you pray about it."

"Do you think I haven't?"

Voriah said, "Then we pray together."

Rachmiel checked on Elizabeth one more time and then he and Voriah opened up, inviting God into their hearts. Voriah backed off as Rachmiel presented his question to God, and then waited. At first, peace filled him, and at that moment he knew that no matter what he decided to do about Tabris, he always would be cherished. Even if no answer came, this was enough, and Rachmiel projected his thanks.

Behind him, Voriah pushed the question.

But for an hour or so—what did time mean with God?—Rachmiel bathed in that attention and let himself return the love poured over him. There were no words, just him and his Creator, with Rachmiel so, so glad to be near Him.

And then, although Rachmiel had forgotten the question, God said, *Compassion, son of Love, will you serve me?*

No words would have sufficed. "Always" and "Absolutely" would have fallen short of the assent that burst from Rachmiel's heart.

God smiled, and Rachmiel drew closer to Him.

In his heart, Rachmiel felt answers:

Be patient.

Tabris needed him to be strong.

Tabris needed him to be trustworthy.

Rachmiel assented. Of course he wanted all these things too. But God continued:

Tabris was by no means out of danger.

A spike of cold stabbed through Rachmiel. Danger. There was only one danger for an angel.

God continued with one final instruction: Before Tabris could be safe again, Rachmiel would have to love him.

The chill went all the way through Rachmiel. *But he killed Sebastian!*

God said, *Loving him doesn't mean approving of what he did.*

Rachmiel's heart hammered. *I have a child to protect!*

God replied, *I need to protect My child too.*

Rachmiel curled over himself, aching. Voriah drew near and helped Rachmiel open up again to apologize.

I'll try," Rachmiel promised. *But he's not making it easy for me to like him. I don't think he likes himself anymore. He won't even accept Your love.*

God replied, *I need you to love him for me, as me, until he'll come to me again.*

If God had asked Rachmiel to move the Pacific Ocean to Jupiter with a slotted tablespoon, Rachmiel would have found a way. In fact, he wished God had asked that instead. The earlier communication, though: *Tabris is by no means out of danger.* Forgiveness meant nothing if you didn't ask for it—less if you didn't accept it. God could unlock the cell door, but the soul had to step out of prison.

The Holy Spirit churned over Rachmiel and through him, the pieces fitting together in His wake: patience, because it couldn't happen now, but God also had time; strength, because God was asking something tremendous, and yet Rachmiel had been the one angel in all Creation He'd asked it of; trust, because God had gifts to give, and Rachmiel didn't have to struggle alone.

More than that: he should be ready; he needed to be ready to respond.

Grasping to regain the calm he'd lost, Rachmiel flailed until Voriah's touch grounded him. The Spirit wrapped him in warmth, and Rachmiel let the emotions recede from him like the tide over a beach, each wave leaving the sand smooth in its wake, until he'd come back to himself. The moon had set. The sky began brightening, and Rachmiel returned to Elizabeth.

Twelve

On the first clear Saturday of the spring, the Hayes family had a picnic. The boys played Frisbee with Andrew while Mithra studied how the Frisbee's spin made it more dynamic. Connie and Bridget set up food on a red picnic table that had chips gouged from the paint and pale shoots of grass forcing itself awake under the benches.

Elizabeth read a book beneath an apple tree, Rachmiel at her side reading it with her. Images from the book filled his head, and he lay like a filter on her imagination, catching the ideas and emphasizing what was good.

A wingspan away, Miriael bowed before Tabris. "I've just given you a mortal insult."

"How awful." Grinning, Tabris called his sword to his side. "I suppose I'll have to battle you to defend my honor."

Miriael laughed out loud, and the pair took off.

Contented by the story unfolding in his mind via Elizabeth's imagination, Rachmiel watched Miriael and Tabris locked in combat. Although they'd started by joking, they each picked up a singular focus, like Michael and Lucifer. As often as they'd sparred since Tabris's arrival, Rachmiel had never watched them in action. Miriael had mentioned his work prior to guarding Kyle, but it had never occurred to Rachmiel to think about the combat he'd seen.

The two of them broke apart to gather themselves. Miriael called, "I'm pretty sure that can't have made up for the severity of the aspersions I cast upon—"

Tabris interrupted by renewing the attack.

Miriael's charge Kyle jumped his brother Martin, unnoticed by Miriael. Rachmiel checked on Elizabeth, but she was still concentrating on her book.

The "sound" of spiritual battle echoed off the hills, not clangs and crashes as much as a death-like intent radiating for miles around. By now, both angels' swords were in flames, and they trailed light wherever they struck. Several angels showed up, armed.

One of the outsider angels said, "Isn't that—"

"Yes," said Rachmiel. "It's friendly fire."

The newcomers stayed. Rachmiel couldn't tell from their projections whether they thought Tabris might pose an actual threat, or whether they just wanted to watch a duel between two highly-skilled angels.

Elizabeth put down her book, staring at Kyle and Martin's wrestling match.

Hadriel said, "Should we stop them?"

Josai'el said, "Let them finish."

Voriah flashed up close to Rachmiel. "You could never defend Elizabeth against that."

"Then you'd better pray I don't have to."

After ten minutes it was apparent to everyone that the pair was evenly matched. By now they knew each other's styles and could anticipate one another's moves, so they might fight for hours before either made a slip in judgment that would cost him the battle. Surrounding Elizabeth and drawing off as much restlessness as he could, Rachmiel realized winning wasn't the point. Ending the match too quickly would be a shame; they wanted combat for the sake of combat.

Voriah said, "Was Tabris a soldier?"

"Yes. And a good one," Mithra said.

Rachmiel leaned forward, watching Tabris's style, the spareness of his motions, the way he never left an opening. Tabris's awareness was focused not only on Miriael, but also spread out over the entire field so that the breeze, the clouds, the motion of the tree limbs all contributed to the fight. If Miriael flashed to another location, Tabris reacted with a speed Rachmiel had to call instinct, and Rachmiel wondered if Tabris was fully conscious of all his moves. The control said yes. The speed said no.

"He's amazing," he whispered. And to Mithra, "Did you and he ever fight together?"

Mithra assented. Rachmiel felt Mithra direct his thoughts to the power behind every strike.

Tabris landed a blow on Miriael, and Rachmiel flinched at the force.

Sebastian, on the other end of that, would have been blown to pieces. No chance. No chance whatsoever.

95

Power went out from Tabris to Miriael, who remained in position a moment before a crack resounded across the field, and Miriael charged.

Mithra leaned forward. "Ooh! Nice!"

"What was that?"

"Tabris pinned him. It's like a Guard, where your will keeps someone out of a space. This is more like a fishhook: you can keep someone anchored to one spot so he can't run away."

Rachmiel straightened. "That's what you did to Katra'il."

Mithra nodded.

Voriah said, "It sounded like Miriael broke it."

"Oh, they can be broken, but a demon who's trying to run won't normally move toward the one he's trying to run from. Miriael broke it by moving toward him instead of trying to escape." Mithra folded his arms. "I'll show you how to do it later."

The game ended when three demons arrived to investigate. Tabris and Miriael changed focus to drive them away. Battle-warmed, within seconds they forced the demons to run.

Josai'el flashed between the pair before they could regroup. "Miriael! Look at Kyle!"

Miriael's eyes rounded, and he flashed to Kyle and Martin, streaming apologies to Josai'el.

"And Tabris—" Josai'el said, turning to him.

But Tabris had already flashed to Elizabeth, dropping to his knees and wrapping arms and wings around her. Rachmiel projected reassurance, but he felt Tabris taking himself to task. An image flared in his mind: Sebastian's mother refraining from wine while pregnant because of the life within. "You're right. I'm sorry. Sparring while she was awake was unprofessional. We won't do that again."

Josai'el returned to Bridget.

Tabris put his head against Elizabeth, frowning.

In the silence that followed the reprimand, Rachmiel said, "You were very good. I never watched you fight before."

Tabris snapped, "For all the good it did Elizabeth."

The family continued their picnic once the boys had finished their wrestling match. Elizabeth returned to her book. Katra'il summoned her guitar, made from her soul's substance the way Tabris's and Miriael's swords were fashioned from theirs, and she played Tarrega's *Recuerdos de la Alhambra*. Hadriel and Mithra formed a light sculpture, calling up a solid block of light and then spinning it as though it were pottery on the wheel; wherever they touched it, the light changed color and shape.

Rachmiel watched their sculpture altering as it spun, and he extended his fingers to graze the outside, leaving a swath of orange. Listless, Tabris remained alongside Elizabeth.

Rachmiel called him. "Do you want to try this?"

Tabris looked right at him, and Rachmiel felt what Tabris wasn't saying: *Light shouldn't be dirty.*

"You're welcome to try," said Rachmiel, but Tabris focused away. Fragments of anger clung to him, but Rachmiel wasn't sure at whom.

When Connie gathered everyone to eat, the angels pulled in their wings and bowed their heads while Andrew said grace for the family. Then the children began squabbling over how many hot dogs they deserved and who got the only can of orange soda.

Tabris retreated from the noise, looking at the tree crowns where birds had begun building nests.

Rachmiel was about to call him when power washed over the field. All eight angels turned toward Jesus where he'd appeared. Seven of them bowed; Tabris had thrown himself to the ground.

Josai'el said, "My Lord."

Jesus stood before Tabris, looking at him in silence. Rachmiel moved closer, hands clasped at his chest and wings trembling. *Love him,* God had said during prayer, and he hadn't. Had Tabris run out of time because of him...? But surely God wouldn't have given Rachmiel instructions for helping Tabris only to end his probation now with fire.

Jesus said, "Tabris."

Rachmiel's spirit twanged like an overtight violin string. The cold light in Jesus's eyes was nothing Rachmiel wanted to see directed at himself, ever, nor at Elizabeth. It was hard enough standing near Tabris when his Lord looked so angry. But Jesus sent him reassurance, and Rachmiel tried to unkey himself. Voriah appeared at Rachmiel's back.

Tabris drew up to his knees, but he kept his arms crossed over his chest. He bowed his head.

Jesus said, "You haven't expressed any concern about Sebastian."

Tabris pulled his wings tighter to his back.

"It's time you visited him."

Tabris's head snapped up. "No!"

Amplifying Tabris's own emotions, Rachmiel was speaking before he realized. "He's not ready!"

Jesus looked at Rachmiel, and Tabris said, "I can't."

Rachmiel dropped to his knees, unsure if it was worship or weakness. "Please don't force him. Don't give an ultimatum." Tabris's desperation had grown to a whine in his mind; it hurt to think. Options. He needed options. He needed space to figure out what to do. Tabris's distress had shot up through Elizabeth (mercifully too young to feel what she conducted) and out her heart into Rachmiel, who formed it up as the loss of everything valuable, everything but God torn away—and maybe God too. Maybe even Him.

Rachmiel raised his wings. "My Lord, send me instead."

Tabris cringed.

But if Rachmiel could stand in his place, it made sense. If someone had to visit the boy, it could be him. He could prepare the way. Buy Tabris more time.

Behind him, Voriah said, "Please. Have mercy."

Rachmiel could feel the prayers of the other household angels, and laced around them, a sensation he could feel only because it backwashed through Elizabeth: Tabris's fear. Not fear of God. Fear of the household angels. Their loyalty frightened him more than condemnation.

Rachmiel pumped strength into Elizabeth, hoping it would overflow into Tabris.

Jesus said, "Why are you doing this?"

Rachmiel closed his eyes. "Please. He needs more time."

"Sebastian needs him."

Rachmiel closed his eyes. "Let me be Tabris to Sebastian. I'll stand in his place. Please. You're all-powerful and all-knowing. You must know some way I can help."

A long pause. Then Jesus said, "Granted. Rachmiel, you can visit Sebastian for now. Tabris?" His voice sharpened. "He's won more time for you, but you need to face Sebastian eventually. Use it well."

Tabris closed his eyes.

Jesus looked back at Rachmiel, who shook with relief. "Tonight I'll send a messenger for you. Thank you." He vanished.

Those parting words—thank you—as if Rachmiel had done him a favor. They made no sense. God had done him a favor. Done Tabris a favor. God had told him to be ready to respond, and Rachmiel hadn't done anything more than asked.

Across the field, the family was eating potato salad and pretzels, talking about the NCAA basketball tournament and other important things.

Thirteen

Rachmiel didn't have long to be nervous that night: a messenger angel came for him as soon as Elizabeth fell asleep. The white-winged angel bowed, projecting that he would escort him to Sebastian.

The messenger scanned for Tabris. He wouldn't find him: Tabris had made sure he was out of the house the moment Elizabeth turned off her light. The messenger projected a question to Rachmiel, who opened his hands and shrugged. "I don't know. I didn't ask."

The other angel frowned, and Rachmiel felt his scorn. Stray ideas: replacements; murder; lack of love.

Looking down, Rachmiel bit back a rejoinder. Let the other angel think what he would. He only said, "If he didn't love Sebastian, I think he would have gone immediately."

The messenger angel blinked, second guesses clouding his eyes.

Second guesses. Rachmiel had been enduring a lot of those on his own, uncertain whether Tabris would be angry with him for going (although to be fair, there hadn't seemed any choice) and then wondering whether he shouldn't have let God force the issue. Tabris might not have persisted in refusing if refusal meant Hell, and maybe Sebastian did need to see him. Maybe he needed to see Sebastian.

As Elizabeth had brushed her teeth, Rachmiel had said, "Do you have anything you want me to tell him for you?" and Tabris had said no.

No. Just no, like Connie telling Andrew she didn't need anything from the store. It didn't feel right to leave it at that. "I could say you want him to forgive you," Rachmiel had added, and Tabris had only said, "I would prefer you didn't mention me at all."

As if that would be possible. Sebastian would have questions. A thousand questions.

The other angel flashed Rachmiel to a grassy field. Limbo. Nearby they could see two figures, and they walked in that direction.

On the sloped terrain, Rachmiel felt a stabbing homesickness for Heaven. As Heaven's outer layer, Limbo resembled it in so many ways: the distant mountains, the air so clean it could mesh with his own essence and remain tinged with angelic spirit for a few minutes. Rachmiel could sense other angel-human pairs at a distance, individuals completing their development before presenting themselves before God. Their guardians would know what they needed and spend the time productively.

Tabris could have done the same for Sebastian. For the first time, Rachmiel wondered why keeping the pair together was such a bad idea.

"Sebastian's caregiver is Casifer," said the messenger. "He's been given charge over the boy's upbringing until he's ready to enter Heaven."

Remembering the other angels' speculation about the child having committed a capital crime, Rachmiel said, "What's holding him back?"

"Casifer will fill you in, but he's got plenty of company, and he's happy." A bird passed overhead, and the messenger watched the path of its flight. "He knows Casifer isn't his original guardian, and he knows what happened, but he doesn't know about Tabris or Tabris's name."

Yeah, that would be a recipe for mutual misery, if the boy were able to repeatedly summon Tabris while the ex-guardian refused to respond.

"He's still wearing the body of a twelve-year-old, but at some point Casifer will teach him to modulate his appearance."

The angels crested the final hill before meeting Sebastian, and Rachmiel gasped as he saw—Tabris!

It had to be Tabris, only he wasn't. He was much younger, his spirit not weighed with the experience of eons. Physically, he was shorter, stockier, less athletic, and of course he had no wings. He still bore an adolescent off-balance Rachmiel had seen come and go in each of Elizabeth's older brothers, when they began growing faster than their minds could adjust to their bodies.

In every other way, the resemblance gave Rachmiel shivers. It was the soul that resembled Tabris exactly, as though God had photocopied the angel, reduced him in size, and inserted him into a human frame.

The boy's eyes glimmered with the same depth Tabris's had, and he kept his face under the same control—a practiced blankness. Confronted by this imitation, Rachmiel found himself attempting to read the boy the same way he read Tabris all the time, ready to either help Tabris or protect Elizabeth from him.

Relax, he told himself. *Of course he resembles Tabris. They were paired in God's mind from before Creation. Elizabeth's soul will resemble mine too.* Well, his and Tabris's both, in some way. Which led to an interesting question, whether that meant Tabris had always been destined to guard Elizabeth as well as Sebastian? File that one away for future pondering. Right now, he needed to talk to a boy with the same mannerisms and the same tightness about his hands and eyes.

The kid was studying him, so Rachmiel inclined his head and opened his wings. "Hello, Sebastian. My name is Rachmiel."

The boy's eyes narrowed. "Were *you* my guardian?"

Wow, the anger there. "No, I'm not. He and I work together now."

The kid spun toward Casifer, a tall angel with white wings. "But you said Jesus was going to invite him to come."

"He sent me instead," Rachmiel said, glad for the ambiguous pronoun. "I'm going to talk to you ahead of him."

For the first time, Rachmiel realized how redundant his position was. Any other angel to Sebastian still wasn't Tabris. The messenger departed, and Rachmiel looked to Casifer for a cue.

Casifer responded with warmth, his eyes green and welcoming, and Rachmiel's tension dissipated. They had worked together in the past, and Rachmiel had been struck by Casifer's generosity even back then. Casifer touched his wings to the tips of Rachmiel's feathers, then hugged him angelically, a contact of the soul rather than a physical action.

Sebastian watched with wide eyes as their souls coiled around one another. "Whoa! How did you do that?"

Casifer put a hand on his shoulder. "Souls are pliable, and when they contact one another without restraint, it feels welcome."

Rachmiel backed up a step to watch them interact. Casifer wore a startled delight whenever he spoke to Sebastian—more of *That Look*. During their first job together, Casifer had confided his one regret: that he never would be the guardian of a human being. God had revealed that to him during the early years, when Casifer had seen the bonding between angel and charge and grown eager for his own.

Having Sebastian was so close to the actual thing. Casifer could finally have what he'd desired.

Sebastian reached for Casifer in his first attempt at a spiritual hug, and Rachmiel grinned as the boy fumbled without being able to grasp Casifer, only touch him. Casifer laughed, and the boy said, "Wow, could I do that any clumsier?"

He flopped down on the ground, looking up at Rachmiel. "Would you like me to stumble all over you too?"

101

"It'd be my pleasure." Sitting at his side, Rachmiel found himself drinking in the boy's smile. When had he ever seen Tabris that able to joke about his own shortcomings? Or that unselfconscious?

Sebastian sat up on his knees. "Can you tell me about home? How are my parents doing?"

No one from Sebastian's life had visited Tabris. Not even once. Rachmiel said, "I'm afraid I don't know."

"Oh. I hope they're okay. I pray for them a lot." He looked down. "I suppose you don't know how my dog is doing?"

No, nothing like that.

Sebastian looked up. "I'm worried about my friends. I'd borrowed a book from Mikey, and I never gave it back. Did my parents know to give it back to him?"

Rachmiel didn't know that either.

Sebastian shrugged then, and he looked right at Rachmiel, waiting.

Casifer said, "Sebastian has been doing a lot of exploring," and turning to the boy, "Why don't you tell him?"

With his eyes large, Sebastian narrated a rafting trip where he knew a little bit of how to raft, and Casifer knew nothing about it, and they finally discovered their mutual inexperience halfway through the trip. Rachmiel laughed out loud. "We kept going, though," said Sebastian. "I figured, what's the worst that could happen? It's not like I'm going to die again."

The longer the boy talked, the more Rachmiel felt himself wanting to remain with him, a feeling he hadn't experienced since the first moment he'd seen Elizabeth. Like Elizabeth, Sebastian loved to read, so Casifer had fetched him an assortment of books from Heaven's libraries, and Sebastian spent some afternoons reading aloud to him.

Sebastian said, "Oh, and do you want to make your ears bleed?" and then stumbled through a badly-pronounced prayer in the angelic language.

"That's not *terrible*," Rachmiel said.

Sebastian said, "No, because Heaven is perfect and therefore some linguist is busy inventing a new word for worse-than-terrible!" He laughed. "But that's okay. The whole thing about projecting your emotions and concepts without speaking at all? Whoosh!" He made a motion of something flying over his head. "Casifer says eternity is a long time, but I'm not sure it'll be long enough for me to get that!"

Casifer made a complex projection to Rachmiel, that as a human, Sebastian expected to be in control of what he said and did not say, or that he could project happiness when he wasn't feeling it. Rachmiel chuckled: someday he'd have to explain the same to Elizabeth, assuring her that in God's light no thoughts were shameful; you could always broadcast anything without cloaking your soul against the horror of knowing and being known.

Sebastian grimaced. "Yeah. Just like that. Thanks for rubbing it in."

"Any time," said Rachmiel, and the boy threw a handful of grass at him.

"It's a language without grammar," Rachmiel said. "Sometimes I think humans invented language because that way it was easier to lie."

Sebastian said, "Angels have language too."

"Several languages," said Casifer. "There's one for worship, one for everyday speech, one for more formal speech, and so on."

"But they're all coupled with emotional affirmation," said Rachmiel. "Demons use the same languages, but they remove the emotions from the communication."

Even as he said that, Rachmiel realized Tabris had done the same.

Feeling Rachmiel's shock, Sebastian welled up with concern, and Rachmiel said, "There! That was a perfect instance of projected communication."

Sebastian glanced with an asymmetric smile at Casifer, who nodded.

Now that they'd become comfortable, Rachmiel found himself wanting to hear more of Sebastian's stories, and the boy obliged, talking about making himself tiny enough to ride a dragonfly and then exploring all the crags of a waterfall.

What he'd tell Tabris, Rachmiel didn't know, but he could say without reservation that the boy was thriving. The laughter, the delight—it was evident in everything about him, and always Casifer was at the ready to provide an explanation to bring the boy closer to Heaven.

As they talked, Rachmiel tracked the time until Elizabeth would awaken, and predictably, it was when he said he'd have to get back soon that Sebastian said, "Before you go—tell me about my guardian."

Rachmiel glanced at Casifer, who darkened.

"Please." Sebastian traced his finger over a grass blade. "I want to know about him. What he's like. If he's—What he's doing now."

Sebastian couldn't have realized how many questions he'd projected beyond the words, but innocent as he was, they'd all bombarded Rachmiel at the same time, and Rachmiel's soul amplified them. The need, one need: an answer to *why*. And also, was Tabris sorry?

As Rachmiel struggled to get his heart under control, his wings purpled at the tips. "He's back at home, guarding my charge." What was worth saying? And what was best unspoken? "He's her co-guardian with me. Her name is Elizabeth, and she's ten."

Sebastian looked up, eyes wide.

"Yes, I trust him." Oh, to soothe the friction coursing over Sebastian's soul. "We work well together."

"But—" Sebastian's soul vibrated with fright. "What if he hurts her?"

Rachmiel lowered the pitch of his voice. "There are other angels nearby. But I trust him, and he won't want to hurt her."

"Why not?" Sebastian said. "Does he love her?"

Rachmiel said, "Yes—" before realizing what Sebastian was really asking. "Guardians always love their charges. We see God in you so strongly."

Sebastian uprooted a fistful of grass. "You love her, but you'll leave her with him?"

"I do, and I did." Rachmiel tried to project calm, but the boy's distress kept making him edgy. "She's safe. I wouldn't have come if I'd doubted that."

Sebastian closed his eyes, breathing heavily.

And behind those eyes, Sebastian pumped out a question continuously, projecting it either without knowing or despite knowing, a question Rachmiel didn't feel free to answer because that night on the rooftop, Tabris had told him not to say anything at all—and in this language without grammar, Rachmiel couldn't pin the boy's sense of abandonment to the present or the past. Worse, Sebastian's feelings weren't the only chronologically ambiguous ones. Tabris had said he loved the boy. He didn't say he still did. Or that he did at the moment he killed him.

Sebastian wrenched his soul around with a violence that made Casifer's feathers flare, and he asked about baseball. Fortunately, after hearing Martin and Alan arguing endlessly over which team stank the most, Rachmiel was fluent in this year's stats. Sebastian settled down, but Casifer stayed very near, his hand on Sebastian's shoulder.

Just before it would be dawn in Vermont, Rachmiel stood to go. Reluctantly. It didn't make sense, but he didn't want to leave the child.

Sebastian scrambled to a stand, and he hugged Rachmiel with his arms. "I can't do this yet with my soul. I might injure you."

Rachmiel ruffled his hair. "You're a good kid. You'll learn quickly."

Sebastian looked up at him. "Will you visit again?"

His eyes were bright, so much like Tabris on the brink of a painful moment.

"Absolutely. I was hoping you'd want me to."

The sheen vanished from his eyes, replaced by a mahogany that wrung Rachmiel's heart. "I would. I'd like that a lot." Sebastian tried to affirm that with a projection, awkwardly mimicking what soon would take place naturally. Casifer gave his shoulder a squeeze.

Rachmiel gave him a promise with his heart, and as Sebastian flashed him a lopsided smile, he returned home.

Tabris was stretched full-length alongside Elizabeth, his two-toned wings spread over her like an extra blanket. The night had grown chilly, and he warmed the air around her to keep her sleeping.

Rachmiel popped into the room, and Tabris clenched his jaw. He waited.

"Did anything happen while I was gone?"

Tabris said, "No. I would have called you."

Of course, then Rachmiel examined Elizabeth's soul and body anyhow, to make sure. She was fine. Dreaming about cotton candy. Rachmiel chuckled.

He turned his attention to Tabris, so Tabris sat away from the girl. The cold air would awaken her, but he'd let it. In the face of Rachmiel's aura of expectation, Tabris said, "Did you meet him?"

Rachmiel nodded, emanating eagerness, worry, and excitement. The combination hit Tabris like a punch to the gut. "Is he doing all right?"

Rachmiel nodded again, and this time Tabris felt more specifics. He recoiled, trying to force away the images that came to him of a child exploring Heaven for the first time. No, not Heaven. That was the calm undulation of Limbo in those images, not the ferocious beauty of Heaven. And then, inexplicably, the sense of a second angel. Tabris blurted out before thinking, "Who's staying with him?"

"Casifer."

"Oh." Up until now, Tabris had hoped—well, almost hoped—Sebastian had spring-boarded into Heaven and gotten private tutoring sessions with God Almighty, received a final dusting-off of his soul, and then sprinted off to the registration center at Heaven's university where he could learn from the finest faculty creation had to offer. Jewish mysticism, taught by Abraham himself. A dozen human friends exploring the mansions of Heaven. Maybe a saintly adviser to sign some kind of report card. He hadn't wanted to think about a substitute. But of course Sebastian would need an angel. It just couldn't be him.

He locked down his emotions. "Casifer will be devoted to him. He never had a charge of his own." He turned away, and the only thing worth looking at was Elizabeth. "I'd hoped you would return before she woke up."

He could feel Rachmiel's inner gasp and knew the other angel's eyes would have gone purple. But Rachmiel wouldn't have understood—in a thousand years, he'd never have understood, and if he thought Tabris indifferent, that was better than thinking the truth.

Tabris turned to him, forcing himself to look blank. "I know you like to be the one who wakes her. I can't imagine a morning where she awoke without you calling her Sleepyhead. She'd be disoriented all day." Rachmiel still seemed shocked, and Tabris flailed for a new subject. Anything. Just get Rachmiel talking about something else. "Of course, you can't substitute for God."

May God forgive him for that. Murdering a child was one thing. Making use of God for his own ends: that was an entirely different category of crime.

Rachmiel said, "No, of course not. God's grace is far more pervasive than our presence."

With an angel, you could always, always, change the subject to God. Fallen or unfallen: it would work every time.

Rachmiel said, "She doesn't detect our presence either, but God's working at such a low level with her, in so many ways at all times."

So long ago, Sebastian had surfed the waves of his first crush. He was six. The object of his affections was a nine-year-old on the school bus, an unreachable third grader who wore a sparkling pink backpack and whose black ponytail swung free to her waist. She could sing in Spanish. Every day for a month, Sebastian had worked with all the stealth a first grader has in his arsenal, getting close to her in order to memorize anything she said, maybe smile at her, and once he even dropped his pencil and she picked it up for him. He'd saved the pencil. He learned to write so he could print her name with it in the margins of his notebooks.

The adults had said it was ridiculous, but this was Sebastian's First Love, a narcotic powerful enough to leave even Tabris giddy. The adults' First Love had been dimmed by experience, by betrayal or tears. But to Sebastian it had been unique, untarnished, and brilliant.

As Rachmiel talked about how God worked in Elizabeth's heart, Tabris realized Rachmiel remained neck deep in his First Love, and Tabris had lost that. Lost it when he'd betrayed God.

His ears rang. *I'm probably the only angel who could listen to Rachmiel without jumping into the conversation.*

Well, for that matter, he was probably the only angel who would have baited a conversational trap with God-talk to begin with.

"*But God,* he thought, *you know I love you...don't I?*

No answer. There wouldn't be. Tabris cleared his head and checked on Elizabeth, who'd curled tight under the sheets to ward off the cold.

Rachmiel leaned over her and laid his head against hers. "Sleepyhead, you need to wake up now. Let's see what God has in mind for you today."

He looked up at Tabris, eyes warm, and when Tabris saw an angel wrapped around his chief delight while snug within God's love, he fought the urge to sob.

Fourteen

After church that day, Tabris sat on the roof rather than stay near Rachmiel. The other angels kept asking Rachmiel questions about Sebastian, but even though he deflected them, he couldn't stop the emotions from bubbling up as he kept recalling the visit. And Tabris kept picking them up. It was already obvious there'd be more visits.

When Elizabeth didn't come out of the garage or go into the house with her brothers, Tabris focused through the roof to find her battling the snow blower, lawn mower, garden hose, six folding chairs and a bag of fertilizer to secure the release of her bicycle.

Tabris went icy cold.

She talked to the bike the whole time she dragged it out, assuring it she'd meant no harm by the winter-long abandonment. She pumped up the tires and cleaned a cobweb off the seat.

Tabris called down to the driveway. "Is that safe? She should have her father check the bike."

Rachmiel flexed his wings in the sun, craning back his neck to look at Tabris. "There's no way we're stopping her. She's been thinking about bicycles all day. Come on down. This will do you good."

"What?" Thinking about bicycles all day—? What had Sebastian told him?

But it wasn't accusation in Rachmiel's voice as much as teasing. "I thought you loved to fly."

Tabris flashed down to him. "Are you saying her bicycle can fly?"

Rachmiel laughed. "When a kid is biking, you fly a little above and behind. Didn't Sebastian ride a bike?"

Tabris's insides corkscrewed. Rachmiel was going to begin talking about Sebastian in everyday conversation. He'd leave tidbits of information like a trail of breadcrumbs and see if Tabris followed.

Tabris only said, "Sebastian rode a bike."

Rachmiel brightened. "Did he enjoy it? Maybe I should see if he wants to do that the next time I visit."

Tabris flinched. "Are you sure you need me? I'd rather not go."

Rachmiel's eyes dimmed. "Do you want some time alone?"

Tabris's heart jumped. "No, it's not like that." He remembered a demonic voice like a zephyr winding its way through him. *You desert Elizabeth far too easily.* "I'll stay, but—"

Elizabeth buckled her helmet. Tabris fought the urge to wrap his wings around himself.

"What's wrong?" Rachmiel looked at him like a linguist cracking a code. "Do you need a break?"

"Leave me alone." Tabris glared away from him. "I'll go biking with you. I'm not *deserting* her."

Rachmiel backed off. Elizabeth mounted her bike and pedaled down the driveway. He steadied her as she wobbled to a start, then guided her tires over the gravel where the driveway met the main road. Tabris followed.

Rachmiel streamed confusion. Tabris clamped down on his heart and said, "I'm sorry. I shouldn't have snapped at you."

"I'm sorry I mentioned Sebastian. Was that why you're upset?"

Tabris shot ahead of Elizabeth down the road and moved a carpenter bee out of her path, then checked the road surface. He alerted Rachmiel to some loose gravel, then went high and scanned for oncoming traffic. A neighbor in a gray pickup truck would pass in a few minutes, probably after Elizabeth had veered off onto another road.

He went in close again. *You desert her far too easily.* Rachmiel and Mithra lying to him, running to Raguel to tattle that he'd done what they'd told him to do, and wasn't Tabris evil?

Rachmiel whispered, "Tabris? What do you think I did?"

With that sharp cut of a confirmed rumor, Tabris knew right then that Rachmiel had betrayed him after all. Demons could lie, but they told the truth when it was worse. This was worse.

He had no time to collect his thoughts. No time to get his head together because Elizabeth was biking and it scared him half to death.

It was almost—almost—bearable if he concentrated on the interlocking rhythms. Her pedaling motion, her breath, her heartbeat, the chain's clicking. Up, down. In, out. Forward. Forward. They all looped together like an elaborate Celtic knot. He could get through this. He stopped scanning for dangers and just kept pace. Keep pace and ignore the question mark flying at his side.

Until the moment Rachmiel burst with a warning, and Tabris focused too late on the trap: a demon shot across the road through the spokes of her tires. The front tire hit a rock and skidded. Elizabeth squeezed the brakes, and as the front tire locked, the bicycle flipped, catapulting her over the handlebars.

Mid-dive to protect her, Tabris pulled back.

She slammed into the ground, bicycle landing on top of her, her arm scraped, blood pouring over her right temple and cheek.

Tabris blazed in pursuit of the demon, snaring him and then attacking with a ferocity he'd never neared when sparring with Miriael. With the demon down, he held out his sword and blasted him with soul-energy, leaving nothing but a slick demonic residue that Tabris gathered up and scattered in three different oceans. But his heart ached: the demon would reconstitute given time, and Elizabeth had been hurt anyhow. Hurt.

Hurt.

He'd failed her.

Standing on an ice floe in the Arctic, Tabris tried to get calm enough to return to Rachmiel.

One heartbeat later he realized that no, he had no need to return. He was much further than a few miles from Elizabeth now, but there was no dizziness, no numbness. The tether was broken.

And so ended probation. They'd proven he was a failure. They'd released him from service. It was just a matter of time before a couple of Archangels dragged him to the Judgment Hall to finish his sentencing.

But they would have come by now, surely, and he wondered if maybe he was just free. Free to go as far as he wanted from a girl sobbing on the gravel because her guardian angel had failed her. Tabris could sit on a mountain top, explore one of Saturn's moons, bury himself in a star a thousand light years away, or even return to Heaven. He could go anywhere he wanted. Anywhere at all. Where did he want to go?

Yeah. It figured.

He returned to Elizabeth.

Several angels had gathered. Elizabeth was on her feet, and the neighbor driving the pickup truck had given her a towel. The cut was at the top of her ear, Tabris realized with relief, not her forehead. The neighbor was chucking her bike in the bed of his truck.

Tabris turned toward Rachmiel and got hit with his fury.

"What did you think you were doing?" Rachmiel shot toward him, wings flared. "I thought you had her and then you backed off! What kind of guarding is that? Better if you'd just let her fall! Then at least I'd have gone after her, but you left her unprotected the first time she really needed you!"

Tabris backed away, but Rachmiel followed. Shaking, he looked around as if there were an escape, but the disdain of the other angels surrounded him like ice. They could keep him from Elizabeth. They could pin him here with their will. They'd probably already called Raguel and this really would be the end. All the explanations died in his mouth, transfixed as he was by the red of Rachmiel's eyes.

He shook his head. "I didn't—"

"That's right, you didn't! You didn't grab her, didn't cushion her, didn't make sure she fell well! You didn't do a thing!" Flames curled through Rachmiel's hair. "You're great at deflecting snowballs, but where were you when she needed you?"

Eyes clenched, Tabris fought the images, fought but couldn't stop the overflow he knew was streaming from him: a boy on a bicycle, a boy flipping over and over, a boy lying dead in his hands with a bicycle jack-knifed between his legs. A snap that broke the world, broke the child, broke Tabris's connection to everyone around him and to God above.

Tabris fled. He shot away from Rachmiel without thinking, and he landed face-down on Elizabeth's bed, fingers clutching the mattress springs. He walled up the room with a Guard and then doubled it. Two kids, two guardianships, two disasters, and he was done for. Something was wrong with him, something he needed to hide. *You desert Elizabeth far too easily,* except that all along, he should have deserted the first one. Or he should have deserted Elizabeth earlier than he had. It was all over.

Still. Just go still. Stay here. Don't move.

He felt another angel in the room. Scared. Sorry. Tabris curled around himself, but a hand touched his shoulder, and the other angel projected that he should stay still.

Rachmiel.

Again from the other angel: be still. Reassurance. Nearness.

Tabris tried to pull away, but Rachmiel leaned over him, and their heads touched. Rachmiel covered Tabris with his wings, and Tabris shuddered. *I'm sorry. I'm sorry. I'm sorry. I'm sorry.*

More calm from Rachmiel, followed by a sense of peace. They breathed in unison, and Tabris tried to clamp down on that grief, shove it to the bottom of his soul, but Rachmiel wouldn't let him. Instead, it chewed on him until Tabris felt very much like fear, only it was something worse, something hot to the touch and sharp with teeth, weighing down in his grasp like tons of ballast.

I'm sorry. I'm sorry.

Prayer: Rachmiel was praying. For himself. For Tabris. Asking God to forgive and ease his own anger, then asking God to comfort Tabris. No, no comfort, Tabris thought. How could there be? That could never be. It just wasn't right. He couldn't ask for what he'd never deserve.

I'm sorry.

Rachmiel wrapped around the grief, the thing with spines and thorns, trying to gentle it away from him. Tabris clutched it, and the weight tore at his hands, but then Rachmiel was supporting it too. The weight eased; the stabbing diminished. The grief ebbed, and Tabris let it wriggle away to swim into the darkest corners of his soul. Relief. Coolness. Softness.

He wanted to ask Rachmiel why he'd done that for him, needed to tell him how sorry he was, but his mind was too sluggish to form the words, and then he gave up trying.

Rachmiel sat away from Tabris, still tingling with God's touch. Tabris lay asleep on the bed.

Leaning against the wall, Rachmiel shuddered as the vestiges of the Guard faded off the room, its creator unconscious. God had gotten him through the Guard. He'd never have made it in otherwise, at least not until Elizabeth had entered.

He sent a question to God.

She's fine, God replied. One of the angels on-site had offered to spot him while he went after Tabris. He didn't know how much the others had picked up when that projection ruptured out, but enough to know Tabris needed him more.

Ten minutes later, he heard Elizabeth in the hall, then in the bathroom with her mother. Rachmiel imagined the routine: the wash cloth, the antiseptic, the Band-Aids. Then Elizabeth's steps neared her room, and Connie brought her in holding an ice pack, told her to stay still with the ice on her ear. Bandages decorated her elbow and hands, and there was a rip in her new jeans.

The other angel returned her care to Rachmiel, and Hadriel stared at Tabris. Rachmiel waved them away. Connie left the room, shutting the door at her back.

Naturally unaware of Tabris, Elizabeth laid down on the bed, curled sideways with the ice pack balanced on the side of her head, and picked up a book.

The wind breathed over the outside of the house, and Rachmiel watched the clouds. Elizabeth was reading a sad story, one of those small gifts you were never quite sure God had given you. If she picked up Rachmiel's emotions, she'd attribute them to the book. As images came to him from her reading, they mingled with those horrifying projections from Tabris: Sebastian, the bicycle, the angel curled over the boy as they flipped over, and the snap of a life extinguished.

Rachmiel reached with his heart for God. *I should have trusted his judgment.* When he'd gone off in pursuit, he'd expected to find Tabris at the pond, but instead he'd run here. Run for home.

Five minutes later, with Rachmiel still numb, Raguel appeared in the room. Rachmiel regarded him, dull. Raguel crouched alongside the bed and touched Tabris's hair. "What exactly happened?"

Elizabeth stopped reading and stared out the window.

Rachmiel couldn't meet his eyes. "You didn't tell me Sebastian died on his bicycle."

"I thought Tabris would tell you everything you needed to know."

"He didn't. I told him to watch Elizabeth biking, and she fell." He looked up. "She's hurt, but not because he hurt her. He didn't touch her at all. That's why she got hurt. I was angry at him." Rachmiel swallowed hard. "I'm sorry. I just don't know what else to say."

The clouds drifted past, and Elizabeth watched them. Rachmiel watched too, letting them drift over the memory of a fallen bicycle. Two fallen bicycles.

Raguel sighed. "I'm sorry this happened. Call me as soon as he's awake. I'll talk to him."

"Actually—" Rachmiel shook his head, but he didn't look away from the clouds. "Let me do it. I was the one he talked to. I'm part of the reason this happened. If I can't handle it, I'll call, but let me try."

Raguel assented, and then he vanished.

Elizabeth closed her eyes. Rachmiel touched the scraped elbow, noting as he did how Elizabeth and Tabris had cuddled against one another, as though consoling each other for a common loss.

Well, in a way, that happened. Rachmiel traced a hand over the girl's arm. *Tabris lost his charge, and she lost—*

Rachmiel's heart pounded.

—her husband?

113

He shot off the bed to the far wall, staring at the pair. Their souls fit with one another perfectly—perfectly, fitting to one another for their differences the same way he and she were bound through their similarities. She and Sebastian would have fit to one another, and now—oh, and now it made sense why he felt so linked to Sebastian: because *he should have been*. They were all supposed to be together, and now they were, except one of them was missing.

He huddled up, tears in his eyes for Elizabeth, Elizabeth who deserved every good thing the world could have given her, first among those someone to love with all her heart. And instead this? Because of Tabris—widowhood? Permanently single in a world of families?

She and Sebastian would have fit together the same way he and Tabris did. They'd have met, maybe in college, and Tabris would have sized her up, hand on his sword, but over time the two angels would have talked on the rooftops, planning for each other, working things out, helping the kids work things out, and now—none of that. Nothing at all.

And in all this, Tabris kept up the charade that he wanted to do right by her, when in reality—

Tabris doesn't know, said God.

Rachmiel trembled. Didn't know? *So why does he think he's here?* And he felt inside that Tabris thought he was with this family because the guardians were such a strong unit.

Terrific. Rachmiel huffed. *So in twenty years when he wonders why no one wants to marry her, do I tell him then?*

God's touch came again, and Rachmiel relaxed as God soothed him: His plan wasn't a projection into the future, a long list of occurrences that might or might not take place, with a single goal at the end. Rather, God had designed a dynamic scheme. They weren't puppets acting out a script.

Well, that made things marginally better. Years from now, Elizabeth would hold another man in her arms, and she would tell him they belonged together, that God had planned them for each other. Only it wouldn't be true. The man God intended for her was dead.

What about their children? Rachmiel asked. If Elizabeth and Sebastian should have had children, would they still be able to be born? Could the father be so easily substituted? Would she suffer decades of infertility because of Tabris?

Again came God's reassurance: Elizabeth could still have children. She could still be married well. Tabris had crossed the Divine plan, but he could never destroy it.

Rachmiel touched Elizabeth again, looking at her and an angel both healing from their injuries. He kissed her forehead. So young and already robbed of a husband.

So many people had been hurt. Sebastian himself. Elizabeth and her unconceived children. The boy's parents. His friends.

Anger coiled like a wire around his heart, and he fired his disgust at Tabris, knowing that while asleep Tabris wouldn't feel it. But awake, Elizabeth moved.

"He widowed you, and he injured you too," Rachmiel whispered. "He doesn't deserve—"

He caught himself.

God blossomed like a flower in Rachmiel's heart. *I love him.*

Rachmiel curled over Elizabeth, but he raised his wings so he didn't touch Tabris. *I'm sorry.* And then, *What he did was awful.*

This God didn't dispute. Rachmiel opened his churning heart. *You'd better take this anger away from me, or I'm going to hurt him more.*

Rachmiel opened his senses to take in the image of God within himself. He lost hold of time, suspended in a moment or in an hour—it made no difference because he was here, and He was here, and they stayed together. Rachmiel held out his anger to God, and God acknowledged it before Rachmiel let it go. He wasn't the one injured. He would forgive before the anger distorted him.

As the fury blew away on the wind, Rachmiel felt God offer him thanks, and a gift. Rachmiel accepted, and God allowed him a glimpse of Tabris's heart.

Rachmiel's spirit brightened, fascinated by the spirals and twists of a crepuscular conscience, the sense of duty combined with the keenness of failure, and something else. A longing he'd never expected.

As God closed away that glance, Rachmiel scrambled for more, but the vision retreated. *That's for Tabris to give you.*

Rachmiel breathed his thanks, then rested back into his sense of God in all. He imagined himself and God in the same position, knocking at the outer gate of Tabris's heart while the inhabitant huddled inside at the back of his closet. But God could see through the walls; Rachmiel couldn't—only once when the figure had thrown open the gates, shown himself mortally wounded, and then retreated.

God eased Rachmiel out of the prayer, and Rachmiel found himself again crouching beside Elizabeth on the bed. He held up his wings as if Tabris were something disgusting he didn't want to brush against.

I'm going to need help, Rachmiel thought to God.

I made you, God replied. *I'll be with you.*

Rachmiel traced a hand across Elizabeth's forehead, lingering over the cut on her ear, and he breathed a blessing over her. Then, again to God, *Thank you for her.*

From God to him: *Thank you for you."*

Fifteen

The ice pack became a sloshy mess at about the same time Elizabeth got bored with reading, but Rachmiel hesitated at the doorway when she went into the hall. Kyle started ribbing her about ditching her bike, and while she told him to shut up, Miriael approached Rachmiel.

"I don't want to leave him." Rachmiel frowned. "Maybe I should call another angel to watch her."

"Or maybe you should ask me for advice." Grinning, Miriael formed a miniature Guard between two fingers. "Do you know what this is?"

"Useless?"

"This is freedom. Ask me how."

Rachmiel folded his arms.

"Fine." Miriael laughed. "A Guard formed like this in midair won't hold anything out, but you'd feel if it got jostled. Make a dozen and position them over Tabris so they're close to touching but not quite. When he awakens, he'll brush against them, and you'll feel the Guards bump one another."

Rachmiel laughed. "That's brilliant!"

Miriael grinned. "Special Ops trick. A smart demon can detect those and avoid them, but you're not trying to outwit a demon."

Rachmiel shook his head. "It's a Godsend that you're here!"

Miriael nodded. "Tell me about it—I haven't had this much fun in years."

Rachmiel formed a dozen grape-sized bubbles and positioned them over Tabris, Miriael showing him just how far apart to leave them so they'd collide if Tabris moved. That done, Rachmiel returned to Elizabeth.

In the living room, she sat in the slanting rays of 3p.m. sunlight, looking through her sheet music. Heart trilling, Rachmiel sat at her side, noting her serious expression as she paged through her book for the piece she was supposed to be working on now. She set the book on the Steinway upright—used by both her father and grandmother—then warmed up for an entire thirty seconds before beginning the piece.

Rachmiel kept her cupped in his wings while she played. Her skinned elbows were stiff, and he frowned, trying to ease them. Poor kid. Such a needless accident.

She worked through the exercises until she got bored, changed pieces, then got bored again. Rachmiel closed his eyes and encouraged her to keep playing. She'd been taking piano for three years. Just a little longer and she'd be good enough that it was fun again.

As soon as humans had begun making music, Rachmiel had tried to learn the language, the way notes could embody emotions. Angelic music created what it represented, but human notes imitated instead of incarnated, and for that reason, human music pulsed with struggle.

Elizabeth closed the book and reached for a Chopin piece she'd learned last year for a recital. Chopin had always excited Rachmiel, and his excitement had increased exponentially when Elizabeth had come along and heard the same things he had in the music. Rachmiel had shadowed the man during his lifetime, trying to discover where the mystery came from, and after the man's death he'd asked him, only to find that sometimes the questions are more powerful than their answers.

Elizabeth hadn't yet heard the great questions, still young enough to see in life only answers, but she didn't need to know them in order to play the notes as written. In the future, Rachmiel hoped, she'd begin emoting through the music as the questions became clearer. Her occasional mistakes made the piece dearer to him, and he watched as she opened her soul to embrace the piano. She turned pages without realizing as she played, concentrating hard enough that she stopped thinking about the music as something separate from herself.

Rachmiel brimmed over with love for Elizabeth, only for her, always for her. He embraced her, then slipped inside her so his form moved in tandem with hers, as though her hands were gloves over his to move his fingers, and then he too could play Chopin. Pictures sprang to his mind through the girl, and the love of God burst like fireworks in his heart. Innocence played the questions free will had raised, that compassion alone was unable to answer.

Rachmiel knew why the author of Genesis had said the sons of God had fallen in love with the daughters of men. It wasn't physical but rather the attraction of an untarnished spirit accepting God and the world as it was, making no demands on either. What the union of a guardian angel and his charge would produce were courage, sensibility, devotion...a saint. Anything else would be redundant.

When Elizabeth stopped playing, he separated from her, heart pounding.

Elizabeth poked around some of her piano exercises for a few minutes, then put them away and turned on the television, deadening any contact Rachmiel had with her soul. Disappointed, he sat beside her staring at the moving pictures, but he found them stale, so he closed his eyes and prayed.

Then God played music in his soul. Not Chopin.

Sixteen

That evening Casifer sent a message to Rachmiel inviting him to visit Sebastian again. Voriah offered to call Rachmiel the instant Tabris awoke, and Rachmiel double-checked those Guarded spheres. When Elizabeth had gone to bed, Tabris had shifted in his sleep, touching his head to hers and laying a wing over her. He'd jostled the spheres, and they'd rung in Rachmiel's mind.

He blessed Elizabeth, and after another look at Tabris, flashed to Limbo.

Sebastian greeted Rachmiel with a hug—the spiritual kind. Rachmiel congratulated him, but he hardly needed to: the boy gave him a self-congratulatory high-five.

"I practiced all day!" He laughed, then paused. "I think Casifer's all hugged-out. He said he'd ask for a few dozen friends to stop by so I could squeeze them."

Rachmiel made a serious face. "Is that why you called me?"

Sebastian mimicked the expression. "I think his ribs hurt, and I might have poked him in the eye."

They both laughed, and Casifer rolled his eyes. Rachmiel felt the boy's warmth suffusing him: Sebastian looked so much like Tabris had that night on the roof. And then Rachmiel thought of Elizabeth, widowed, and Tabris lying face-down on her bed.

Sebastian hesitated. "Did I upset you? I didn't really poke him in the eye. Was that lying?"

"No, you're fine." Rachmiel forced down the wistfulness. "You remind me so much of your guardian."

Sebastian's face tightened.

Casifer said, "Are you all right?"

Rachmiel shook his head. "I probably won't stay the whole night this time. If Elizabeth wakes up," or Tabris, for that matter, "I'll just take off."

Sebastian grinned. "That's *so* sweet. You'd be in such a rush you wouldn't even say goodbye?"

Rachmiel said, "Probably not—" and then he smirked. "You guys are making fun of me."

Solemn, Sebastian nodded.

"You can think it's cute if you want." Rachmiel shrugged. "So does he."

Casifer said, "I make sure I'm right here whenever Sebastian wakes up."

Rachmiel drew back. "He needs to sleep?"

"For now, but not on a regular basis."

Sebastian made his eyes round and his face seem younger. "It wouldn't be Heaven if it had bedtime."

Casifer said, "Staying up all night is something of a thrill. But he's still growing."

"I sleep less often the longer I'm here." Sebastian giggled. "I guess in Heaven, you don't need to sleep at all."

Rachmiel flinched, thinking of Tabris out cold on Elizabeth's bed.

Casifer's heart jumped, and he projected a question. It was more than a little unfair to do this, knowing Sebastian couldn't understand projections, but Rachmiel compacted the whole of today's incident into one pellet of information and sent it to Casifer.

Casifer sent back a response: anger. Anger that Tabris had hurt Elizabeth, that he'd hurt Sebastian, and that he couldn't be bothered to come to see the boy when given the chance. That this child was a treasure and Tabris was treating him like worse than an annoyance. Then one final opinion flung with the force of a dart: that because Tabris hadn't wanted to see the result of what he'd done to Sebastian, now he had to see the result of what he'd done to Elizabeth.

Rachmiel tried to backpedal, but Casifer let Rachmiel know he considered it part of his job to protect Sebastian from Tabris.

Sebastian's eyes darkened, so much like Tabris. "Is it about my guardian?"

Casifer said, "Elizabeth fell off her bike today, and afterward, your guardian was very upset."

Smooth. Rachmiel wouldn't have thought of editing the incident that way, yet Casifer had done it despite his outrage. "He's asleep right now."

Sebastian said, "If you're that worried, maybe you should return."

Rachmiel looked at the ground. "I'd like to stay here, and the other angels in the house will call me if he or she wakes up. I'm sorry I'm so distracted."

Casifer said to Sebastian, "When angels sleep, it's for recovery. It's a last-ditch means of saving yourself from an emotional breakdown."

Sebastian's eyes flared. "Are you kidding? How bad was the bike accident?"

"Elizabeth is okay. He—" Rachmiel sighed. "It reminded him of you."

Sebastian was breathing fast. "Did he hurt her?"

"No, not at all." Rachmiel began wishing he hadn't even come, but Casifer rested a hand on Sebastian's shoulder and nodded to him. Maybe he could take a page from Casifer's book. "Tabris didn't even touch her."

"Oh, okay." Sebastian kicked at the ground. "Why would he be upset about it, then? I mean, if she's not hurt and he didn't do anything." His eyes darkened. "Or is he just upset that he missed his chance?"

Casifer fired a reprimand at Sebastian, and Rachmiel exclaimed, "No!"

Sebastian hunched his shoulders and put his face in his hands. "I'm sorry. I'm sorry."

So young, so brittle. Rachmiel said, "I forgive you."

"It's not charitable to assume the worst of him." Casifer pulled Sebastian closer. "Elizabeth's fall might have been God's way of bringing Tabris to think more about what he did to you."

Sebastian pursed his lips. "But you said he'll feel better when he wakes up."

Rachmiel shook his head. "Sleeping just postpones the problem. Angels don't dream, so we wake up in the same condition we went to sleep in, only strong enough to deal with the problem. You could sleep and feel better, but if an angel falls asleep sad, he wakes up sad."

Sebastian's mouth tightened. "How will my guardian wake up?"

"Probably sad," Rachmiel said. "But sometimes, now especially, I feel I don't know him well enough at all."

Tabris awoke instantly, his sword in his hand and ears straining after the sound he'd just heard. Out. He needed to get out. He needed to get Elizabeth out of here.

Tabris, came the hiss again.

He couldn't find the source. "Show yourself, Irony!"

Wake up Elizabeth. Get her away from the danger. Something wanted her dead.

Tabris tried to reach out with his mind to find Rachmiel or Miriael, but the room was Guarded—Guarded to keep him inside, and for a moment he panicked that he was under house arrest. But no, that Guard was evil. And keeping him here. Trapped. He needed to get out.

The voice came from everywhere. "I have a new name now. You can call me—"

"I'll call you damned!" he shouted, slashing his sword around the room. "Leave!"

"Please." The voice shifted around the room: at one moment the walls or the carpet could be speaking, and again Tabris pushed against the Guard, but he couldn't get out. "Come with me," said the ceiling. But then the bookcase added, "What use is this little anchor? She has another angel to take care of her, one capable of loving her. Come with me."

Go with him. Get out of here. Get out. Just go with him and he could leave...

"No." Tabris sent his awareness through the room, but the presence was too dissociated. "I belong here."

"You belonged with Sebastian," said the desk, but the carpet responded, "even though Sebastian hates you."

"I belong here now."

"Sebastian wants you in Hell. I was at the trial."

"I was there too." Tabris focused on the corners, the shadows, but in the preternatural dark he couldn't nail down the demon's hiding place. "He made no such request."

"It was internal."

Tabris said, "Then there's no way you'd know."

"The boy told me himself when I visited."

Tabris screamed, flinging himself into a corner and slicing with his sword until the tip met with resistance, and he dragged the demon into the open.

"You leave him alone!" Tabris grabbed the demon by the neck. "Just leave both of them alone! He's not yours!"

"Soon she won't be, either! Rachmiel's with Sebastian right now, gathering evidence, looking for patterns—"

"Shut up!"

The demon's eyes glittered. "They talked about you for hours. Why do you think Rachmiel said nothing about his visit?"

"I didn't ask." Tabris still clutched the demon by the throat, but his hold slackened.

"Exactly what he wanted. Could *that* angel really keep a secret if he didn't want?" The demon gasped, and Tabris loosened a bit more. "He's afraid you'll blow the game once you discover how much Sebastian hates you. Your Tyrant wanted to arrange a sticky-sweet forgiveness scene, but Sebastian's mad, and he made Rachmiel mad too. Sebastian demands every day that you be retried. That's why your bond to Elizabeth is looser. When they sever the bond, Rachmiel doesn't want there to be a shock to the girl."

Tabris forced his voice low. "You're lying."

"I'll go on. Raguel came here after you knocked Elizabeth off her bicycle."

"That was your doing." But even as he spoke, Tabris extended his mind and detected traces of Raguel's signature in the room. Not very long ago.

The demon opened his hands. "All Rachmiel told him was how she got hurt because of *you,* and he insisted it's stupid to keep you with a brat so close in age to Sebastian because eventually you'll punish her with one hug too many. Raguel's waiting for you to mess up just once more, and then he's going to reassign you to shoveling brimstone into the fiery furnaces."

Tabris rolled his eyes. He hoped it looked disinterested.

"You're not listening to me! I'm warning you because I'm the only one you have left." The demon became plaintive. "I can't stand to see you dog-piled. They're humiliating you. When it all goes down, you're going to look like creation's biggest idiot because you trusted them when it was obvious they wanted you gone."

"You're lying. You're only friends with yourself, and I have God." Tabris released the demon and folded his arms. "No one can take away that consolation."

The demon looked him in the eye, then smothered a laugh. "That's rich. You don't believe it any more than I do. If you did, you'd send me away. When two liars know they're lying to each other, it's an awful lot like truth, and I'll play that game if it's easier for you to talk that way. But you're covering all the bases, and God doesn't share. I would know." The demon stepped closer. "He'll settle for nothing less than all of you. Rachmiel's a lot happier not having to think, but you—you'd never be happy that way. It would be untrue to your name—Free Will."

Tabris tried to steady himself.

"I'm not lying," the demon said. "Rachmiel was furious. Sebastian can't forgive you. Raguel investigated this afternoon. And Rachmiel is trying to get you transferred because he can't guard you *and* Elizabeth."

Tabris glanced at the girl. Elizabeth had grown restive, and Tabris said, "Go back to sleep, little lady. It's midnight."

"You know enough of what I'm saying is true that you can trust me for the rest. Come with me. I was Unbridled," the demon said. "Now my name is Windswept. You can truly be Free Will, but you have to come with me."

Tabris trembled. "No."

"But, Free Will—"

"I'm exercising it now. A refusal is a choice, and I chose once. *Irrevocably.* You're not God to me. You're not omnipotent or all-knowing, and you didn't create me."

The demon shook his head. "If the only reason you're staying with God is for what He gives you, then give up. He's insatiable, and He's not going to let you keep refusing to pray. He'll want you to be with Him for who He is, not just what He does."

Tabris leaned closer. "The way He loves me?"

The demon snorted. "He claims He loves the essence of His slaves and not what they do, but I know better. I was condemned for what I did." The demon looked up. "And what about what you did? You murdered a child."

"But you wanted separation. I wanted—"

The room went silent. Tabris looked back at Elizabeth.

The demon sounded puzzled. "What *did* you want?"

Tabris's eyes narrowed.

"Did you get it?" The demon chuckled. "I doubt you did. But I think I have it for you. You just need to grasp it in your blood-covered hands, and I'll give you everything."

"Out." Tabris pointed his sword at the demon. "Go. Now."

Before he was finished, Tabris's voice echoed in the spiritual emptiness of a room minus one demon, and the Guard came down.

Out. He could get out now, but instead he listened.

Still. The house felt so incredibly still, and Tabris probed to detect which angels were where—and Rachmiel wasn't anywhere. No one was watching Elizabeth.

That's odd— Tabris thought before he realized it wasn't odd: it was exactly what the demon said. Rachmiel wouldn't leave Elizabeth lightly. He'd have Guarded the room if he needed to, or had another angel

125

checking in on her. Instead, he'd left her alone with an unconscious angel—and for what?

He huddled at the head of her bed, wings wrapped around himself, and wondered how people did this. There wasn't an angelic precedent, but many humans returned to their churches after long absences. They'd fumble, wondering which shoulder you touch first in the Sign of the Cross, how to navigate the hymnal, and then realizing when they looked around that no one cared if they were clumsy, least of all God. They'd come home, and no one would mind the muddy shoes on the porch steps.

Please help me, Tabris thought, knowing he didn't deserve help. Alert to all the locks on his heart, he wondered if they really locked out God, and if not, why they'd gotten there in the first place. But one at a time, he'd find each lock a little too scary to turn the key, the phantom behind the door something he'd rather not risk. Not now when he was already shaken.

And finally he stopped trying because if he wasn't willing to unlock the door, no one was going to get inside anyhow, and maybe the demon had a point. God wasn't going to let this stalemate stand forever.

The instant he slackened his concentration, Jesus appeared—and caught Tabris before he could prostrate himself. "Don't be afraid of me," he said.

Tabris pulled back and dropped to his knees, crossing his arms over his chest and pulling up his wings. "I'm sorry. I'm not ready."

Shivering, Tabris tried to get under control, and he couldn't look up.

A touch on his head, and he went still. Jesus said, "You're not ready, but I am."

Please don't force me. Tabris couldn't form the words. He closed his eyes, and then the touch vanished. He looked up, again alone.

Briefly. Only seconds later, Josai'el appeared in the room, startled. "You're awake?"

Apparently so. Tabris flashed to Elizabeth, who slept deeply, and when he looked back, Miriael was there, then Voriah, and in a moment the rest of the household. Minus Rachmiel, whom he felt Voriah calling at a long distance. Not on Earth.

"You're shaken," Josai'el said. "Are you all right?"

"Of course he's shaken," Miriael said. "There was a demon in here. Can't you feel it?"

Mithra said, "I can feel the presence of the Lord too."

Josai'el said, "What happened?"

Tabris looked at her, lost for what to say. The demon's Guard was down, but he still felt trapped, and he thought longingly of the pond. Or further, since he no longer had a tether. But Elizabeth, how much longer might he be with her...leaving when they might take him anyhow felt wrong. He could imagine them Guarding the house at his back. And then—nothing.

Rachmiel reappeared, and the first thing he said was to Miriael: "You said I'd know if he woke up."

Miriael said, "I said a smart demon could outwit that kind of device, and a smart demon faced him down."

Tabris shuddered as Rachmiel's awareness filled the room, and the orange-winged angel summoned a dozen tiny spheres to his hand, scattered in different places. "Terrific."

Miriael said to Tabris, "Whatever attacked you—ask for help next time. You shouldn't fight that alone."

Tabris said, "I drove him off."

"You have allies." Miriael cocked his head. "You're hogging the action to yourself. Not nice."

Tabris laughed, but softly.

"Crisis over," Mithra said, and the angels dispersed. Miriael waited a moment, then looked Tabris right in the eyes, a penetrating glare that made Tabris catch his breath. Miriael murmured, "Don't play with them. Throw them out. You can call me." And then he returned to Kyle.

Tabris found himself alone in the room with Rachmiel, who checked over Elizabeth and projected satisfaction that she was unhurt. He turned back to Tabris, shedding concern as he studied him.

Tabris recoiled, and Rachmiel got himself back under control. "Are you feeling better?"

Tabris stared at the floor. "I'm sorry I let her hit the ground."

"You said that before, and it's all right. I'm sorry I over-reacted. She'll be a bit stiff in the morning, but that will be the last of the matter." Rachmiel started projecting something else, but cut himself off.

Tabris walked to the window. "Where were you?"

Rachmiel hesitated. "I was with Sebastian." And then, "He asked for me to come. Miriael said I could set things up so if you woke up, I'd know and could come right back. I didn't—"

"That's not a problem." Tabris turned back. "You didn't tell me about him."

A burst of surprise escaped Rachmiel.

"Or were you hoping I wouldn't ask?"

Rachmiel projected hurt, but also irritation. "What did you want to know?"

Well, there was the rub. The only way to prove Rachmiel was willing to talk was to hear things he didn't want to hear. Even then, Tabris wasn't going to sift through the details to spot the tiny gaps where half-truths tried to take up the space of a full. "What do you think of him?"

Rachmiel's grin hit Tabris harder than a punch to the gut, and his eyes shone like a sunrise. "He's so smart! He's funny, but with a self-deprecating sense of humor. He's determined. And in so many ways, he's exactly like you!"

Tabris's heart pounded. "Which ways?"

"Do you want a list?" Rachmiel laughed out loud. "He feels like you, he thinks like you, he reacts like you. He even looks like you!" When Tabris recoiled, Rachmiel nodded. "His eyes. They're exactly like yours. And his face is similar too. He laughs the way you do. It's startling sometimes."

Tabris walked to the window and looked out at the grass. "What about his hands?"

If Rachmiel had been eager to talk before, he was confused now in equal measure. "Small?"

Tabris flashed in front of Elizabeth's mirror, then concentrated so he reflected.

"Tabris!" Rachmiel flashed between him and Elizabeth. "What are you doing?"

"She's sleeping." He was visible now in both the human and angelic planes of existence. "What's she going to see? Even if she did, she'd think it was a dream."

Unreassured, Rachmiel placed his hands over her eyes. Tabris ignored his stare while scrutinizing himself in the mirror. His eyes. His face. Dark eyes. Small hands.

He tried to smile, and it was perfect symmetry. Sebastian smiled like him. Lovely.

Rachmiel said, "What's going on?"

Tabris gave a laugh sharper than a switchblade. "Our souls are alike. Of course he'd be just like me after he died." He turned to Rachmiel. "He hates me."

That should have come out dark, or broken, or flat. Or sardonic. Instead the words were just...words. *He hates me.* There's one person I loved more than anything else, and because of what I did, he hates me.

Rachmiel whispered, "He's never said that."

"He doesn't need to say it. God wanted me to meet the boy so he could forgive me, right?"

Rachmiel opened his hands. Translate that as, *I don't know the mind of God.* Secondarily translate that as, *I'd rather not admit it.*

Tabris looked again into the mirror. "It's better for him if I don't go. I think that's obvious."

Rachmiel swallowed hard.

Tabris made himself invisible again, vanishing from the mirror, and saw how Rachmiel's eyes had picked up a pink tint. "Please keep visiting since he wants you there. But I'm not going to ask anything more, and please don't tell me about him."

"But—"

"I don't want to know the things he says, and you shouldn't be forced to lie to me. So just—don't talk about it."

Rachmiel's eyes widened. "I wouldn't lie."

Tabris stilled, and he looked across the room. How to respond to that? With it right out in the open, and Rachmiel saying one thing and reality saying another.

Rachmiel said, "Why would I lie? It would offend God, and we're on the same side."

"We're on Elizabeth's side." Tabris's voice was thin. "You'd do anything for her."

Seventeen

Five nights later, right after Kyle went to bed, Miriael tagged Tabris for a midnight death-match down in Antarctica. "I'm afraid to tell you," said Miriael with solemnity, "that a demon is impersonating me there, and you'll need to fight him."

Tabris grinned. "I'd heard the opposite, that it looks like me. We'd better head down and check it out."

Four hours later, they'd been fighting on the ice so long that each had been wounded several times, but never conclusive enough to declare a victory. They'd gone for close fighting this time, and Miriael had called a knife to his free hand.

As they grappled, Tabris wrenched the knife free. He slashed at Miriael's throat—and missed.

Miriael flared with disgust, and he hurled Tabris to the ground, then flung his sword into the snow. "Are you playing to win? Or not?"

"I am." Tabris sat up, gasping a white cloud. "I was, I mean. I thought I was." He curled forward, leaning his arms on his knees and letting his breath heave. "I'm sorry."

Miriael sat facing Tabris. They were both throwing off heat, and Tabris noticed Miriael deflecting it upward to keep the ice unharmed.

Miriael glared, waiting for an answer.

Tabris looked down. "I hesitated."

"Because you broke Sebastian's neck?"

So casual, the same way you'd say "Because you're attending the morning liturgy?" Tabris looked up with half a smile. "You're direct."

Miriael kicked some snow through Tabris. "You're trying to kill me. The least I can do is not stand on ceremony." His brow furrowed. "You're not offended by that, are you?"

Tabris rested his chin on his wrists. "Everyone knows everything anyhow. It's more than a little weird when they don't talk about it."

Miriael frowned, surprising Tabris with the strength of his negation. Raising his wings, Tabris picked up his head. "What about me don't you know?"

"Just about everything," said Miriael.

Tabris shook his head. "You should be thankful for that."

"I'll be the first in line if they ask for people who don't understand you." Miriael chuckled. "Until Rachmiel pushes me out of the way, that is."

Tabris huffed. "Rachmiel's been a lot less curious lately." That kind of thing happened when you had all the answers you needed.

Miriael's eyes flashed.

"Or he's gotten more controlled," Tabris admitted. It sounded more charitable that way. "The effect is the same."

"Do you want to go back?"

Tabris shook his head. "I'd rather wait until they wake up. It's cold here, and I love the open spaces."

Casifer appeared in Elizabeth's bedroom where Rachmiel was praying. "Sebastian wanted to see Elizabeth, and I came ahead to make sure it would be all right."

Except that they would have been married, Rachmiel thought this would be a great idea. "I don't—" But with his mind still half in a prayer-state, he felt God assuring him it would be fine. "Sure, bring him."

Casifer returned in a minute with Sebastian. The boy looked around, grinning. "I haven't been back to Earth at all before now! This is so awesome."

"I'm sorry your first visit has to be a mess." Rachmiel nudged a discarded t-shirt with his toe. "I'd have inspired her to clean if I'd known."

Sebastian shrugged, then walked to Elizabeth's bed. "Cool." He looked closer. "You said last time that angels can't dream. Can you tell what she's dreaming?"

"Come here." Rachmiel rested his hands over Sebastian's eyes and concentrated, showing him Elizabeth's soul as he saw it: a pastel swirl of grace and mercy, of compassion and love, understanding and faith. Innocence.

Sebastian whistled. "Are all our souls like that to you?"

"Everyone is different," Casifer said. "Your soul has sharper colors and more contrast, but yes, without sin you're all that beautiful."

Voriah entered the room and did a double-take. A moment later, the rest of the household clustered nearby.

"Sebastian?" said Josai'el. "This is a surprise."

"Um—hello." The boy backed into Casifer. "Rachmiel talked about Elizabeth enough that I thought I might come see her."

Voriah gave him the spiritual equivalent of a handshake, which Sebastian struggled to return. "Glad to meet you. Rock, he looks just like Tabris!"

Sebastian's eyes flew open. "Tabris?"

Casifer said, "Your guardian."

"*Tabris.* I like the sound." Sebastian seemed as if he were tasting the name, and he studied each angel in turn. "There have got to be like a hundred angels here! Do you all live in this one house?"

Rachmiel said, "Elizabeth has three brothers—" and then noticed Voriah had flashed from the room. "Plus her parents and her grand-mother. Even so, a visitor is the only entertainment at night, so every-one's going to come see."

Sebastian saluted. "Thanks a lot, folks—you've been a wonderful audience." He laughed. "I'm not even going to start asking who everyone is. Maybe you guys should get name stickers." He hesitated. "And... Tabris...isn't here?"

Ah—had there been an ulterior motive? "He and one of the other guardians are out tonight." Rachmiel watched Sebastian's face, but the boy didn't look disappointed. Nor did he appear relieved. "Have you visited your parents?"

Casifer said, "I opted to visit you first because you're three time zones ahead of them. They might not be asleep."

Rachmiel said to Sebastian, "He was supposed to say he was honoring us with your presence because we were so important."

Sebastian laughed out loud. "Yeah, of course!" He looked at Casifer. "Can we go see them?"

"In a while. You can stay out all night, so there's no rush." He shrugged. "Let's visit a few other places first."

Sebastian took Rachmiel's hand. "You come with us. And your friend, too. The one who told me my guardian's name."

Rachmiel didn't bother saying that after a slip like that, Voriah wasn't likely to let any other sensitive information slide. Instead, he projected agreement and told Casifer to go ahead.

In Alan's room, he found Voriah in urgent prayer tinged with apology. Josai'el joined them. Voriah turned to him, wings flared. "I'm sorry. I didn't mean to mess that up."

"He'd have learned his name at some point." Rachmiel sighed. "They want us to go on a mini world tour."

"Call back Miriael and Tabris." Voriah put a hand on Alan's shoulder. "Four on seven isn't good defense."

Josai'el said, "I'll ask for outside help. I'd rather not have Sebastian stop back here and find Tabris, and Sebastian's energy is going to be all over that room for a little while."

Voriah and Rachmiel flashed away after Casifer, landing on the crown of the Statue of Liberty.

"You're joking!" Voriah turned to the boy. "All the world to visit, and you chose New York?"

"I've never been here." Sebastian looked at the skyline. "Where would you suggest?"

"Australia. It's as far from New York as you can get without having to float."

"We could go underwater, though!" Sebastian's eyes brightened. "Let's go under the ice floes in Antarctica!"

Rachmiel said, "No."

Casifer looked at Rachmiel, and he caught Rachmiel's meaning. "Yeah, not there."

Voriah said, "We could try the arctic circle, though. It's just as cold."

Sebastian hesitated. "Would it be too cold? I don't want to go back to Limbo as a Kidsicle, and I'd like to see some fish."

Casifer said, "Oh, that's easy—" and the next moment they were off Ms. Liberty's shoulder and at a coral reef in the Pacific.

Sebastian panicked and clutched at Casifer, who wrapped him in his wings and projected that he was safe; he didn't need to breathe, but he could, and it wouldn't harm him.

Sebastian white-knuckled his hands into Casifer's feathers. Rachmiel projected that they could leave, but Sebastian shook his head. Rachmiel saw in him right then all of Tabris, fighting to ride out the panic to the good things he knew should be there, struggling to trust the ones around him when every instinct told him not to.

Sebastian forced himself to gasp, and then again. When he realized he wouldn't choke, he erupted with joy.

They checked out the fish, even some species that human scientists had never cataloged. The watery life swam near the three angels and

133

premature saint, seeking God in the dark waters but failing to find Him. The lightless currents flowed around the foursome, and they expanded their other senses to compensate for blindness. Rachmiel noted how Sebastian learned to navigate with an instinctual understanding of where everything was located around him.

When Sebastian wanted to leave—it was at least an hour—they flashed to a cliff in Washington State overlooking the Pacific. The horizon offset them as they glowed at the edge of a drop that plummeted to a rocky beach. The waves regularly sounded below while overhead the stars glimmered.

Voriah said, "I bet Elizabeth's dreaming of fish."

Rachmiel chuckled. "Swordfish." He craned back his neck and admired the clear sky, the Sitka spruces towering like the slats of a picket fence.

Sebastian whispered, "What an amazing world. I left it too soon. There were so many places I could have gone and I never did. I'd have climbed mountains and gone deep-sea diving for real."

Voriah said, "You can do that when we have the New Earth."

Sebastian pulled up a grass blade. "I don't think it will be the same."

Voriah said, "It might be better."

Sebastian flicked the grass to the ground. "I should have found out for myself. Sorry. I'll shut up now. I know you're on his side."

Voriah burst out laughing, and Rachmiel huffed. "Sebastian, I promise you this: no one thinks what Tabris did was right."

Sebastian's head picked up. "But—"

Voriah said, "Don't believe Tabris thinks he was right either. I'd be surprised if he's *stopped* regretting it for even a heartbeat since it happened."

Sebastian sought out Casifer's eyes. "Then why'd he do it?"

Rachmiel said, "I have no idea. But he'd un-do it if he could."

Frowning, Sebastian said, "Then why won't he visit?" His voice broke. "I figured he hated me all along, and that you let him stay with Elizabeth because he liked her, because she was cute and sweet, so she was safe, and I wanted to see—"

Rachmiel grabbed the boy in a hug. "No!" An ulterior motive? *This* had been Sebastian's motive. He'd wanted to see the kid who was good enough that Tabris loved her. "Don't think for a minute he loves her more than you."

"Then what did I do?" Sebastian blurted out, and Rachmiel wasn't prepared for his tears. "What did I do that deserved him killing me? Casifer won't tell me—"

Rachmiel said, "You didn't do anything!"

"—and God's charitable and won't hold it against you once you've been forgiven, so He won't tell me, but I must have done something so awful—"

Rachmiel looked at Casifer, helpless.

Sebastian pushed his face into Rachmiel's shoulder. "Whatever I did—just tell me. I'll deal with it. Just tell me."

Casifer moved right next to them. "I'm not holding anything back."

Sebastian kept his fingers in Rachmiel's wings, his face down.

Rachmiel held him, his heart vibrating with the boy's grief but feeling shock from both Voriah and Casifer. In the swirl of feeling, he realized Casifer hadn't known Sebastian was thinking this at all, that the boy had hidden the doubts, and maybe the first question he'd planned to ask Tabris was, "What did I do?"

Rachmiel said nothing as Sebastian's soul fit against his with an ease that broke his heart: Elizabeth's husband. They were so compatible.

Finally Sebastian said, "If only I'd been a better charge, he wouldn't have done that."

Rachmiel said, "You were a wonderful charge. It wasn't your fault."

Sebastian clutched him tighter. "That can't be true."

Rachmiel said, "Absolutely true. I promise."

Pulling back, Sebastian frowned. "Then what's his deal? He should be here." He clenched his fists. "Although you know what? I'm kind of glad he kept his distance because even if it's my fault, I'm still pissed off at him. Casifer said I need to forgive him, but you know..."

Rachmiel sighed. "You were hurt. Feeling angry isn't wrong. It's normal, and I'd be worried if you weren't angry." He put a hand on Sebastian's shoulder. "You do need to forgive him. But it doesn't have to happen right now."

Sebastian shrugged him off. "Maybe I can just work real hard on it and get the divine brownie-points, but not succeed."

Voriah said, "Pray about it. Pray for the grace to want to forgive him. If you can't, then back it up a step and pray to want to *want* to forgive."

Sebastian laughed out loud, but it sounded to Rachmiel as if it hurt. "So when I'm praying to want to want to want to want—"

Voriah said, "Before it gets to that point, maybe one of us should pray with you."

Sebastian tensed. "But—really?"

Rachmiel said, "Surely you've prayed with Casifer."

"Yeah, but he kind of has to." Sebastian swallowed hard. "You'd be praying with an unforgiving kid who wasn't even good enough for—"

"No." Rachmiel's voice had dropped. "Quit thinking that. Of course we'd pray with you." He touched Sebastian under the chin so the boy looked up. "Would you like to do it now?" Teary-eyed, Sebastian nodded.

They sat, Casifer behind Sebastian and the other two angels before him. Casifer began first, silent and earnest.

Sebastian closed his eyes. His hands were fists.

"Don't expect anything specific." Voriah kept his voice low. He rested his hands on Sebastian's. "Open your heart and invite God inside. Once He's in, He'll do whatever He wants. You may want to hide parts of yourself, but try not to because those are the parts you most need to show God"

Sebastian nodded.

Rachmiel joined the prayer Casifer had begun, a low-stress, repeating praise, an invitation. Muted. Rachmiel didn't understand at first until he realized Casifer didn't want Sebastian overwhelmed. Start slow. He could ramp it up later.

Sebastian tried to open up, but he'd left his heart locked tight.

Voriah was praying now too, an adoration/meditation mix which imbued Casifer's steady prayer with a sense of peace. He projected to Sebastian: *Relax. Trust. He's not going to hurt you. He made you.*

Rachmiel opened his own heart to God. *I'm sorry this is so mercenary,* he prayed, *but I want to show him how.*

God replied, *It's not as if I mind being with you, no matter what your reason.*

Rachmiel grinned.

Voriah was still projecting, *Relax.*

Sebastian said, "I'm trying, Coach. But it's tough."

"Then we can stop." Voriah backed off. "There's no need to rush. Eternity's a long time."

Rachmiel felt God stream from his heart like water flowing back to the sea.

Sebastian sagged against Casifer. "Why is that so hard? I prayed all the time when I was alive."

"This is different." Casifer rubbed his shoulders in slow circles. "Back then you prayed with words and thoughts, but souls pray differently. You're asking that He enter your heart and see your soul from the inside. To increase the difficulty, you're asking Him to see a flaw, and one you're not ready to correct. But keep trying. God will come in when you're ready."

They remained on the cliff, Sebastian lying with his cheek against whatever grass had defeated the wind to find a foothold in the rock. The angels talked among themselves until Casifer decided it was late enough that Sebastian's parents would be sleeping.

The four arrived in a bedroom, dark and tinged with pollution that took Rachmiel by surprise. He forced himself to get used to the thinner atmosphere, changing his eyesight to make out the square shapes of furniture and the form of the couple cuddled beneath the blanket.

Sebastian whispered, "Hi, Mom. Hi, Dad."

The parents' guardians cried out with surprise, embracing Sebastian and looking him over, each one saying "I'm so sorry" and voicing a wish that they'd predicted the danger and somehow averted it.

The two guardians introduced themselves, and then Sebastian introduced everyone else. Sariel, who guarded Sebastian's mother, thanked Casifer for everything he'd done with Sebastian so far.

Sebastian crouched alongside the bed, then touched his mother's face. His fingers didn't make contact, but he stopped as if they did. "How are they doing?"

Sariel said, "Surviving, I suppose. Your mom misses you terribly. She's been working hard at her job, and she's not crying every day anymore, but it's going to take a while before she makes peace with losing you."

Sebastian kissed her cheek as if brushing her skin with a rose petal. As Sariel watched, Rachmiel picked up from her a stream of projections: her joy that Sebastian had gotten into Heaven, but also grief raw like an acid burn, the image of a mother holding her son's body and talking to him long after he couldn't hear her.

Sebastian didn't try to hide the tears. "And Dad? How's he doing?"

The father's guardian, Neraya, said, "It hit him hard. He doesn't have the same support your mother has, although your great-uncle Carlos took him under his wing right away because he'd lost a son too. At least he has someone to talk to. But he still comes across daydreams he hasn't removed you from yet, all the things he'd planned for you, and he realizes again that you won't be there."

Sebastian knelt alongside the bed, resting his head near his father's. "I'm sorry," he whispered. "I'm so sorry. I would have lived if I could have."

Casifer wrapped around Sebastian as he rested his hand over his father's.

"Can I talk to them?" Sebastian said. "Could I leave a message in their dreams?"

The angels looked at one another. Sariel said, "It would be tricky, but I think we could manage it."

The angels conferenced, all projected and at a speed Sebastian wouldn't have been able to understand anyhow. The decision: they could slip a communication into one parent's dream; it would be better to use the father than the mother because the mother would be more likely to believe it, and the father would be less likely to discount it if he were the one who'd felt the communication.

"This isn't something we do all the time," Voriah said. "But let's go ahead. Do you know what you want to tell him?"

Rachmiel stayed out of the way as Casifer and Neraya set up a conduit between Sebastian and his father. "They can't keep it open long," Voriah said, "so you'll need to get in, give a message, and then get out again."

Sebastian looked flustered. "I didn't realize this was so difficult."

Rachmiel said, "You asked for your father to have a vision in his dreams. We can simulate that. But it's not easy."

Voriah smirked. "It's easy for God."

Rachmiel said, "And if Sebastian's father dreams about seven fat cows coming up from the Nile, then we'll know whom to credit."

Casifer signaled, and Sebastian closed his eyes.

Rachmiel felt the boy's concentration shift, and he backed up the process with prayer, asking God to bless their work and approve it. *He's a father whose son died,* Rachmiel prayed.

God replied, *So am I.* And then, *I will bless this work.*

Rachmiel shifted to praying for Sebastian as the boy radiated grief, and momentarily Rachmiel felt himself amplifying and trembling with it too. And then, rage. Rage that this was necessary at all, that a boy should be reduced to saying one or possibly two sentences to his own father after six months, from across the divide between life and death, and why? Because an angel had taken his life instead of protecting him.

God— Rachmiel prayed. *God, help me—*

Casifer and Neraya thinned out the channel and then pinched it off so the communication ended, and Sebastian dropped to the ground, his face in his hands.

Voriah said, "It worked."

"We got through." Casifer crouched beside the child. "I'm going to take him back now. Thank you for everything."

Sebastian didn't look up, didn't say goodbye, just stayed coiled tight. All Rachmiel wanted to do was wrap around the boy, but just now, struggling so hard to keep it together, he resonated exactly like Tabris. Exactly. And with Casifer between them, and with that anger still brimful in his heart, Rachmiel stayed still.

Tabris caused this. Tabris.

Casifer vanished with the child.

The four remaining angels said nothing for a minute, and then Sariel said, "I hope he'll be all right."

Voriah said, "I never realized— You know, with Tabris in our household, I never thought about what he'd left behind."

Rachmiel forced himself not to add, "You mean the trail of devastation?" He'd thought about what would happen if Tabris killed Elizabeth; he'd never thought about what her death would do to her parents; her brothers; her grandmother.

Sariel looked up. "How is Tabris? He's never visited."

Yeah, funny that. But they'd never visited him, either, and Rachmiel wondered if they were just as angry. Or angrier, since they'd lived through the parents' every single second since then, every question, every middle-of-the-night crying jag.

Voriah said, "Until a short while ago he was tethered. I think he's pretty well settled with us."

Sariel said, "That's good, at least. You guys were brave to take him in."

Rachmiel shifted his weight. "Bravery had nothing to do with it. Divine orders. I wanted him gone."

She picked up her head. "That's not how the story got back to us. Interesting."

Voriah said to Rachmiel, "Well, we didn't exactly advertise that you tried to hack him to pieces."

Rachmiel's eyes narrowed.

Voriah said. "Doesn't Sebastian look just like him?"

Sariel shook her head.

Both Rachmiel and Voriah started.

Neraya said, "Not at all. A slight similarity, but not as close as some I've seen."

Voriah projected confusion.

Rachmiel said, "The eyes? The mannerisms?"

Sariel said, "Not especially, no. But that's just my opinion."

Just her opinion as someone who'd spent twenty-five times longer with Tabris than he had, and far more with Sebastian.

Voriah said, "Would you like to visit Tabris?"

It was an odd enough segue that it took Rachmiel a minute to realize what Voriah had: Mithra had said the changes in Tabris were obvious but would never elaborate. Bring these two, and they might.

While Rachmiel prayed for help to diminish his anger, Sariel decided she would go, and Voriah spoke long-distance with Josai'el to find out if Tabris had gotten home yet. He hadn't, so instead of flashing back to Vermont, Voriah brought them all to wherever Tabris was.

They landed in Antarctica, as far south as they could get without going north again. Snow dusted them on the wind, and they adjusted their vision to compensate for the brightness after so long in the dark.

Miriael and Tabris were seated on the ice, and Tabris looked up with his wings flaring. Sariel flung her arms around him, and he closed his eyes. "Tabris, I'm so sorry. I wish I could have done something."

Rachmiel sat on the snow, keeping his wings raised, trying to figure out Tabris's very, very, very careful non-reaction to Sariel. When she sat back on her heels, he said, "How are you guys doing?"

It was then Rachmiel realized the emotional stream from Sariel had dried up too. She wasn't projecting anything at all.

Sariel gave an abbreviated version of the update she'd given Sebastian, but she also included information on some other angels she and Tabris had worked with. All the while, Rachmiel sensed Tabris probing her: he had to be able to detect Sebastian's presence, and yet he said nothing. Nothing like, "Why are you here with Rachmiel and Voriah?" When Sariel paused, Tabris said, "Did Sebastian's death destroy their faith?"

Sariel hesitated. "No, not Lilia's. She found her faith comforting. Luis—well, he's numb. He's going through the motions, but for now that's okay because at least it keeps him in place. I'm worried about the long term. The questions."

Tabris looked down, and Rachmiel fought a new anger: if Tabris couldn't pray for himself, he at least should have been praying for them.

Voriah felt Alan wake up, and he excused himself to go home.

Tabris introduced Miriael, adding, "We've been sparring."

Sariel smiled. "We never liked to mock-fight."

Miriael's eyes flashed a negation. "Not a mock-fight. This is to the death." He grinned. "Tabris won last time."

She asked about the household, about which other angels were assigned there, and she wanted to know about Elizabeth.

Rachmiel paid attention here. What did Tabris really think of the family? Or Elizabeth, for that matter? But Tabris gave only an overview, *there are three boys and one girl, and the grandmother lives with them, and they live in Vermont*—and Rachmiel felt himself missing the details that would have set his family apart from any other. The chaos, the interactions, the alliances between the children, the feel of them. The laughter.

If that was all Tabris thought of them, then what did it matter which household he stayed in?

"I need to get back to Lilia, but it was good seeing you again. I'm glad you're doing all right." Sariel hugged Tabris, then said, "Rachmiel, can you come back with me?"

Well, that put the B in 'subtle.' Rachmiel said, "You guys can get back to beating each other senseless."

Miriael said, "Swords are so much more elegant than a beating."

Tabris laughed. "If we're going to kill one another, we're going to be civilized about it."

Sariel put a hand on Rachmiel's arm, and then she brought him back with her to Los Angeles.

As soon as they arrived, she dropped onto the bed and cupped her face in her hands. Neraya rushed up beside her, one wing over her shoulder, and let Sariel cry.

Rachmiel's wings flared. "What—?"

"He's so different." Sariel looked up. "You were right: he does look just like Sebastian. Dark-eyed. Face all tense." She closed her eyes as if she could wipe away the memory.

Rachmiel said, "What did he look like before?"

Sariel said, "His eyes were hazel, fading to green on the edges just like his wings, but even his wings are darker now than they were. More like honey on the covert feathers and emerald on the primary ones." She shook her head. "It's not just the way he looked." She turned to the father's guardian. "He was always a bit stiff, right? But now he's rigid. His bearing is all wrong, like he doesn't want to move. And he's silent."

Neraya said, "Silent?"

"He speaks. But he's not projecting, and there was always a steady stream of that from him. He'd be watching—" Sariel shivered. "He was a watcher and a thinker, but today, he was...speaking."

Neraya whispered, "That's deep damage. He needs help."

Rachmiel said, "How was he as a guardian?"

Sariel gave a half-laugh. "I thought they were going to send a camera crew in any day to create a new manual on how to be a guardian angel."

Rachmiel sat up: a chance to add to his mental portfolio on Tabris. "How so?"

Sariel said, "His reaction time was astonishing! I'd have barely registered a threat and he'd already diffused it."

Difference number one, then. Rachmiel had always considered Tabris's reaction time to be slow...except when battling Miriael. He said, "Was he hands-on?"

Sariel nodded. "Absolutely. Sebastian didn't so much as skin his knees when he learned to walk, and Tabris was all over him, helping his balance."

Fascinating. Rachmiel had learned early on to shoulder all the work when it required contact with Elizabeth. Projectiles and insects and fractions were in Tabris's column, but balance, walking in the dark, base-running in kickball—those were Rachmiel's job.

Neraya said, "He kept the boy on a tight rein, always alert for things that might potentially become problems." That, at least, Rachmiel had seen. Tabris, telling Elizabeth to eat an apple rather than open a bag of chips. Or the daily (and futile) routine of telling her to do her math homework first, instead of letting it drag on until bedtime.

She continued, "Sebastian stayed free of significant sin until he was about twelve. And then one day, Tabris shut down. He stopped communicating. We assumed Sebastian had done something, but we couldn't get from him exactly what—"

Sariel added, "—and of course, that's not any of our business, but we wanted to help—"

"—and we tried to reassure him that this happens to every human being because of their free will. After a day or two, Sebastian made things right, but Tabris stayed quiet. And about a week later, he killed him."

Shuddering, Rachmiel closed his eyes.

Sariel said, "Does he talk to you at all? What about the angel he was sparring with—Miriael?"

Rachmiel said, "If he talks to Miriael, I don't know about it."

Sariel bit her lip. "He's got to be getting an emotional outlet somewhere. It should be you. You're his partner."

Partner and guardian of Sebastian's intended wife. That ought to have counted for a certain degree of compatibility. Rachmiel said, "He doesn't trust me enough. The other day, he even asked me not to lie to him."

Sariel said, "He can't keep that much pain locked inside."

Neraya muttered, "Yeah, because if he did, it might make him silent and broody and make his bright spirit go dark."

"Good point." Sariel folded her arms. "He's got a really strong will. He probably could control his whole soul if he had to. No comfort, no sympathy. He knows he was wrong, and he knows everyone else in the world knows it." She looked up. "Has *anyone* tried talking to him?"

"Of course I've tried talking to him!" Rachmiel's eyes narrowed. "He shuts me down. I don't think he even talks to Raguel, and Raguel's in charge of his probation. He doesn't want help."

Sariel said, "Maybe he wants to get what he deserved. It sounds like sabotage."

Rachmiel recoiled. "I don't want that."

"As well you shouldn't." Sariel flinched. "I'm sorry. I keep forgetting that if you get him to open up, you're going to feel his emotions as acutely as he does. That's not going to be pleasant."

Rachmiel said, "And it had better be while Elizabeth is sleeping. I don't know how she'd react to all that." He reached out with his mind. "Speaking of which, she's starting to wake up."

Sariel hugged him. "Thank you. Thank you for looking out for Tabris. There's no way I could have done that." She stepped back. "Just remember, when he does project his feelings, it's powerful and precise. He could rip out your heart. You want to help him, but you're going to need God helping you."

Eighteen

After an entire day of enduring Rachmiel's hunger to ask a thousand questions, Tabris answered only one question: *Yes, I'm going out tonight.* And five seconds later, he floated over the postcard skyline of New York City. He made his subtle body a little more solid, adjusted it a bit to compensate for the air composition, and then beat his wings once. Perfect.

Vermont was too oxygen-rich for rapid flight. On the spectrum's other end, New York's pollution wouldn't suspend a hovering angel who made himself semi-corporeal. Los Angeles had dense air but with less abundant oxygen, although not as oxygen-deprived as the air over Berlin and Moscow in the seventies and eighties. In the search for the perfectly polluted city, only Reykjavik and Denver had answered Tabris's criteria: Denver because of its elevation and Reykjavik for its longitude.

A crime for every streetlight. He spread his wings to hover with difficulty in the thin air. No better place to be alone. Within moments he felt himself coated in atmospheric grease that left him slippery in the sky and would boost his maximum velocity. He warmed up with some spirals to acclimate himself to the sky's consistency. His eyes itched, but that was good: it meant he'd gotten the balance of substance to soul just right.

Tabris sliced through the air and spun, no more than a green blur as he corkscrewed down the streets of midtown. He skimmed the heads of New Yorkers walking beneath the streetlamps, watching the pavement.

He approached the Empire State Building and made a ninety degree turn to race straight up the side, skimming the silvery windows that reflected lights and traffic but not himself. He opened his wings as he passed the scalloped top floors and snagged the broadcast antenna, spiraling around and around until his momentum diminished and he slid down it like a fire pole.

Almost as good as L.A., he thought out in God's general direction.

Leaping from the top, he cannon-balled to street level, breaking from a curled position just past the twentieth floor, then flexing his back and spreading his wings into gravitational forces that would have blown the feathers off a real bird. He pulled up before plummeting through the cement, twisting to redirect his momentum and blaze along at street level.

All around him were other guardians, but them Tabris ignored while he streaked, a green-winged fury through the corridors left by the buildings, rows of dominos that made the perfect playground for someone who'd turned around to find he'd left childhood far behind, the games too real and the toys more serious than he'd anticipated.

He circled the Citicorp building, knowing that if he slammed into it he could level the whole area of Manhattan—there was nowhere for a building of that size to fall—and then the resemblance to dominos didn't seem as funny. Ten million souls. It was all so fragile.

From there he rose above the city, soaring with his feathers spread, letting his own momentum carry him as far is it could before leveling off. Once he'd mounted the cloud cover, he angled eastward over the Atlantic. So silent. So alone. But beneath him, the song of a sea with her barely-chained chaos, the power of an appetite that never sated itself on just the shores, as though all the seaboard was an hors d'ouvre to sharpen her hunger for the Midwestern plains. The ocean grasped for the moon with its tide high, yearning for the orb with a famished patience.

He used to pray at times like this, that afterglow following a rough flight. *Wait for me,* he thought toward God. *Please wait for me.*

And then, *I wish I knew if there were any point to all this. I wish I knew if I could be forgiven.*

No answer. God would have recorded his comments in His files as all self-reflections must be. Pushing down the ache, Tabris lowered his altitude into the clouds, allowing the mist to swallow him so he was at times visible and at times not.

In a moment, he felt another presence.

"Show yourself, Windswept."

The demon said from somewhere, "And do more than you've done?"

Tabris didn't join him, but when he ran out of cloud, he just kept going. The demon kept pace, flying with their wingtips nearly touching. He smiled, and it looked kind until Tabris forced himself to remember it was an act. The demon's amber eyes radiated gladness, and he brushed the hair from his forehead. "What a lovely night. If by *lovely* you mean banal and lifeless."

Tabris said, "If you leave out the *love* then yes, that's what it means."

The demon laughed. "My favorite verbalist is exercising his pun nature! You make me miss you so much when you do that."

"Whatever you want to believe."

The demon looked stung. "Please don't lie. We *were* friends. Now that I'm in Hell, pretty much all I have to hold onto are the memories, since I know you won't get close to me anymore."

Tabris pointed to the demon. "Speaking of which."

The demon had been drawing nearer while talking. Windswept retreated, but rolled over so he was flying on his back underneath Tabris, the pillows of cloud around him like a feather bed. "Please don't fight with me. Not now. I just want to travel with you since they've cut that stupid tether. Let's go wherever the wind takes us."

Tabris made no answer, but Windswept was gazing up at him, yearning. The demon stretched, then fixed his eyes on the moon. "Isn't she beautiful?" the demon murmured. "So round and misty, so distant. It's cold. And alone. No one's there now. Let's go."

Tabris shook his head.

Windswept drew closer. "I missed you, and I still miss you, and now you're here and you're so close it's driving me crazy." He reached up his wings to touch him with the tips, and Tabris looked into eyes softened in the darkness. "You're everything. You're everything to me, and I would do anything for you. You have no idea how magnificent you are, how I used to plan my days around when I'd see you and then afterward I'd spend the rest of the day thinking about the time we spent together."

Tabris shook his head.

"No one loves you like I do. Does Rachmiel love you? Does Sebastian? How about Sariel? Certainly not Miriael, who gave you and keeps giving you the most explicit warning I've ever seen."

Tabris looked into the demon's eyes. So close now. The demon began projecting awe; projecting shock that no one else recognized Tabris's beauty; projecting fascination. Fascination with him.

"You could do anything." His voice trembled. "You could change the moon's orbit. Why are you watching a child? Why two angels to do that—when you alone could rule continents? An angel with your power...could build a universe."

He reached up a hand and touched Tabris's, and he projected joy that they were close enough to do that. Projected disbelief that Tabris might actually like him. He whispered, "I hadn't been happy in thousands of years. You're making me happy."

He wrapped his hand around Tabris's. "I love you."

Tabris flared his wings and yanked backward. The demon shot toward him, trying to entangle his wings in Tabris's, but Tabris shoved him away.

The demon's eyes glittered with tears. "I don't understand!"

Tabris streamed humiliation and reluctance, but he couldn't clamp down on it. "Leave me alone! Just leave me alone! You're damned and you want me damned too—and that's love?"

"And it's love to murder a twelve year-old-boy?" The demon's eyes smoldered. "And is it love for God to burn the souls He built with His own fingers? I'm being just like my dear old dad—I want to own you, and I'll make you lose yourself to have you, just the way you'll lose yourself if you stay His. Is that love? To love something so totally it ceases to exist?"

Tabris wanted to cover himself, but the demon stared straight into him as if he knew, knew everything. "That's all wrong! God isn't like that!"

Windswept opened his hands. "God is exactly like that. Otherwise, I'd still be in Heaven."

Tabris wrapped his arms around himself and turned away.

"You love me, don't you?" said the demon.

"I don't know. I don't see how. I remember how you used to be. I loved that."

The demon said, "I'll be that way again. For you I'd do anything. I'll change my name to whatever it was, and I'll be your darling, and I'll follow wherever you want me to go."

Tabris looked over his shoulder. "Except it wouldn't be you following me. If I did that, I'd be following you. And I'm not prepared to leave God."

The demon's eyes flashed. "You're preparing. You've been preparing. And I'm waiting."

"You're not waiting. You're pushing."

"And God isn't. Which one of us loves you more?"

Tabris flashed away, landing in a field where the heather and wildflowers slept in the starlight. For miles around were only more fields and one two-lane highway, a straight gash through the land.

"Don't run from me." The demon reappeared behind him. "Once was enough to break my heart."

Sitting, Tabris tucked his wings around himself.

The demon dropped beside him. "Within three days, God's going to order you to visit Sebastian. That's obvious to everyone. The angels at Elizabeth's school are even placing bets whether you simulate a happy reunion or refuse outright. The pool is leaning toward you not wanting to see what you did to the poor little brat. His soul's in shreds."

Tabris shuddered.

"I have to admit, I'd never have been able to incite as much hate in his soul as you did." The demon chuckled. "Has Rachmiel blown his secret yet?"

Tabris closed his eyes.

"I knew he couldn't keep it. Which one—about going to Raguel, or about the kid hating you?"

Tabris projected the latter.

"Oh! You haven't lost that!" The demon's eyes illuminated the nearby flowers like a flashbulb. "Rachmiel said you'd lost your capacity for higher emotion."

That didn't sound like Rachmiel at all. Rachmiel would twist himself into a pretzel rather than voice judgment on someone. Tabris tried to ground himself on that: the demon was lying. And he thought about Miriael leaning close and saying, *Don't play with them. Throw them out.* What was he doing? Not playing. But—but what?

"I thought you were finally growing a bit," said the demon. "You know how they say suffering prompts growth? Well, you've seen what God's really like, just a big kid smashing His toys together to see which ones survive."

The demon made an image over one hand of a die-cast yellow cab, and a green tractor-trailer over the other. He brought his hands together, and the images collided. "Yeah, loads of fun, huh?" He snapped, and the images disappeared.

Tabris said, "We're not toys."

"You might as well be. God took this magnificent angel who commanded one of the best units in Heaven's army and stuck him in a dirty corner of North America like a potted plant, and He waited to see if you'd wither. Instead, you turned into a venus fly trap." The demon sighed. "He set you up for failure. And you know it, which is why you won't pray. *Oh sweet and loving Father, thank you so much for kicking me in the head! I love it when you do that! Maybe next you can punch me in the gut! Hallelujah!* The demon snorted. "Yeah, how could I have walked away from all that? Boggles the mind."

Tabris looked at the stars. "Is that how we sound to you?"

"I'm toning it down so I don't hurt your feelings."

Of course he was. "Then in that case, the prayer should sound more like this: *Thank you, all-holy and loving Father, for giving me free will so I could choose to screw up enough that I deserve a kick to the head.*" Tabris shrugged. "Hallelujah."

"It's a farce of free will to put you in a place where you had no choice."

No choice. Interesting idea: if he'd been set up then it wasn't his fault at all. No guilt. Just acceptance that this was what God wanted, and now he had to wait for the next thing God wanted. You might hate Richard III or Iago; you'd never hate the actor playing the role. God wrote His characters so much better than Shakespeare—so much better that after a while, the actor could hate himself. How could that be fair?

Tabris sighed. Because it wasn't. It wasn't real, wasn't true. It was a way out, but that didn't mean it was the right way.

The demon said, "I love it when you think so deep like that. Share it with me."

"I'm thinking you're a liar." He looked up. "Leave. Go. Don't make me force you away."

The demon vanished, but not without saying, "I'm the only one who loves you. You need me."

Tabris huddled around himself. Grimy. Unwanted, unfit for contact with other angels, let alone contact with God. *I can't do it,*" he thought to God.

Inside he felt a touch, a turning of his mind toward an orange-winged angel with sunset-colored eyes. Although the push was gentle, Tabris shuddered.

Tabris thought again, *I can't do it alone.*

Again the thought of Rachmiel.

I can't do it with him either. Tabris put his face down and covered himself with his wings. *I won't trust him again. All he needs is more ammo.*

Inside: a question of why God would place him with a co-guardian who would betray him.

Tabris worked his fingers into his feathers. *I don't know. I don't know.*

And inside a sense: go home. Elizabeth. Rachmiel.

Shaken as he was, Tabris knew if he went home, Rachmiel could get any information out of him that he wanted. Anything at all.

He returned anyway.

Nineteen

Tabris arrived in the middle of a battle—demons all over the house, the kids' bedrooms Guarded off as strongholds. Miriael, Katra'il, Mithra and Josai'el were fighting a contingent of demons in the hallways, on the roof, and even in the basement.

Tabris's sword appeared in his hand, and he reported to Miriael. "Why didn't you call me back? Don't you trust me?"

Miriael blew apart a demon. "We did call! Clear out the garage."

In the garage, he found a cluster of demons, and based on the feel, they were causing havoc, nothing more. Attacking in force at night—ridiculous. What were they going to tempt the people to do? Sleepwalk? At worst they'd cause nightmares, like the anti-angels they were: instead of *Do not be afraid* it was *Boo!*

Tabris started driving them from the house. When he'd fumigated the garage, he swept the outside of the house, then set a Guard to prevent more from entering. Now it remained only to dispose of the dozen inside.

Miriael had laced the interior walls with a Guard, and Tabris took half a second to admire the work before coursing through to flush out the intruders. Josai'el reported that one had gotten to Bridget, appearing in her dream. Tabris snagged that, and as he pulled it off, the demon said, "I made her dream you killed Elizabeth."

Tabris pushed it through his own Guard with enough force that it would land on the driveway unconscious, if still semicorporeal at all.

It took half an hour to track down the final three demons, every one of them an unexploded bomb with a message for Tabris.

He knew—he knew it in the back of his mind, that this whole thing was a trap to ensure he'd come home and be unable to regroup. Push him and push him until he ended up divulging everything to Rachmiel, who then would carry the information back to Raguel, and Raguel would remove him. But knowing that, he still couldn't get away, and he couldn't unhear the things they said whenever he grabbed one from wherever it had ensconced itself—Sebastian hated him; Rachmiel feared him; Rachmiel had brought Sariel only to assess his fitness.

Miriael stationed Tabris and Mithra to watch for more demons, then he and Katra'il conducted a final sweep. After that, he cleared Rachmiel, Hadriel and Voriah to open the rooms they'd Guarded from the inside.

The guardians gathered in the hallway, Tabris struggling to stay put rather than run away. He garnered a precious minute alone by checking on Elizabeth. Rachmiel would think he doubted him—fine, but at least he'd stolen time to get himself together.

When he returned, Josai'el was congratulating the household team on a good defense. Mithra conducted a debriefing on how their strategy could have improved. Out of patience with the rundown, Tabris interrupted with, "No one called me."

"I did," said Rachmiel said, and Miriael added, "So did I."

Or so they said. Then they could tell Raguel he hadn't come back.

Miriael said, "If they put their own Guard over the house, they could have blocked our communications. This was clearly an orchestrated attack. But then why did you come back?"

Tabris smoldered. "God told me to."

Voriah laughed. "Well, He would know!"

The other angels discussed the early warning signs, the way they'd responded to the initial salvo, and how they could prevent a communications blackout in the future. The whole time, Tabris ignored how Rachmiel studied him. Not burning with curiosity. Just studying. Ten minutes later, Josai'el dismissed everyone, and Tabris went back to Elizabeth.

Rachmiel restrained himself from drinking the thin ribbons of emotion trailing off Tabris's heart. He entered Elizabeth's room to find Tabris stroking her hair and looking at her with desperation.

Rachmiel said, "She's fine." The room felt like a dark gymnasium with a high ceiling and empty bleachers. He realized the sense emanated from Tabris only when the two-toned angel looked at him with gleaming eyes.

Rachmiel said, "You're hurt." Then, "What happened?"

He moved close to Tabris, who for once didn't back away. But with the struts around his heart vibrating, Rachmiel forced himself to hold back. He could force Tabris to open up. He hungered for it. But do that and he'd lose everything.

Tabris looked only at Elizabeth. "I went to New York for some flying. It shouldn't have been a big deal."

He caught an image from Tabris: that demon with eyes bright as amber, and a gut-wrenching feeling Tabris managed to squelch before it resolved. Rachmiel acted as if he hadn't sensed it. "Except you got attacked there at the same time we did?"

"I don't know if it was simultaneous." Tabris swallowed hard. "Maybe you guys only got hit when I didn't— I don't know."

Rachmiel could sense every part of Tabris about to collapse, and to be honest, it frightened him. Frightened him more than standing over Elizabeth supporting the Guard over her room against the demonic attack. He didn't know what Tabris was capable of when fully in control; the idea of Tabris out of control—

He raised his wings. "You're not doing well. Let's call Raguel."

Tabris's eyes flashed. "And get rid of me for good?"

"I'm not getting rid of you, and it wouldn't be for *good*. You need help." Rachmiel opened his hands. Tabris was sitting right on top of Elizabeth; his knees were through her shoulders and his fists lay on his lap, directly over her neck.

Tabris glared at him. "Quit lying to me."

Ice cold, Rachmiel whispered, "What?"

"I said to quit lying." Tabris flared his wings. "I know you're working to get me removed. I may be quiet, but I'm not stupid, and you're a horrible liar."

The emotions pummeled Rachmiel from within and without: Tabris's anger, his own terror for Elizabeth, and shock at the accusation. "I never worked to get you removed. I've never lied to you."

Tabris said, "You've gone to Raguel twice that I know of."

Rachmiel struggled against amplifying Tabris's anger because then he'd return the charges with rage of his own. "You're losing me. When?"

There was no way to get him away from Elizabeth without making him angrier, and calling for help would trigger the explosion he needed to avoid. Of this much Rachmiel was certain. The only way to protect her was to get him calmer.

Tabris said, "You asked me to go into the basement to watch Andrew. Instead, Mithra took your place with Elizabeth and you went to Raguel."

Wracking his memory for any situation that might resemble that, Rachmiel remembered the night Tabris had driven him away from the pond. The fury. The coldness. Had it instead been betrayal? "I didn't go to Raguel. One of my friends needed help. Mithra had just returned, and I asked if he could watch Elizabeth while I took care of it. I'd be gone five minutes. It didn't seem worth the effort to shuffle you and Mithra back."

Tabris said, "And after Elizabeth fell off her bike, I felt his presence in the room."

"He came to me," Rachmiel said. "I didn't call him. I told him I would handle it."

"You had the tether removed so it wouldn't shock Elizabeth when they ripped me away."

Rachmiel kept his voice steady. "You needed the range and you've proven your devotion, and that was God's decision, not mine."

"You told Raguel I desert Elizabeth far too easily."

Rachmiel opened his hands. "If I wanted you gone, why would that be a problem?"

Tabris's eyes narrowed. "You're colluding with Sebastian to get more evidence."

"Sebastian saw Elizabeth once, while she was asleep. What evidence could he have that wasn't brought out at your trial?"

Above Elizabeth, Tabris still stared through Rachmiel. Logic wasn't going to win this one. Suddenly Tabris's words, *You'd do anything for her,* encompassed a whole lot more territory than Rachmiel had ever anticipated. And with Tabris still angry, and her right beneath him, it made no sense to delay using the biggest weapon he had.

Rachmiel raised his hand toward Heaven. "I swear by Him who lives forever and ever, who created Heaven and Earth, I am not trying to have you removed. I did none of those things."

The same way a little liquid will spread out through a liquid of a different color, the emotions dispersed through Tabris: anger like red, and then through that a trickle of clear. Tendrils of confusion, a surge of denial, then more questions, then another surge of anger. As Rachmiel waited, he felt the confusion winning over the anger. He kept his silence. Let Tabris settle it out.

That demon. That demon, feeding him lies. And Tabris, listening for no reason Rachmiel could comprehend, but listening nonetheless.

If emotions had color, then humiliation burned brilliant yellow, and Rachmiel felt it searing around the edges of the emotional waters.

Rachmiel swallowed. "You're fighting the wrong enemy."

Tabris rocked back to sit against the wall. Away from Elizabeth. Rachmiel shot close to her, near her head, heart pounding with relief.

Tabris whispered, "I'm sorry."

Rachmiel raised his wings. "I know I've gotten angry at you. That's my fault, and I'm sorry. But I never did anything to have you removed. If I didn't think she was safe with you, would I leave her with you while I went to do something that would make you angry?"

Tabris hugged his knees to his chest, dropped his head and brought up his wings around himself. The picture of that demon again came to Rachmiel's mind, and Tabris said, "Enough of what he told me was true—I believed the other parts."

He jerked up, a streak of light splitting his multicolored emotions. "Then Sebastian—? He doesn't really hate me?"

Rachmiel flinched. "Well—"

Tabris's head dropped again. "Blast."

"He's talking about maybe forgiving you. We prayed with him during the last visit." Rachmiel touched Tabris's wing. "He needs time."

He settled himself beside Tabris and enfolded him in his wings, casting a Guard around the room. "Easy," Rachmiel whispered. "Let it out. The demon was trying to get you away from us. But we're a team."

Tabris shivered. "He said he loved me."

Rachmiel snorted. "Well how could that be possible?"

Tabris recoiled, and the loneliness seeped from him like juice from a broken fruit. "Yeah." He felt smaller. "I guess it couldn't be."

He went limp under Rachmiel's touch, and Rachmiel projected reassurance as best he could. "I wish you'd told me sooner."

"What good would it have done?" Despair's straw-like color tinted the emotional waters. "I'd still be the same."

Rachmiel said, "You've lost me." And in the next moment he caught his breath. "You're not unlovable! That's not what I meant. I meant demons can't love—"

Despair gushed from Tabris, and Rachmiel felt the overwhelming-ness of his situation: what he'd broken, his inability to make it whole, the conviction that angels don't get second chances, and that one wide-open question—whether he'd broken the final link that mattered.

Rachmiel grabbed him by the shoulders. "God loves you. Don't question that."

"No one else does."

"That's not true!"

"Name one," Tabris shot back.

Rachmiel quivered.

"Let's see." Tabris glowered into the dark. "Any guardian of a person who knew Sebastian is furious because of the unnecessary grief I subjected his charge to. Raguel looks at me as another burden to lug around, but he put his name on the line for me so I had better come through for him. Sariel dutifully visited the wretched soul, got her service points, and went home again. Sebastian hates me, and rightly so."

And the obvious name left off that list: Rachmiel's own, even though God had told him that before it was over, he'd need to love Tabris.

Rachmiel offered, "Miriael?" It sounded weak.

Tabris shuddered. "Have you ever thought maybe Miriael spars with me as a shot across the bow? A warning that if I harm Kyle, he'll personally see me in Hell?"

Rachmiel gasped. "Are you kidding?"

"I realized tonight he's the only one in the household who's never asked me to stand in for him." Tabris sighed. "The guardians are far angrier than the ones who never guarded. Non-guardians imagine it must be an awful job. The ones who've guarded a person don't understand how I could have done it." Tabris put down his head. "For that matter, neither do I."

Rachmiel fingered his hair. "Why did you?"

Tabris shook his head.

Rachmiel projected an apology. "Sebastian will want to know."

"Reason number one I'm not going to visit him."

That made a lot of sense, actually. Rachmiel said, "But if you visit him, he might find it easier to forgive you."

"I don't deserve his forgiveness, and I'm not going to see him until God forces me."

"Who deserves forgiveness?" Rachmiel sighed. "It's mercy because it's undeserved. If we deserved what we got, it would be justice."

Tabris shook his head. "I cannot comprehend that."

"Only because it's you." Rachmiel chuckled. "I can see it." He hugged Tabris, then pulled back. "Are you okay with me now? Or were there other things that demon told you, like that I planned to write and illustrate my own line of greeting cards?"

As Tabris raised his head with a smile, Rachmiel's breath caught. "You'd be good at that."

Rachmiel raised his eyebrows. "I should hope so! *Script font and fourteen words to say / I hope you have a special day.*"

They both laughed, and then Tabris made an image in the air of a half-open rose bud in watercolor, dewdrops on the petals, inscribed with

Insert Sentiment Here. Rachmiel said, "We need a logo," and Tabris replied, "We need a life."

They laughed until Elizabeth stirred, and Rachmiel bent over her. "Go back to sleep. We're just being silly."

"It's not like we have your soul in our hands or anything," Tabris added.

Rachmiel looked up. "Hey, you said before that God told you to come back. You were praying?"

Tabris frowned. "I'm not sure. I mean, I was talking to God. And He was talking back to me. But it wasn't real prayer."

"It's a start, right?"

Tabris huffed. "It might be a finish, too. I'm afraid to find out."

At that moment, unseen power took form in the room. Rachmiel and Tabris both dropped to their knees.

"Relax," said Jesus. He gestured that Rachmiel stand. Tabris stayed with his arms crossed over his chest and his head down. "I'm going to take you up on your offer."

Tabris's head jerked up. "What offer?"

"That you wouldn't go to Sebastian until I ordered you. You're now under orders to visit him tomorrow night."

Rachmiel felt Tabris's soul groping for his, and he met the grasp, sending power back through him. Was this a solo trip?

Jesus turned to him. "Yes, you can accompany him, and Casifer will be there too." He turned back to Tabris. "You should try to pray before you go."

Rachmiel said, "Does Sebastian know?"

"I'm telling him," said Jesus, and vanished.

Tabris closed his eyes.

Minutes ticked by. Tabris didn't move.

Rachmiel touched Tabris's wingtip with his own. "So, eighteen hours." He sat beside him. "Do you want to pray now?"

"You pray," said Tabris. "I need to think."

Twenty

Last night, Tabris had needed him. Rachmiel wanted to grab random angels and tell them this, jump in place and laugh out loud. But today, Tabris needed him quiet. Needed him not to go exulting that he'd seen a little into the mazy interior of Tabris's soul.

All the same, they got looks. Rachmiel noted the puzzlement from the guardians of Elizabeth's classmates when Tabris and he bantered with one another. Although tense and with an eye for the clock, Tabris initiated conversation. He'd make ironic remarks in a low voice, and Rachmiel would laugh, and the angels would look.

Not everything had changed. During the course of the day, Rachmiel learned about many, many reasons to delay praying. While he didn't want to nag, he also didn't want to ignore a divine recommendation. "You should pray," while not a command, also felt stronger than a suggestion.

He did seize every opportunity that came up. One of Kyle's classmates had broken his leg on a camping trip, so in the car on the way home, Rachmiel suggested they pray for him. One by one, all the family angels did. All but Tabris, who Rachmiel could feel was saying the words but keeping his heart shut.

Rachmiel even touched their wings together, but Tabris resisted. Instead, Rachmiel opened his heart to God, and God gave him strength.

Rachmiel gave God the image of what he feared most: of Sebastian coming toward Tabris, needy for any sign that his guardian cared about him, and meeting only the cold eyes of a former-guardian. Rachmiel showed God his alternate thoughts: that the love was there, only buried beneath sheets of denial and pain. Love replaced by shame.

God suffused Rachmiel's soul, and when the car stopped, the prayer ended.

Hours later, as Elizabeth propped herself on her pillows to read before bed, Tabris settled on the floor. "So: game-time. What do you know about me?"

Rachmiel's attention peaked. "You mean about you and Sebastian?"

Tabris nodded. "You deserve not to be surprised by whatever comes up, but there's no need to duplicate information."

Rachmiel sat forward. "For starters, Sariel says you were an amazing guardian."

Tabris exclaimed, "She said that?"

Rachmiel nodded. "She said you protected him from all physical harm and kept him free of serious sin until he was twelve."

"Go figure." Tabris's eyes narrowed. "What was that sin?"

Rachmiel shrugged. "Not that it's any of my business, but I don't think it was something so bad you killed him in retaliation."

His wings flared. "What?"

Rachmiel pulled back. "Some angels speculated that Sebastian committed a crime deserving of death."

"What on earth could a kid do that would deserve that?" Tabris's eyes were huge. "Who could even imagine such a thing? Of course it wasn't retaliation!"

Rachmiel raised his hands. "I didn't believe it was. His heart and soul didn't seem that hardened."

Tabris huffed. "Not hardly. He stole an MP3 player from his best friend. He was over the kid's house, and he pocketed it. Later, the kid asked if he'd seen it, and Sebastian said no." Tabris frowned. "His friend didn't have much money, so losing that was huge. It wasn't like he could just replace it, and Sebastian didn't seem to care that he might lose a friend."

Rachmiel winced. "And you got him to turn back to God after a few days."

Tabris sighed. "He didn't own up to what he'd done, but he put it in the bottom of the kid's backpack as if it had been there all along. I made him confess it to God." He shook his head. "I didn't know what more I could do."

Rachmiel said, "At which point, your fellow guardians told you that there was nothing you could have done to prevent it because Sebastian had free will, but you felt guilty anyhow."

Tabris traced a finger over the carpet. "I failed the kid. An angel as powerful as I am shouldn't have let my own kid steal an expensive piece of equipment from his friend. I lost some of my sight into his soul when that happened—it'll happen with Elizabeth too at some point—and that was awful."

Rachmiel leaned forward. "But it wasn't about you *letting* him. It doesn't reflect on Katra'il or Mithra when Martin or Andrew does something awful."

"They're not as high-ranking in their choir, though." Tabris bit his lip. "Lesser angels were doing a better job than I was, and I needed to get my act together in a hurry or the kid was going to end up in Hell. So one day Sebastian proved he had free will, and three days later, I did the same."

"How did it happen?"

Tabris looked down, fists clenched. "You tell me."

"On his bicycle. You told me that. Sebastian hit a rock and flipped over, and you didn't break his fall."

Tabris kept staring at the carpet. "Don't sugar-coat it. I killed him. He biked over the railroad tracks and his front tire got turned into the groove of the track, but his back tire didn't. Two tires going in two different directions, so he flipped. He went over the handlebars—" Rachmiel could see it like a movie advancing frame by frame. "—and I curled over him with my hands on his shoulders to protect his spine, and then, just as he hit the ground—I broke his neck." Again that snap in Rachmiel's mind, a sensation he'd never quite exorcised after the first time he'd felt it. "Not negligent homicide. Murder one. And I stopped. I thought—*Lord*. I couldn't think anything else. I threw myself on top of him and stayed there until two Archangels chained me, and another lifted Sebastian's soul away from his body to bring it to judgment." Tabris had gone pale. "You know the rest."

Rachmiel said, "Had you planned it?"

"No." Tabris shut his eyes. "That's how Raguel asked for mercy. He said I hadn't meant it. I did mean it, just not for too long before it happened and not for too long afterward. I regretted it before the bicycle hit the ground, but by then I couldn't take it back. I couldn't resurrect him. I couldn't reverse time."

Rachmiel had gone cold. "You didn't run?"

"Where could I have gone?" Tabris choked out a laugh. It hurt to hear. "I belonged with him."

Rachmiel looked at Elizabeth. "I think I would have."

"It was such a shock, I'm not sure anyone could predict his reaction. Once you do something like that, nothing is sane. I just stopped moving because I was afraid that—"

After a moment, Rachmiel said, "Go on."

Still he didn't speak. Rachmiel could feel it anyhow: the moment frozen between 'fight or flight,' Justice bearing down on himself like an oncoming train, staring into its headlamp, the world vibrating all around, but at the same time, no sensation at all.

Rachmiel lowered his voice. "If you didn't plan on it, and you regretted it that quickly...why did you do it at all?"

Tabris's eyes gleamed. "That doesn't matter. It's done. What matters is what happens now."

"But—"

"It's not important!" His fists clenched. "Knowing why can't change it."

Rachmiel backed off rather then have Tabris shut down.

On the bed, Elizabeth looked up at her clock, about to close the book. Tabris turned to her. "It's a good story. You'll finish by ten. Stay up until your mom tells you to go to sleep."

Elizabeth returned to reading, but her eyes were half-shut.

Rachmiel's mouth twitched, but he let it go. An hour's lost sleep wouldn't harm her, and Tabris needed the time—or the delay. He said, "Whatever the reason, wouldn't you do it differently if you started again?"

"But isn't that the point?" said Tabris. "We'd all make the same choices if we were returned to the first moments. Damnation and election were decisions, not chance. That's why it's so horrible. Every step was our own choice, each building on the next toward the conclusion we were writing for ourselves."

Rachmiel said, "But just that one thing—"

"That's what I mean. It wasn't *just that one thing*. There had to have been bad decisions I was making all along that led up to it, only I don't know what they were." Tabris hunched forward. "I wasn't right, and I regret it every minute. And I have no idea how I can love and protect *this* kid—" he jerked his thumb toward Elizabeth, "—when I slaughtered the first one. It's not fair to Sebastian."

Hadn't Sebastian said almost the same thing? Rachmiel circled the issue. "You mean you aren't sure you have the ability to protect her, or that it's not fitting?"

"Not fitting." His eyes narrowed. "I'm not sure what meeting Sebastian is supposed to accomplish. Anything I say or do is going to make him resentful. It's better for him if he can just forget me." He closed his eyes, and Rachmiel wondered how often he'd mistaken grief for unconcern. *Forget about me.* Just let the memory go, and in eternity

Sebastian could be happy while a grieving Tabris stayed away for his former charge's sake, an unhealed wound in the spiritual body of Christ.

"I think he needs you." Rachmiel glanced over Tabris's head to find Elizabeth stretched out and breathing deeply, her book tucked under her arm. He didn't wake her, but now they had a ticking clock. "Tell him what you told me. That you're sorry, that it wasn't his fault, and you want him to forgive you."

Tabris clenched his fists. "How can I ask for that? I'm never going to forgive myself."

Rachmiel shook his head. "God forgave you. Are you holding yourself to a higher standard than God?"

Tabris glanced sideways. "God's got omnipotence on His side. I don't. Neither does Sebastian. What I did deserved Hell, and you expect the one I hurt to be able to forgive that?" He bit his lip. "Dark-eyed like me."

Rachmiel said, "I owe you an apology. I didn't realize you weren't dark-eyed by nature."

"He shouldn't be, either. He's angry. It clouds him."

Rachmiel bit his lip. "Are you angry?"

Elizabeth's deep breaths created a rhythm for Rachmiel's heart, but Tabris didn't notice. "Not angry. Unforgiven. This is a gorgeous world, and I've ruined it."

"You," Rachmiel said. "You, personally."

Tabris gave a half-smile. "Me, personally. I've ruined Sebastian's world, his parents' world, your world, my own world. But there's so much here. Cold nights, polluted cities, occasional chats with the Creator. I feel like I'm leap-frogging from one peak to the next trying to avoid all the pits in between, and I've run out of peaks." He sighed. "I'm going to need a cold night over a polluted city when we're done."

Rachmiel extended his wings. "Would you settle for a chat with the Creator?"

"He'll refuse to chat back." Tabris closed his eyes. "Right before I go see the kid— I'll lose everything at once. I can't."

And with that denial, time was up. Casifer arrived.

Tabris and Rachmiel stood while Casifer scrutinized Tabris with no warmth.

Rachmiel blessed Elizabeth before calling Voriah to watch her. Miriael came into the room and leaned on the door.

"Not yet," said Tabris. "Bring Sebastian here."

Casifer said, "I will, but I'd prefer he doesn't have an audience."

Casifer vanished. Miriael grasped Tabris's hand and nodded, and Voriah wished him well. They left the room just as Casifer returned with the boy.

Twenty-One

Rachmiel couldn't get a good view of Sebastian's face, half-hidden by Casifer's wing. From his position, Tabris would be able to see even less.

Tabris stayed a step behind Rachmiel, giving a tentative, "Hello, Sebastian."

The boy nodded. "Hi."

Sebastian's soul emitted streamers of emotion: fright, anger, curiosity. But from Tabris, sensation bubbled up through a sleeping Elizabeth and back into Rachmiel, relief like cool water to a burn. When Rachmiel turned to Tabris, he found *That Look.*

All along he'd assumed Tabris didn't want to see Sebastian, but instead, all along Tabris had yearned for it the way two notes of a chord stay unresolved until they find their third.

Tabris inched forward. "You look well." Actually, Sebastian looked upset, but Rachmiel could tell Tabris was scanning the interior of Sebastian's soul, comparing it to the last time they'd been together. There, again, the relief. Tabris didn't see the damage he'd imagined, the pain the demon had talked about. "Casifer's taking good care of you."

Sebastian only nodded again.

Tabris took a step forward, and it was as if the gray of the world eased back to reveal light and the sharpness of shadows, the boy before the angel. "Do you— Can I show you around the house?"

Casifer folded his arms. "Actually, since we'd stopped here once before, I'd planned a field trip for tonight."

And with that the clouds returned. Tabris went still, and Rachmiel stepped forward, saying, "If that's what Sebastian prefers. After they talk for a bit, I thought we'd visit someplace exotic, maybe even off this planet."

"I've planned a trip to a place Sebastian will find interesting, and they can talk afterward." Casifer looked at the boy still shielded by his wings. "Are you ready?"

Tabris hadn't reacted, but his hands were clenched.

Rachmiel said, "Maybe we should let them talk first."

Although with Casifer acting as Sebastian's gatekeeper, there was no way Tabris could apologize. His presence dominated the room.

Casifer said, "I'd rather give Sebastian a chance to get comfortable." He flashed the four of them to a dark place where the scent of dirt and leaves imbued the air, and insects sang around them. The air felt rich, clean. He turned to Sebastian. "Can you guess where we are?"

Sebastian said, "The Amazon jungle?"

Casifer nodded. "Yes, but the Amazon isn't a jungle. It's a moist broadleaf forest."

As if Tabris weren't trying to stare him full of little holes, Casifer began showing Sebastian the varied insect species, the adaptations they'd made to better suit the microbiomes within the rain forest. With Sebastian checking out Tabris over his shoulder every few seconds, Casifer showed Sebastian ground-level plants that had adapted to survive with nearly no light, and harmless bugs that mimicked poisonous bugs in order to escape the birds. He called over birds to show him how their beaks had changed shape over the generations in order to better open the seeds they found.

Tabris and Rachmiel followed, tourists in this leafier part of the world. Tabris projected a picture into Rachmiel's head: Casifer sitting in a library with an encyclopedia open on his lap, taking notes.

Rachmiel remembered Casifer declaring it his duty to protect Sebastian from Tabris. Keeping that stuffed down, he returned a question.

Tabris replied with a wish for open sky and flight. The damp heat felt oppressive to an angel who used to race down the side of Rockies and then glide as far as he could across the Great Plains, usually clearing Kansas and sometimes Missouri.

Rachmiel touched his wing to Tabris's.

Sebastian turned to look at them.

Tabris said, "Are you having a good time?"

The boy nodded. "I've never seen a place like this!"

Tabris said, "I know."

The emotions had cut off, with Tabris clamped so tight that he might not have been able to feel whatever Sebastian and Casifer were projecting.

"I mean including even after I was alive." Sebastian forced a pleasant expression, and Rachmiel had to look away. "I've been undersea, and I never went scuba diving. I'd never been to the northwest either, but we visited that cliff with that other angel, the one I called Coach."

"Voriah," said Rachmiel.

"Yeah, him. He was cool." Sebastian waited a beat. "But we never came here."

Casifer said, "About a tenth of all the species on Earth are right here in the Amazon."

Tabris said, "Fascinating."

Rachmiel shot him a look.

For a while they wandered, never at a loss for something to examine: different types of trees, plants, animals. Rachmiel crouched close to a bush and took a juvenile macaw in his hands.

Sebastian tried to touch the bird, but he couldn't manipulate his density enough to get any sensation. Casifer tried to explain, but when Sebastian tried again, the macaw could sense him. It looked right at him and squawked.

Tabris laughed. "He told you off!"

Sebastian smirked. "Well, I guess that makes the decision for me."

Rachmiel breathed over the bird. "I can keep him calm."

"It's fine. Don't worry."

Sebastian took a step back while Casifer looked at the bird, and he ended up standing beside Tabris. Sebastian said, "Those two are a lot alike."

Tabris was studying Sebastian again, getting a look at the interior of his soul. "You may be right. *Rachmiel* means *God's compassion.*" The sense of cool relief overcame Rachmiel a second time, and he released it into the bird. It settled down in his hands.

Sebastian said, "And what does *Casifer* mean?"

Casifer started to say something, but Rachmiel projected at him to stand down. *That's an opening.* Rachmiel thought it, but he didn't project it. *Take it, take it, take it.*

Tabris said, "That one I don't quite get. It means solitude or temperance, depending on which language you're using as the base. I've also seen *Casifer* referred to as the Angel of Tears."

Sebastian huffed. "But how can someone be the angel of a bad thing?"

165

Rachmiel started when Tabris said, "Solitude and tears don't have to be bad things."

"Oh." Sebastian looked puzzled. "So what does *Tabris* mean? What are you the angel-of?"

Tabris said, "Free will."

Sebastian frowned. "I'll have to think about that."

Casifer glanced at Rachmiel, who met his eyes and projected calm.

Sebastian was saying, "How does it work? Does Rachmiel *have* to be compassionate?"

Tabris looked brighter than moments ago. "The names were given by God, so they express our natures, and in turn our natures express different aspects of God."

"That went straight over my head. How can your name express your nature?"

Tabris chuckled. "Our potential is the highest expression of what our names mean. It's not like when your mom and dad sat down with a baby name book and tested them out with your last name. Your soul has a name too. You'll uncover it over time."

Sebastian looked up at him, his head cocked, for the first time appearing unguarded. "How long did it take to uncover yours?"

Tabris shook his head. "We got our names. You guys have to earn them."

"Unfair!" exclaimed Sebastian, and Tabris surprised Rachmiel by smiling. "It'd be helpful to have a road map. Anything else?"

Tabris tensed. "I'm sorry. I shouldn't have gone on like that."

Sebastian looked at his feet. "You can teach me things too. It's okay."

Speaking low, Tabris emitted a feeling that went through Rachmiel like a blade. "I think Casifer's done a better job than I did."

Sebastian said, "He told me you did a good job, until the end."

Rachmiel felt Tabris flinch. At the same time, Casifer said, "Sebastian, let's try this again. Come here."

While Tabris watched, Casifer stood behind Sebastian and took his hands in his own, then helped Sebastian concentrate until he became more corporeal. "We can practice this later," he murmured, "and you can get a bit more solid or you could discorporate completely. But for now, you need just a little substance. Like this."

Rachmiel held the bird over Sebastian's cupped palms, then moved his hands through Sebastian's, becoming less corporeal so that by the time he let go, Sebastian was holding the bird.

The boy grinned. "He's so soft! Is he really this light, or is it because I'm not real?"

"You're real," Casifer said. "He weighs about three ounces."

Sebastian didn't take his eyes off the bird. "Does he trust me?"

"You're from God. Of course he does."

"He's so fragile." Sebastian turned to Tabris. "Do you want to hold him?"

"He's happy with you," Tabris said.

Rachmiel thought, *Take the opening.*

Sebastian extended his hands. "But he's so sweet."

Tabris said, "I know. You should enjoy him until he flies away."

Rachmiel fought disappointment. Sebastian looked down, his mouth tight.

Casifer gave Sebastian a quick rundown of avian anatomy, but Sebastian didn't ask questions, and then he let the bird fly away. "Let's keep walking."

Sebastian remained silent. Even their passage made no sound.

Casifer said, "A mosquito on that leaf is the size of a thimble."

Tabris said, "Did we come here to see mosquitos?"

"They grow 'em bigger in New Jersey," Rachmiel said quickly. When Sebastian looked at him, Rachmiel made his eyes glimmer so he'd realize how much to trust this 'statistic.' "Moms have to chain down their strollers so the mosquitoes don't carry off their infants."

Sebastian said, "You read that in the *Weekly World News*?"

"Elizabeth saw it on the internet," Rachmiel said. "It must be true."

Sebastian laughed. "Of course! But I have to say, insects are a lot cooler now that I can't be bitten or stung."

Behind Rachmiel, Tabris said, "Dragonflies are awesome either way."

Sebastian perked up. "I love them! They're so beautiful and perfect! I remember one landed on me once and I was freaking out because it was so awesome to have it right there on my hand!"

Tabris laughed. "I remember calling over a dragonfly and getting it to land on you."

Sebastian got a queer look, a struggle. He choked out, "Thank you."

Casifer said, "Are you getting tired?"

"A little." The boy looked up. "Could we go somewhere and pray a little? I liked doing that last time, and you just showed me so much. There's a lot to assimilate."

Yeah, Rachmiel thought, *a lot to assimilate.* The boy was transparent: an angry core overlaid with sensitivity, mistrust and yearning. The difficult thing wasn't the macaw he'd been shown; it was the two-toned bird.

Tabris said, "There's a pond out by Elizabeth's house. I wanted to take you there."

Casifer said, "Actually, I'd planned to bring him back to the cliffs we went to last time, on the Pacific coast."

Rachmiel said, "There might be dragonflies at the pond."

Casifer said, "I'm thinking of what's best for Sebastian. He was doing pretty well praying at the cliffside, and we ought to take advantage of that."

Tabris's feathers stood out. Casifer flashed Sebastian back to Washington State, and Rachmiel followed with Tabris. Once there he tried to get Tabris's attention, but Tabris turned his back and glared out over the pounding of the ocean.

Rachmiel couldn't tell which he was feeling: the sea or Tabris. Fierce, formless. Deep. The straight spruces stood like pikes on a rack, and on the other side, Sebastian was reaching out to the waters with a nonhuman sense he was still struggling to control. As the ocean beat the shore with the steadiness of a pumping heart, Tabris inhaled and then folded his arms.

Rachmiel felt Casifer opening the prayer, and he joined him, spreading his wings and reaching out with his hands in mimicry of his heart's actions. As the tension in his soul increased, he vibrated with expectancy until God dissolved the walls around him. Rachmiel momentarily felt himself connected to all creation, seeing it as God saw it, and feeling the joy God had in what He made.

In that moment, Rachmiel extended his reach for Sebastian and helped him let down the fences around his mind. The boy drew back on himself, but Casifer surrounded him and gave reassurance. Afraid, Sebastian nevertheless invited God to come into his heart.

He cried out, and all three angels moved closer, but he remained suspended in a moment of adoration, amazement winding him round. In that deep communion, Sebastian brimmed with an awareness of God in every iota of creation, as though every cell glowed to form an impressionist painting. He was projecting the images even as they came to him. The sea gleamed like a sun, and the cliff sparkled. The angels towered heavenward like shafts of light with tendrils lacing them to one another.

God asked if Sebastian wanted a gift. And Sebastian replied with a request: he wanted to want to forgive.

Rachmiel closed his eyes and reached for Tabris, realizing only then that he had dropped back from the prayer framework when they'd opened up. Battened down, he hadn't felt Sebastian's request. Rachmiel couldn't tell if it was his own feelings or Tabris's or Sebastian's, but he kept sensing desperation: *when he was alone, then he'd break down, then he'd cry. Maybe for weeks, but not now.* And he couldn't sort out whose feelings were whose any longer.

Below them the water kept ramming into the rocks. Casifer invited Tabris into the prayer.

Tabris pulled back, but Casifer insisted. This time Tabris stopped praying at all, not even with words. Casifer looked up long enough to glare at him, and Tabris glared back.

Rachmiel touched Tabris with his wing, and Tabris projected into Rachmiel's heart, *Not now.* He didn't want to shatter in pieces in front of Sebastian and the new guardian.

Rachmiel let him go. Casifer emitted an air of disgust.

When the boy was ready, Casifer transitioned him back from an ecstatic state to his normal level of perception. Sebastian shook, and he rubbed his hands on his arms, as if grounding himself in his own form. "I could have stayed that way forever."

"When you're capable, you'll have that all the time," said Casifer. "That's the Beatific Vision. Angels have that level of awareness and higher."

Tabris watched and said nothing.

Sebastian's mouth opened. "And you can still function? What's your prayer like?"

"We meet God soul to soul, not just face to face," said Rachmiel. "It's a more total union."

Casifer added, "When you're ready, God will take you into Heaven, and then the experience will be easier for you to bear—and eternal. Your capacity will deepen and your endurance will become greater. But first you'll need to complete your development."

In mid-nod, Sebastian's eyes widened, and he held his breath, clenched his fists. Casifer started, and the shock went right through Rachmiel: Sebastian realized that if he'd lived his full life, the experiences, suffering and choices he made during his lifetime would have changed the facets of God his soul was capable of seeing. His relationship to God would have deepened, and so would his experience of the Divine.

169

The rage blew from Sebastian like steam venting from a volcano, and he glared at Tabris.

Rachmiel moved between Sebastian and Tabris. "Thank you for visiting." He couldn't get Sebastian to look at him, and the boy shifted sideways to keep glowering. "Will we see you again soon?"

Casifer sounded shaken. "I'm going to leave that up to Sebastian."

Sebastian glared at Rachmiel, and when Tabris moved closer, he stared away. "Thank you for agreeing to see me." His voice was a wasteland. "I'll let you know if I decide to see you again." He turned to Casifer. "Let's go."

Casifer took Sebastian's hand, and they returned to Limbo.

Twenty-Two

Tabris stood straight for a moment, then turned toward the ocean.

Rachmiel couldn't read any feeling off him. "Are you all right?"

"I'm thinking... No, I'm not all right." He picked up a rock and hurled it across the water. Rachmiel altered its trajectory so it wouldn't reach escape velocity. "I'm not all right, and I won't ever be."

He sat at the cliff's edge, swinging his legs so his heels hit the loose stone without dislodging any.

Rachmiel sat beside him. "It's going to take time."

"Time?" he snarled. "Time is my enemy. Immortality is a curse. It certainly is in Hell. One mistake, and I'm wearing a scarlet M for all God's creation to see." Tabris rubbed his forehead. "How nice for Sebastian to have a travel-agent angel with an iron-clad itinerary."

Rachmiel said, "Casifer wanted a plan in case things got awkward."

Tabris wasn't listening. "And that child is so angry there's no way he can keep controlling it."

"Just like you." Rachmiel looked at the waves. "But he's young yet. He doesn't have your control."

Tabris put his face in his palms. "I didn't teach him that."

Rachmiel shook his head. "What's under his anger?"

From Tabris: irritation; a reprimand about playing psychologist; the boy didn't have to have anything underlying the anger.

Rachmiel said, "Is he ashamed?"

"Stop it!" Tabris angled away from him. "Don't push. Let me get my head together."

"Maybe you need to let go just once? It's unreal to deny that much—"

Tabris flashed back ten feet from the edge. "But not here, not with you. I'm going somewhere alone—"

"—so I don't have to see what you're really like inside?" Rachmiel followed him, and before Tabris realized, Rachmiel had him pinned the way Mithra had shown him: he wouldn't disappear this time. It was simple enough as long as he concentrated. He'd just never imagined he'd need to use it on a friend.

Tabris struggled. "Let me go! You already know everything—you already know I'm the kind of angel who'd put my hands around a child's neck and snap it when he hit the ground—what more do you want? You know it all, and I'm never going to be the same—not with you, not with God, not with—"

Tabris went still. No thoughts, no emotions, no words.

Rachmiel said, "Not with Sebastian?"

He didn't relax his hold. One flicker and Tabris was out of there.

"Or is it with yourself?"

He might as well have been talking to a tree. Tabris couldn't escape, so he was locking down on the spot—not what Rachmiel had intended. He pushed. "You haven't lost Sebastian completely."

Rachmiel caught a stray feeling: he'd lost Sebastian's trust and any hope the kid would ever like him; whatever remained wasn't all that much.

Rachmiel said, "God loves you."

Tabris said, "God tolerates me."

They stayed that way during a silence Rachmiel couldn't figure out how to break—two angels on a cliff against the speckled dome of the sky: the peacemaker, a son of God, and another who mourned and would not be comforted. Things couldn't stay that way. "You know about the prodigal son."

Tabris folded his arms. "Do you have the expanded director's cut anniversary edition, where the older son goes in to the party and kills the younger son? I do. Let me go and I'll get it."

Rachmiel said, "In my version, the younger son got the fatted calf."

"And in mine, the older son got chewed out." Tabris bowed. "Allow me to introduce the older son. And the other stories in the collection are just as exciting: the lost sheep, devoured by wolves. The lost coin, buried."

Rachmiel frowned. "I don't think it works that way. You're the younger son in as many ways as the older. And *you* could be the coin God finds. You could be the sheep he carries home on his shoulders."

Tabris's shoulders slumped. "How can you say that?"

"He's forgiving."

"Only if you're human. Lucifer was never forgiven."

Rachmiel huffed. "He never asked."

"Neither did I."

Terror flitted through Rachmiel, as if God might snatch Tabris off the cliff's edge right now. "Don't you want forgiveness?"

"Of course I do!" Tabris's voice broke. "But I deserve the worst He can give. No prayer, no child, no friends—I could never ask forgiveness because I can't balance all the scales."

"God can."

"Can, sure." Tabris turned his head. "But under the rules He's set, no. He can't make Sebastian fulfill His plan in the way only Sebastian with his background and his personality could have. If Mary had said no to Gabriel, would he have gone door to door? No one could have mothered Jesus the way she did, and no one else can be Sebastian." Tabris closed his eyes, and Rachmiel got an image of withered flowers. "And now Sebastian doesn't get to be Sebastian either. He'll never go to college, hold a job, get married. His potential children no longer exist. His future wife will either stay single or marry the wrong man. Why don't we track down *her* guardian angel and see what he thinks?" Rachmiel got another image from Tabris: a series of ever-expanding circles on a pond's surface. "Over time, the repercussions are infinite."

Rachmiel said, "Many people die before their time."

"Not murdered by their guardians."

"Well, no." Even from a distance, the tension of unshed tears crawled over him like spiders, so he kept his voice soothing. "God's plan is more dynamic than that anyhow. You've heard about free will, I assume?" He forced a smile, but Tabris didn't settle. "He took bad choices into account. Sebastian's parents and friends, yes, worry about them. But not the wife, not the potential children. We aren't cast in roles, and there's no script. When we improvise, God rewrites the play and doesn't keep forcing us back into the abandoned channels. So Sebastian's intended wife can still marry, and it's not going to create a chain of divorces and children who should never have been born."

Tabris said, "You've thought this through. Why would—"

Rachmiel didn't react fast enough. Tabris shot toward him, and until the moment he tackled him, flames in his wake, Rachmiel had been concentrating on keeping Tabris from escaping. He took the hit square in the chest.

Tabris towered over him, sword in hand. "You lied to me! You've been lying in every way that mattered!"

Back against a rock, Rachmiel raised his hands. "She's going to be fine!"

"I killed her husband! You knew it! Everyone's been watching this charade of me protecting her when you knew I hurt her in the worst way possible!"

"I never told anyone!" Rachmiel wanted to project calm, but he couldn't reach it past his own fear. Energy pulsed off Tabris, betrayal and rage, but beneath both those frothed hatred. Rachmiel knew absolutely that first Tabris was going to strike him, and then he was going to damn himself. And for that reason, when Tabris struck, Rachmiel didn't defend.

God made Rachmiel incorporeal like light. Tabris's sword swept through him and lodged three inches deep in the stone.

Petrified, Rachmiel could only watch. Tabris heaved up his sword and swung again, but he could no more hit Rachmiel than a dust cloud. The sword was useless now, but with a heart that couldn't be shielded from emotional weaponry, Rachmiel cringed under the force of that anger.

More fire than angel, Tabris opened his heart at Rachmiel: projected into him the blaze of his anger, his disgust, his fury at everyone who stared at or mistrusted him and the simultaneous sense that they were right, right to be disgusted, right to want him gone. The despair. The hatred. Hatred of the one at the center, the one who had ruined it all.

Rachmiel curled around himself, unable to fight a lightning strike of emotions that left a crater behind. A world in ruins because of him, of him, of him.

When it ended—and Rachmiel had no idea how much time passed before it did—he found himself still clenched on the ground.

Silence. No, not silence. Birds.

A breeze through leaves.

Waves whispering.

Elizabeth? Was she okay?

He asked the ground where he was, and he felt the cliff, the land's edge. The same spot. Next he probed for other angels but felt no one. He opened one eye, then the other. It hurt. Elizabeth. He had to get to Elizabeth.

He raised his wings and pushed himself up, only to find Tabris sitting against a rock a wingspan away. Watching him. Emotionally void.

Rachmiel froze in place halfway up from the ground. They stared at each other: kindness and truth, Compassion and Free Will. Rachmiel wanted nothing more than to leave, to flash to Elizabeth and Guard her room until Tabris promised never to return. The fear clamored on the surface of his heart and Tabris would feel it, but he didn't care anymore what happened to Tabris or if Tabris was sorry. He'd forgive him someday. Right now he just wanted him gone.

Rachmiel sat up as slowly as he could. All the emotions Tabris had discharged into him...they echoed: the despair, the anger, the self-hatred. That last was what rebounded within Rachmiel most often, a deadly pinball with an unpredictable ricochet.

When Tabris spoke, it was low and slow. "Now that you're awake, I'm going to get Voriah and leave you forever."

Rachmiel shook his head.

"I'll take myself off your hands. I've already gutted Elizabeth's future. I killed Sebastian. And now I've hurt you. You have a child who needs you."

"So do you. Don't leave."

Tabris's eyes were lightless.

Rachmiel tried to find words, but everything kept forming up as Tabris's latent *I hate myself*.

Tabris stood.

"Don't! That doesn't solve the problem." Rachmiel put his hands to his eyes. "You're still on probation. I'd leave her myself before I sent you to Hell." He looked up. "I mean it. Stop talking about leaving."

If Tabris didn't, Rachmiel might well agree to it. *I hate myself*. A little venom spicing up the emotional waters. But he hadn't damned himself yet, and he'd been on the cusp. All those emotions he'd let out—they'd harmed Rachmiel but bought Tabris time. Time and rational thought. Small consolation.

Rachmiel pushed to a stand, regretting it the instant he tried. His vision swirled.

Tabris grabbed him before he toppled. "You're still hurt?"

"Obviously," Rachmiel snapped, trying to get his balance enough to push Tabris away. He closed his eyes against the glare of the daylight and then realized—*Daylight?* And who knew which day's light it was?

"Same day," said Tabris. "You were out maybe six hours."

Rachmiel tried to stand on his own, but when Tabris released him, the vertigo took him once more. He dropped back to a seat. *Don't panic. Just get your strength back and then you can leave.*

And in his mind still, the aftertaste of self-hatred. The chalkiness of despair. The thorniness of rejection.

Rachmiel muttered, "I should have let you go. I stupidly thought I could help, but I'm only a nuisance."

As soon as he said that, Tabris burst with a projection of shame. He was sorry. He shouldn't have reacted that way. He wanted to be forgiven. He wanted to make it right.

Tabris opened wide to let Rachmiel feel his apology. And as he did, Rachmiel bundled up that aftertaste of self-hatred and pushed it back to Tabris like an unpinned grenade.

Rachmiel was half-in and half-out of Tabris's heart, a heart open to apologize with full contrition, and the instant that grenade got inside, Tabris struggled to clamp shut, but Rachmiel stayed put. He kept Tabris's attention on it. *Why? Answer me. You wanted to make it right. I want an answer.*

The urge to pull away tornadoed through Tabris and into Rachmiel, and then with an act of will, Tabris showed himself.

Murderer.

Rachmiel looked past that, but Tabris shoved it front and center again.

Rachmiel slipped around that label and moved into the feelings, each like a beast chewing through its cage: the guilt; the anger; the resentment toward the angels who mistrusted him and the anger against the ones who pretended to understand.

And then at the back of them all, the wall he'd built around God.

Rachmiel let Tabris give it all to him, and etched into every bit of the way Tabris perceived himself was hatred. He'd ruined everything. Everything. Everything.

Rachmiel gave him time to get calm, and then he kindled a light within Tabris's soul. *It doesn't need to be so dark in here.* This spiritual anorexia gave the perception of control, but as Tabris starved himself, his spirit was crumbling. *Let me see what you really are.*

And there, behind the resentment was need. Behind his anger at himself was conscientiousness. Behind the loneliness was empathy. The wall around God was only a wall around himself, and inside was someone who'd lived to please his Father.

Rachmiel beheld the whole of Tabris's heart, the places that still shone and the open wound where he couldn't reconcile forgiveness with the damage he'd done. The purity still gleamed there beneath the control and anger.

Oh, wow, Rachmiel thought. *You're so beautiful.* And on top of that, *I love you.*

Tabris started. "But I hurt you!"

176

I was hurting you too. Rachmiel looked again at the glory of God in Tabris's heart, suppressed but there, definitely there. It was so similar to the glory God had placed in Sebastian's heart and so different from the Godly light in Elizabeth's. Facets of God, spread out over separate souls. This soul, hand-crafted by God, wasn't after all just tolerated by God. It was loved. Loved for who he was: dutiful, conscientious, clever, brave, goal-oriented, and honest. An angel who weighed his decisions and measured his worth by their outcome.

As Rachmiel beheld him, he perceived images without knowing why: sunflowers, children, Ferris wheels, fish, and opals.

Tabris trembled around him as Rachmiel reached another dark area. He tried to shine on that, and Tabris recoiled.

Okay, not there. But he kept going, admiring Tabris's architecture from both inside and outside, and he congratulated God on yet another masterpiece. Inside Rachmiel, inside Tabris, God said thank you.

As if he sensed that, Tabris tried to push Rachmiel out, denying that God had made him specially. He was just one of a trillion angels, named T-A-B-R-I-S like an alphabetical serial number.

Rachmiel projected a refusal.

Tabris put a dark thing into Rachmiel's heart. A scary thing. Hatred. The times he'd wished himself in Hell.

Rachmiel's eyes widened. *Why?*

The self-hatred thrummed again in Rachmiel's heart: in Hell, it would be justified.

Rachmiel grieved.

Tabris pushed another scary thing into Rachmiel's hands: proof that God didn't love him.

Rachmiel held it like a closed box. Would Tabris mind if he opened it?

Tabris opened it himself, spreading a dull dread through Rachmiel's gut: there had been no punishment following the crime. Other angels had been punished for far slighter offenses, the crowning example being the Archangel Gabriel, cut away from Heaven for a year because of a tiny infraction in 600 BC.

Tabris's voice was a whisper. "God loved them enough to reform them. But not me. I got reassigned as though it never happened."

Rachmiel sat with that in his hands, leaden and cold. No answer. He closed his eyes, and his light inside Tabris went dull.

God, I don't have a rebuttal for this one.

Tabris took that for confirmation. "He may still love me," Tabris added. "But not the same way."

But that's not true. Except inasmuch as Tabris was going to be different in the aftermath, of course God's love for them had to change along with the ways they changed; different angels needed love in different ways.

Rachmiel streamed this out even as it came to him, and he realized the Holy Spirit was pumping it through to Tabris. Huddled on the ground, the semicorporeal Tabris doubled around himself and closed his wings like a bivalve shell protecting the soft creature inside.

Of course God would love Tabris differently, but different didn't mean less. New choices formed new facets of character, and Tabris, with his additional perspective and growth, would love God differently too.

The inspiration flowed like a stream on a July afternoon: that God had created His creatures with free will precisely for this end, to give them the opportunity to shape themselves so they could love Him in their own way, and so He could love them not only as they were made but as they became. Like a tree from a seed, the branches would divide where they would, and the leaves appear, but all differently for every tree, and as each soul formed different branches to extend itself toward His light, God loved the result.

The question for Tabris was whether this new branching would lead to new growth, or whether Tabris would allow one bad decision to destroy him.

Rachmiel thought, *Are you saying all things work together for good for those who love you?*

In his heart, and only to Rachmiel, the Holy Spirit indicated He'd heard that somewhere before. Rachmiel laughed.

The communication hadn't reached Tabris, but Rachmiel's joy had, and he shuddered.

May I speak through you? asked the Spirit.

Thrilling, Rachmiel assented.

The Spirit reached for Tabris, who retreated on himself, wide-eyed. The Spirit surrounded him without engulfing him, and the first thing He did was assure Tabris not to be afraid.

Tabris waited.

Like an inspiration, Rachmiel realized two things, and they passed through him to Tabris: first, that a harsh punishment at the beginning would have pushed Tabris over the edge of despair. Part of correction was knowing when too much would make your child lose heart.

Tabris closed his eyes and stayed down.

Next Rachmiel felt that the natural consequences of the crime were severe already: Sebastian had been taken away; Tabris had to live with the memory of his crime; the other angels knew about it. These factors alone had crushed him. A reprimand from God on top of that would have extinguished him.

The Spirit receded from Rachmiel's heart, and Rachmiel released Tabris. The sunlight shone through him as he sat on the cliff, and he realized his energy had returned—or more likely been restored during the contact with God. He flexed his wings and neck, then stretched and got to his feet.

Tabris lay on the grass, exhausted. Exhausted, but relieved.

They would need to return Elizabeth, but not yet. For now Rachmiel waited while Tabris gathered his strength. Below them, the waves flowed over the rocks and out again to sea, rhythmic and fruitful, while the wind above sang of freedom.

Twenty-Three

Listening to her teacher, Elizabeth didn't detect the return of her guardians. An angel stood with her. He greeted Rachmiel, then added, "Voriah summoned me when Elizabeth woke up."

Rachmiel thanked him, then asked if Elizabeth was all right.

"She had trouble awakening. A bit confused."

Remembering how Tabris had predicted exactly that, Rachmiel kept himself from grinning at Tabris. "I'll check her over. Anything else?"

The sub nodded. "Voriah said she woke with a start at three-thirty. Did something happen?"

"Something." Rachmiel focused on a corner of her soul, then looked back at the sub. "She just turned off the light and went back to sleep?"

"Her mother had tucked her in about ten. She's been fine all morning."

Rachmiel thanked the other angel, who departed.

As Rachmiel checked over Elizabeth, Tabris sent him two observations. First, that non-guardians were time-dyslexic. (Rachmiel chuckled.) And second, that other angels always reported to Rachmiel and didn't even look at him.

"Force of habit," said Rachmiel.

Rachmiel grew conscious of the room's emotional flavor: angelic wonder. At first he would have called it curiosity, but it didn't have that peckish feel. This was surprise, and aimed more at Tabris than at the pair of them: Tabris, projecting?

Rachmiel sat on Elizabeth's desk, legs swinging, then wrapped around Elizabeth and apologized for not waking her up. *Did you miss me, kid? Just a little, in your heart, did you realize I was away?*

Tabris stood guard, eyes scanning the room.

Then Rachmiel realized the unsaid half of Tabris's second observation: other angels always reported to Rachmiel, but Rachmiel himself considered Elizabeth his own. Claiming coequality with Tabris meant nothing if his unquestioned assumption was that she belonged less to Tabris than to him. When he thought of the guardianship, it was himself and Elizabeth as a human-angel team, and Tabris and himself as the guardian team. In his mind, they weren't a triad, and Tabris wasn't her partner.

Maybe Tabris realized. Maybe he even understood.

Only to him, Rachmiel projected, *Sebastian will come back to you.*

Tabris turned away, pacing the room in a patrol pattern. Rachmiel forced his thoughts away from the subject. Space. Tabris had said he wanted privacy, and where was more private than the classroom of a public school? When everyone was already watching them? Answer: anywhere.

Then Tabris sent a negation: a denial that Sebastian would ever forgive him, a denial that it mattered, a denial that there could be a happy ending for an angel named Free Will.

The teacher started talking about this afternoon's math test, and the other angels lost interest as Tabris returned to what they expected: an impervious but soulless presence guarding one of the students without that faint spectrum of emotions.

Right before library, the teacher exclaimed, "Oh, Elizabeth! We forgot about the supplies! There's not enough time."

Elizabeth said, "I can do it! I'll run."

The teacher said, "I've got an idea: you go down to get them, bring them back here, and catch up at the library."

Rachmiel looked to the teacher's guardian, who said, "Sylvia had them answer trivia questions for the privilege, and she won."

Out in the hallway, Rachmiel said to Tabris, "I'm not used to being surprised."

Tabris said, "But on the other hand, who can argue with a trip to the supply room?"

Elizabeth skipped over the colored tiles to jump from one white square to the next. Rachmiel said, "Sebastian will come for you tonight. I'm sure of it."

Tabris huffed. "I'm not. You're acting as though he's you. He's more like me, and he's going to mull it over before approaching. Maybe a thousand years or two." He folded his arms. "Most likely, right before he enters Heaven because it's a requirement that he cancel all outstanding debts, and Casifer will want to check off the box on the paperwork."

Rachmiel shuddered. "Tell me there isn't paperwork to get into Heaven."

"There's a mountain of it." Tabris wore the beginnings of a smile. "Why do you think I opted to be a soldier? Michael has a secretarial squad do the army's forms."

Grinning, Rachmiel held his hand over his heart. "I don't suppose my greeting card company will have to file taxes?"

"Better line up your accountant now." They paused at the supply room door while Elizabeth fished the key from her pocket. "That's all a lot of nonsense, of course. Maybe Sebastian won't be able to. Maybe I took out both of us because God won't allow unforgiveness into Heaven. Wouldn't that be a horrible irony?"

"Quit that!" Rachmiel's voice was stern enough that he felt angels around the building suddenly pay attention. Elizabeth popped the lock and entered the supply room. Speaking lower, he said, "You're not serious, are you?"

"I don't think I am." Tabris grew subdued. "But I don't know."

"Don't think like that. The kid will come tonight, and it'll be fine."

Elizabeth started gathering items from the teacher's list: a box of pencils. Twenty-two blue test notebooks.

Tabris frowned. "You know, if he does forgive me, I won't know what to do."

"That's easy." Rachmiel grinned. "You hug him."

Tabris's eyes clouded, the color of honey mixed with blood. "I mean longer-term. What do I do about Elizabeth? She's my job, but so is he, and I can't do both. So maybe it's for the best that he won't do it meaningfully in her lifetime."

"God works quickly. But maybe you wouldn't have to choose."

He thought of a dozen cautionary tales, though, and he found himself mimicking Tabris's frown. The one-person rule existed because if a guardian angel had a second charge, the bond with the first charge could spiral into the bond with the second. If Sebastian got near Tabris and Elizabeth while Elizabeth was awake, Elizabeth would sense Sebastian's thoughts and feelings, effectively hearing voices. Keeping them separated would solve the problem, but that meant choosing.

Tabris said, "In the natural order of things, I shouldn't be here at all, so going back would set things right. Right? Except that I have a responsibility to Elizabeth now, and she needs me."

Rachmiel watched Elizabeth double-checking the test booklets. "I'm not going to dispute that. You work really well with her. But I managed alone before, and I could do it again."

Tabris shook his head, giving the icy smile of an angel who had watched God about to reject him. The spiritual temperature dropped.

Rachmiel swallowed hard. "You had an idea?"

"With two of us around, she's stronger than with one. But remember Milton? 'Sufficient to stand but free to fall'? With two of us, her temptations will be greater because that's only fair, but so will her accomplishments. If I leave, the good she produces will be in proportion to her gifts. If I leave, that will necessarily be less."

Rachmiel's nose wrinkled. "I don't think God would cut off her potential because of choices you made."

Tabris huffed. "You mean Sebastian's potential wasn't cut off?"

Rachmiel paid a lot of attention to helping Elizabeth check over her list. A box of dry erase markers.

Tabris said, "And keep in mind that as Sebastian's wife, she'd have had me around anyhow to help with her formation. For Elizabeth's sake, I have to stay. But if Sebastian decided it was worth the effort to forgive me, I would owe it to him to be with him, even though he belongs to that other angel now."

Dust from the supply shelf got on Elizabeth's hair, and Rachmiel flicked it off. "When I first visited, the one he wanted was you."

Elizabeth found a bottle of antiseptic wipes, and that was the end of her list.

Rachmiel said, "Casifer's a lot like me, and he's giving emotional support. You're like Sebastian, though. He'll need you before the end to finish off his spiritual formation."

"He can't enter Heaven without me?" Tabris's eyes went huge. "That's crazy! What if I'd been damned? God wouldn't have abandoned him to eternal Limbo!"

Rachmiel raised an eyebrow. "I think I have my answer about whether you were joking two minutes ago when you said the same thing."

Elizabeth left the supply room and headed back to the classroom.

"It's about more than forgiveness," Rachmiel said. "You're his role model."

Tabris said, "In that negative-example sort of way. *Here, Kiddo—see all these things? Don't do them or you'll deserve Hell too.*"

Rachmiel sighed.

Tabris snapped, "I'm sorry to weary you with my problems. When you brought up the subject, I figured you wanted to talk about it."

"Stop talking about damnation as if God's just waiting to fire up the barbecue."

Tabris refused to reply.

Elizabeth's class had already left the room, so she set the supplies on the teacher's desk and turned to follow. And then she stopped.

On the desk was a copy of this afternoon's math test. And the answer key.

Elizabeth returned to the desk and leaned over the paper.

"Elizabeth!" Tabris's voice deepened. "Leave that alone!"

She reached for the paper, hesitated, then picked it up. All the multiple choice answers, straight down the page. A, A, D, C, A, B...

Before Rachmiel's eyes, her soul darkened.

"Leave it alone! That's cheating!" Tabris pulled up close to her, his hands over hers, his wings around her. "Elizabeth, you know that's wrong."

Rachmiel could feel her trying to memorize the numbers in the longer questions, and one by one the lights winked out. The fractions. The percentages. The spreading darkness. "Sweetie, don't do it."

Tabris hovered over her. "You might get caught."

Elizabeth looked at the door, and Tabris reached into her heart, raising her pulse and increasing her adrenaline.

Rachmiel picked up her fear. "Whoa—stop that!"

"I'm not letting her cheat," Tabris said. "If she doesn't know the material then she needs to fail."

Rachmiel pushed closer. Her soul felt clammy. "Giving her a heart attack won't help. Calm down and—"

"I'm not calming down about sin!" Tabris said. "Stop her!"

The lights in her heart were going down like dominos. This sin wouldn't take out the whole string, but she was choking off the inlet of grace. In the face of Tabris's urgency, Rachmiel exclaimed, "What do you expect me to do?"

"I can't let that happen again!" Tabris's eyes were throwing light. "She's not listening to me!"

Rachmiel said, "I can't trump her free will!"

"You're not trying!" Tabris slammed his hand into the desk. "How do you expect to get her into Heaven if she starts doing things like this?"

"It's not our job to get her into Heaven!"

Tabris's wings flared. "You want her in Hell?"

"Saving her soul is God's job! Our job is to make sure she's free to choose grace." Rachmiel turned back to Elizabeth and put his head beside hers, as if to say *Wake up, Sleepyhead*. "This is cheating, sweetie. You need to stop. You're not a cheater."

She turned to page two. Tabris began exerting force on her heart, and Rachmiel pushed himself between them.

Tabris's eyes blazed. "Let me work!"

Rachmiel spread his wings, blocking him from Elizabeth. "Back off and stop interfering!"

Tabris shot backward.

Elizabeth turned to the third page, noted the answer to the final problem, and replaced the answer key on the desk.

Angels from the neighboring classroom poked their heads into the room. "Is everything all right?"

Tense like a fault line the moment before an earthquake, Rachmiel kept looking from Elizabeth to Tabris.

Tabris said, "Completely. I'm done interfering." And he flashed away.

Twenty-Four

Tabris landed in Heaven.

He'd gone home. A log cabin empty of furniture and with an oak floor polished to a slippery shine, this was Tabris's homebase, selected ages ago from Heaven's infinite acreage. When he and the Holy Spirit had gone house-hunting, God had teased him along with almost-but-not-quite locations until bringing him to a mountaintop crisp with snow, with an ice-choked stream trickling through the rocks and a vertical drop at the peak's edge. Tabris had burst with joy, projecting, *Here! Here. I want to be with you here,* and the Spirit had begun showing him floor plans.

The demon, whatever he was calling himself today, smirked in the white-blue light shining through a windowpane. "Spar with me."

Tabris's eyes narrowed. "Why?"

"To be rid of me forever. To work off energy. To prove something to yourself." The demon paused. "I don't care what excuse you make. They're all the same to me."

"My damnation."

He huffed. "Not even God is that unreasonable." The demon formed his sword and balanced it in his hand. "Maybe if you'd surrendered to me over New York harbor you'd have to explain yourself, but this would be different. You're supposed to fight demons. It's what soldiers do."

"Get out of here."

"I'm looking for a new name." The demon studied the way the sun glared off the snow. "What do you think?"

"I think I don't care."

"I think I'll do it. Hell's a free country." He looked over his shoulders. "Any suggestions? I'll give you the honor of naming me for a little while."

Tabris folded his arms and leaned against the wall. "How about Damned-By-God?"

"That's taken. Let's see..." The demon stared at Tabris. "Recklessness? Too long. Primrose Path? It works, but too feminine." He stepped toward Tabris. "I have it: *Presumption!* What better name for a creature as unfettered as I am? Brazen, always taking the easy way out, doing whatever I want...but always knowing someone else will bail me out. Relying on it! Running up debts with no inclination to pay. Let someone else pay my way! I love it."

"I'm glad you're pleased. Now you can go."

The demon turned about, examining himself as though modeling a designer dress. "It fits my soul. Come to think of it," and he looked up, "it fits yours too, you short-sighted assassin! Sacrificing your *son* for a second or two of freedom... Living on the back of forgiveness you don't deserve... Reduced to *interfering—*"

Tabris blasted the demon, knocking him to the ground and sending his sword across the floor. He formed up his own sword and struck before the demon could call his back to his hand.

The demon took the first blow and then, armed again, returned the fight. Tabris unleashed everything, everything—not just his sword, but his will, his energy, and although the demon defended, he kept yielding ground. With Miriael, Tabris had always been conscious he battled an ally. It kept things measured. Not now.

Again and again they clashed, Tabris not slacking his pace even when the demon harmed him. He didn't care anymore. Relentless, Tabris focused on the demon with an intensity that kept him pinned to the room, and at that point the demon tried blasting away any number of different ways but failed every time.

Tabris tackled the demon, forcing him to the floor. Green fire coursed along his eyes and feathers.

"You lose," he whispered.

"*I* lose?" The demon laughed. "Not hardly. I know who you are."

"And I know who you are, Zeffar. *Irrevocable Choices.*"

Free Will and *Irrevocable Choices.* Don't those two sound as if they belong together?" Zeffar chuckled. "Head or tail of the same coin, and either way, you lose." He spat in his own blood. "And you chose death."

Tabris kept him pinned. "I've chosen life."

"You've chosen to sacrifice freedom on the altar of obedience." The demon narrowed his eyes. "These name games are garbage. I shed my name because I refuse the pigeonhole God scooped out for me. I want more."

Tabris said, "There is nothing more."

The demon raised his head. "Not for a puppet like you. God knew— God knew all along! Remember His omniscience? He knew you were going to kill Sebastian on his bicycle when he was twelve years old. He *knew* it. And then not only did He go on to create the both of you, but He matched you up as guardian and charge anyway."

Tabris's heart clenched.

The demon relaxed under his hand. "He denied Casifer a guardianship just so He could page the childless angel to the lobby to sweep up the pieces of your victim. He designed a human female to be Sebastian's breeding partner and let her be widowed."

Tabris recoiled. "But—"

The demon sat up. "So tell me about this love and dignity. Talk to me about love and free choice. Because I'm just not seeing it here."

Tabris had gone cold, cold, cold. "But I wasn't fated to kill him."

"That's the worst part! God knew you were going to make that choice, and what did He do? He matched you up anyhow!" Zeffar's eyes widened. "*He gave you a child to kill.* He could have given Sebastian to Casifer right from day one. You'd never have noticed! You might have met the kid someday and thought he was interesting, but you'd never have said, *That should have been mine.* God could have prevented you from doing this just by cutting it off at the pass!"

Tabris let him go. "But then—"

"All He had to do," Zeffar whispered, sitting up, "was give that boy to another angel. You failed Sebastian, but God failed him first. God could have called you up to Heaven for tea on the day you murdered him. Sent a baby-sitter angel. Oopsie, he fell off his bicycle, scraped his knee, too bad. Even leaving him alone would have been better." Zeffar opened his hands. "God could have taken the kid's life the day before. Boom, car crash, no child to murder. But God did nothing."

Tabris said, "God didn't do nothing."

"God did worse than nothing." Zeffar's eyes glinted. "God set it up."

Tabris closed his eyes. Sebastian. God. *I wish I'd never had him.* But a universe without that curiosity, those quick eyes—no, that was wrong, empty. God loved that boy. *I wish I'd never been Created.* That worked better. Because if Tabris never existed, then Sebastian couldn't have been killed by him, and then Sebastian would have been happy, and Elizabeth would have been happy, and Rachmiel would have been happy, even Casifer would have been happy—and maybe God would have been happier too, without one more angel on the dole to leave the world an unfinished symphony.

Zeffar said, "So that's love and personal dignity for you. Sorry. I prefer the irrevocable choices. Put me in Hell. At least I have no illusions that God cares."

If Tabris had been bleeding before from his body, he bled out now from his soul. The betrayal, the futility: if God had known it all along, and still matched them together—but He *had* known it all along, *had* matched them together. Had created them for one another. And from the beginning, there had never been a choice?

"There had to have been a choice," Tabris whispered.

Zeffar got to his feet and dusted off. "If God knows in advance, how much choice could you have had? From where I'm standing, there was one road. He put you on it."

Tabris hit his knees and stared at the blood freezing to the floor. His, Zeffar's—it might as well have been Sebastian's.

Sebastian. And himself. The two best gifts God had ever given him. And now to discover they hadn't been gifts at all. More like curses.

And the only possible response—return a curse for a curse. Nothing left but to tell God it was over, all done playing games with eternal pawns, goodbye forever. Goodbye. I loved you, but goodbye.

Eyes closed, he reached for Zeffar's hand, and it closed around his own. The betrayal—God laughing at him in an impossible situation, giving him a gift in order to snatch it back and still expecting to be thanked for it.

The words formed in his mind: *You never loved me, but you made me love you.* He didn't think them toward God, but they burned to be said. Ready. *I want nothing more to do with you.* The final ones would be, *I reject you.*

After all that, after God did that—no other possible choice.

No.

Zeffar's hand tightened.

No, this was wrong. On a cliff-top overlooking the Pacific, Rachmiel had said something. The Spirit had been inside Rachmiel, and Rachmiel had spoken. Thus says the Lord. But what had he said…? And was it true?

Head tucked down, Tabris slipped free his hand and clutched it to his chest. His voice was hollow. "God wanted me to make a decision."

Zeffar crouched before him. "Right!"

"But—" Tabris raised his head to look the demon in the eyes. "He wanted me to make choices. To shape myself, grow myself."

Zeffar said, "And he wanted *this*?"

"He wanted me to *become*." Tabris shook his head. "The growth was important. My own participation. My responses." He closed his eyes. "I'm not saying they were good. I'm saying they were *mine*, and that's what God wanted when He created Free Will."

Zeffar gestured outside. "And that rotting body in a Los Angeles cemetery...?"

Tabris shuddered as he got to his feet. The poor kid. In a thousand years, he could never make that right. "I offended Him and disgusted Him with that choice. I was wrong. But God taking away the opportunity to grow badly is the same as taking away my identity."

Zeffar said, "And who gets hurt?"

"We all get hurt! The whole Body of Christ gets hurt!" Tabris opened his hands. "Knowing you'd leave, He still gave you the freedom to go. What if God had seen you'd be suffering in Hell and decided not to let you? Just had you get distracted by your music that day, and when you left the practice room, you were stuck in Heaven with a psalm on your lips?"

Zeffar kicked a puddle of blood, spraying it on the walls. "He could make me. It wouldn't mean anything."

Tabris leaned forward, wings raised. "That's what I mean! You decided. I decided. God made us with free will because to make us without it meant He wasn't making us at all. And here we are, the end product of a thousand decisions made moment by moment."

Zeffar said, "But—"

Tabris said, "And I'm making one more decision. An irrevocable one."

Zeffar's eyes flared. "Wait!"

"I'm done with you."

"Tabris, please!" The demon's eyes gleamed with tears. He projected in staccato bursts: don't do this, don't expel him, they were friends. "Please! I can't lose you again!"

Tabris opened his heart, and he shoved forward with the exorcism formula he'd recited so often as a soldier. *Begone, spirit of darkness and enemy of my God—*

Zeffar vanished before he finished. Even the feel of him evaporated from the room.

Tabris crumpled to his knees. *God, that was too close.*

As silence pervaded the room and the blood began vanishing from the floor, Tabris felt Zeffar's argument coming back to him: God had created him and Sebastian both. God had meant them for each other, even knowing the outcome. *God set it up.*

No. Quit that. God had given the gift. It was up to Tabris to do with it what he could. Whatever he decided.

Tabris tilted back his head, looking at the ceiling he hadn't seen in... thirteen years? Longer. While he watched, some demonic residue on the ceiling curled on itself and popped out of existence. The place would get clean in time. Time.

Time had only mattered when it mattered to Sebastian, and after that it had become an obsession. Moments that once had flooded from somewhere into somewhere else had transformed into mystery when inhabited by a changing creature he loved. Seconds meant more to a creature who perished after a finite number of them, saved in the boxes of the mind. Hoarded. Cherished. Feared.

Back then, Tabris had begun counting future moments he could spend with Sebastian. *I wanted to bring him here. I still will, if he lets me.* All the things they could have done together, the milestones as important to Tabris as the oatmeal breakfasts.

How long had eternity been before Sebastian? Creationists argued with evolutionists about six days or six billion years, and Tabris had listened in confusion. He'd forgotten the time it had taken and remembered only that God's hand had manufactured the pieces that made up space and fit them one into the next to create a seamless garment for the creatures He'd called His sons.

But now the future moments couldn't be counted. How long would it be until the next time he saw Sebastian? Or was eternity just too long to measure without him? An enthralling pain had come with seeing him again. Only God could wound him deeper, but because it was him, because it was *Sebastian,* Tabris would let him. If Sebastian needed him there, there he would be.

If the kid wanted him.

"I wish I knew," Tabris whispered to the interior of the cabin. The oak logs shone in the light reflecting off the snow, and Tabris took in the fireplace, the joints in the corners, the hand-knotted rug patterned on one he'd seen while deployed on Earth. With eternity to furnish the place, he hadn't hurried. What did he need, anyway? Even having a homebase hadn't seemed important at first because anything he needed he'd always carried with him. Like God's love. And later, his own care for Sebastian.

"I should undo that dream." His voice echoed. He ought to fill this place with something, make it less empty. A minute after walking in, Elizabeth would have dropped her coat on the floor, left her hat near the window while looking outside, and then dumped a pile of debris from her school bag over in the corner. After she'd left, Tabris would have found pencils and scraps of paper for days even as the plushness of her heart lingered in the walls. But forever after, a specific emptiness always would ghost it. A home never filled with all that should have.

If Sebastian ever stopped by, it would be nice to have a place prepared for him. A place to sit. A place to talk. They didn't need to eat in Heaven, but he could scramble up a table and a couple of chairs. Sit facing each other and then listen to all the reasons Sebastian despised him.

A spotlight focused on Tabris's soul, an attention he'd never fail to recognize. He bowed his head, whispering, "Gloria in excelsis." And then, unable to stop the smirk, Tabris added, "Would you like me to find a chair for you?"

No, here on the floor was just fine.

Tabris lowered his gaze. "Thank you. Thank you for visiting, and thank you for having Rachmiel explain things this morning. I wouldn't have withstood Zeffar's attack otherwise."

Inside, Tabris sensed that God was thankful that Tabris had opened up enough to listen.

Tabris kept his head down.

God asked a question: was he angry at Sebastian?

"Of course not." Tabris double-checked his own heart, but he couldn't find anything resembling anger at Sebastian. No resentment, nothing like that. "I'm sure."

The follow-up question: then whom was he angry at?

"Myself."

And anyone else?

Tabris said, "I'm not angry at Rachmiel any longer. Who else is there to be angry at?"

Was he angry at God?

"No." Tabris closed his eyes. "No. I love you."

"You need to answer that more thoroughly." God's voice became clearer in his mind. "You don't come to me anymore."

"I can't." Tabris looked out the window again. That brittle cliff. The clouds like lines slicing up the sky. "You understand why."

He became intensely aware of the log cabin: tiny; chilly; stained with blood and the residue of angelic power. He got the message: God could enter any place, no matter the size or the dirt, if one of His children needed Him.

"It's not a question of can't," Tabris said. "It's about fittingness. You deserve better."

"I'll decide what I deserve."

Tabris said, "I want to give you more than that, and I'm not a house."

God said, "You're better than a house."

Tabris decided not to dispute that. Better and worse at the same time—houses didn't sin. If a house collapsed, you wouldn't blame the center beam for wanting to kill the owner. You could clean a house. If you tired of it, you could get rid of it. You could leave it alone for thirteen years and come back to find it unchanged. And for its own part, the house would wait for you without becoming impatient.

God replied, "So will I."

Tabris flinched. "Am I that bad?"

"Come home," said God.

"And if I think I can't?" Tabris's voice pitched up, and he realized in his own way he was playing Sebastian to God. "You gave me one ridiculously simple thing not to do, and I did it."

God replied, "You mean like, *Don't eat that fruit over there?*"

Tabris folded his arms and turned his head. "The fruit of another tree resolved that barrier for them."

God said, "Ask yourself why you're so invested in holding out."

"Why did you do this?" His heart pounded. "I sent Zeffar away, but I want to know— Why did you still make both of us?"

God said, "You yourself said the universe would be poorer without Sebastian in it."

Tabris said, "But me? If you'd made the universe without *me*, Sebastian would have been taken care of. He'd never have missed me. No one would have."

God replied, "I would have missed you."

No, You wouldn't— Except God wouldn't lie, so Tabris had to look that uncomfortable thought full in the face: God wanted him. God would have been sad not to have created him.

God pointed his mind back to the last question: why he was so invested in holding out.

Reasons. You needed a reason to build a wall. A boundary. This far and no further. Fences. Neighbors.

"If you want," but it hurt, even that much hurt, "I'll let you in. Just for now. A little."

The spotlight feeling diffused into a sensation through the entire angel. Don't be afraid. Take your time. Don't feel pressured or hopeless. Whenever he wanted God inside his heart, God would be ready.

Tabris swallowed hard because—six months ago was the last time he'd felt that presence inside, and he craved it. How many times had he seen Rachmiel reach for God on reflex and brighten when God responded? He'd held back at first because he didn't want to be rejected, and here God was as good as telling him he wouldn't be. So why not do it? Get it over with. Just reach out and take whatever God returned.

Except for the fittingness part.

Why are you so invested in holding out?, God had asked.

God was waiting. He shouldn't put God through that. It was selfish.

God said, "Don't project your pain onto me. You're identifying yourself with Sebastian and then me with you. I want you home, but when you're ready. Aren't you doing the same with the child?"

Tabris said, "The prodigal son's father ran out to meet him on the road, but he didn't follow him into the distant land. Is that why?"

God said, "If you choose me, I'll help you every step of the way. But if you run, you can leave."

Tabris said, "Free will."

God said, "Irrevocable choices."

"If I asked whether Sebastian will come back to me, would you answer?"

"I would tell you that he's been praying for both himself and for you."

Maybe that was the reason Tabris hadn't succumbed to Zeffar. Prayers for your enemies covered a multitude of evils.

Tabris said, "Tell him thank you for me. If he wants to hear it."

When God didn't reply, Tabris let the throbbing in his heart consume his attention. After six months, God's love left him feeling awkward and Rachmiel's left him suspicious. But he'd loved himself before last autumn, and he'd known himself since the beginning. Sebastian had never met him before yesterday, hadn't known more than his title and the end result of their professional relationship

Tabris had no choice but to deal with himself; eventually he'd reach a state of truce. But if after six months Tabris still despised himself, what were the odds Sebastian wouldn't be doing the same six months from now? Six years?

Tabris closed his eyes, whispered, "I've sinned against Sebastian and against you."

God said, "Come home."

"I no longer deserve to be called your son."

God said, "Come home."

"Treat me like one of your slaves."

God said, "I have no slaves. I have sons." And then a picture came into Tabris's mind, a pair of hands outstretched, cupped, with God pouring something into them.

God wanted to give him a gift.

Tabris shivered, but you never say no to a gift from God; so with bowed head, he crossed his arms over his chest.

Calm settled over him. Tabris examined himself, feeling no different but realizing God had changed him so no other angel could detect him. Confused, he said, "What should I do?"

"You should visit someone," said God. "You can do this once."

Tabris frowned. "Whom?"

God said, "Free Will, make your choice."

Sebastian. Sneak up on Sebastian and watch the boy in unobserved silence for an hour or two, reassure himself Casifer had the child well on the way to Heaven, maybe even overhear Sebastian rail about the unfairness of it all. God was giving him the gift a silent goodbye. Do that and Tabris could release the hope and the grief at the same time. He could cry over the kid if he had to and no one would try to comfort him. Sebastian wouldn't feel manipulated into offering forgiveness. It was everything he needed so he could move on.

And yet... And yet, if Tabris could use this gift once only, there was something more important. Not something he needed, but something someone else needed.

"Thank you." Tabris braced himself. "Thank you, Father."

He flashed to the roof of the elementary school, arriving not fifty feet from the school's guardian. He tensed, but Zohar didn't detect him. Tabris projected toward him, but again, he sensed nothing. Good.

Elizabeth: beneath him, he could feel her in her second floor classroom. At her side, Rachmiel. He opened his heart to catch Rachmiel's projections, and he found him spent but praying. And emerging from him in pulses, encouragement.

Elizabeth's soul seemed dim like a light behind a lampshade. But whenever Rachmiel strengthened her, the lights would intensify, embers under a gentle breath.

Tabris lay on the roof and closed his eyes, spread out his wings, and poured his senses into the classroom, absorbing the activity. He'd never watched Rachmiel, really watched him. Always when they'd been together they'd divided the labor. Even though Rachmiel had most definitely gone "off duty" to observe Tabris in action immediately after his assignment, Tabris never had done the same. Why?

Elizabeth. Elizabeth, sweetheart. You deserve the best there is. And I think you have him. I wanted to give you better than the best. I'm not even sure I was wrong.

Tabris slipped through the roof to the second floor. The fourth graders worked on a reading assignment, their guardians assisting them or defending the perimeter. He watched only Elizabeth, Rachmiel embracing her and shedding encouragement into her heart. Gentle. Coaxing.

Elizabeth's pulse and adrenaline levels were elevated. She fidgeted. Tabris got a reading of her blood pressure, her eye movements, her tension. The way Rachmiel would feed her energy, then back off, and she'd look at the teacher. The way she'd bitten her eraser right down to the pencil. The way she'd go back to work, and then Rachmiel would encourage again, and she would bite her lip.

When the bell rang, the students shut their books. Elizabeth stood from the desk to get her backpack, and Rachmiel breathed into her soul again, fueling those embers.

Before Tabris's gaze, the chokehold of her sin slipped, and grace trickled in faster.

Elizabeth stood at her desk until the other students had departed, then set her bag on the chair. She went to the teacher, who was stacking papers in her messenger bag. Standing before the teacher, Elizabeth said, "I need to take the makeup test with Alex and Ben on Monday."

The teacher looked up, puzzled. "Why? I'm sure you did fine."

Elizabeth stared at her feet, unaware of the light shining again in her heart. "I looked at the answers. You had them on the desk when I brought the supplies."

She had tears in her eyes. Rachmiel had tears in his.

The teacher's breath caught. "Elizabeth, I'm disappointed."

"I'm sorry." She bit her lip. "Math is so hard."

The teacher sat in her chair so she was face to face with Elizabeth. "I'm not sure what's the best way to handle this. I'm glad you came to me, but cheating is serious."

Tabris felt himself becoming more solid. His gift was ending. He had to leave or become visible.

He completed the process, and Rachmiel turned to him, shedding a mixture of pride in Elizabeth and wariness about Tabris.

Tabris bowed his head. "Please forgive me." He reached for Rachmiel's hands. "You're right. I've been fighting the wrong enemy."

Twenty-Five

Rachmiel would have lost the bet, had they bet on it. Sebastian didn't visit that night, nor the next.

Now that he was projecting more, Tabris emitted a cloud of resignation as he worked with Elizabeth. Rachmiel didn't ask where he'd gone or what he'd done, but Tabris had given him the outline. That demon, gone forever. Thank God. And that he'd spoken with his Father. Not prayed, but still, spoken.

Rachmiel had said, "Did He tell you anything about Sebastian?"

Tabris said, "I don't think he's coming back," and Rachmiel felt that stone-dead weight in his stomach.

The nights came and went. Tabris didn't leave for the pond any longer, and although he didn't open up in prayer, he did join the other guardians in theirs. When they asked one another for prayer intentions, he would ask for prayers for Sebastian's well-being. He'd never done that before. He prayed for Casifer too, that Casifer could be the guardian Sebastian needed.

With Elizabeth, Tabris had a new unsteadiness, a wire-walker gaining his balance after stepping off the platform. Although he had the same vigilance, his focus had shifted, and Rachmiel found him less directive, more suggestive. He wasn't forcing her virtue; instead he guarded her openness to the gifts God gave her.

More nights. One night Miriael asked Tabris to watch Kyle, and Tabris seemed first surprised as he agreed, and later sad.

And on the eighth night, after Elizabeth changed into pajamas but before she went to bed, Rachmiel turned around to find Sebastian.

The boy shifted his weight and stared at the floor. "Hello?"

Beside Rachmiel, Tabris had gone still with shock. "Hi."

Rachmiel panicked for an instant before grabbing Sebastian and flashing all three of them a quarter mile away, to where Elizabeth wouldn't sense him.

"Oh, sorry." Sebastian gave a nervous giggle. "I guess I should have asked if now was a good time."

Vibrating with excitement, Rachmiel said, "It's always a good time, just wasn't a good place." When Sebastian relaxed, he said, "How are you?"

"Doing good. Nearer to Heaven than before." Sebastian shifted his weight. "I was wondering if I might borrow Tabris for a few hours."

Rachmiel could feel Tabris's heart pounding so hard it hurt, and he wondered if Sebastian had grown sensitive enough to detect it. In a low voice, Tabris said, "I'd love you to." He hesitated. "Where's Casifer?"

"He sent me, but he stayed behind."

Tabris still hadn't taken his eyes off him. "Do you want Rachmiel?"

The boy shifted. "Well, if you want. I hadn't planned on it."

Sebastian was just as nervous as Tabris, and Rachmiel ached with anticipation. "I'll stay with Elizabeth." Needing to keep calm, he reached for her heart; she lay on her bed finishing a makeup math assignment as part of the consequences for cheating. "Have a good time. Send a post card."

Sebastian looked cautious. "Angels have a postal system?"

"Angels have a silly sense of humor," said Tabris.

As they flashed away, Rachmiel laughed in relief. *Thank you, God. Please help them get through this.* He flashed back to Elizabeth.

Mid math problem, she rolled onto her back and smiled at the ceiling, her gaze intercepting Rachmiel's eyes and warming him to the core.

Tabris flashed Sebastian to a flat field in a flat plain where you could see flat land for about ten flat miles because of the flatness. It hadn't occurred to him until Sebastian arrived that they'd need to go some-place, and on the grounds that Sebastian would never come back, he hadn't planned on a place to take him. But since Casifer had taken them someplace interesting to prevent talking, this time he chose someplace bare like a bald man's head.

Here it was still daylight. Sebastian took a look around. "I love this world."

Tabris said, "Are you being sarcastic?"

Sebastian giggled, an infectious laugh that came from his belly. "Well, kind of. Even here, though. I didn't care for the world much when I was here, but now I see it in more detail, all the different animals and bugs, and it's neat."

Sebastian started walking, and Tabris kept pace. "What parts do you like best?"

"So far, the oceans." Sebastian's eyes widened. "They're wild, but they're under control by the moon and all this other physics I don't understand yet. I keep bugging Casifer to teach me natural science, but he got me a book and taught me theology."

Tabris laughed out loud, fighting a hope he didn't dare feel.

Sebastian said, "How many stars are there?"

Tabris said, "You want an actual number? Wouldn't that diminish the drama?"

"I suppose." The boy shrugged. "It would be handy for Angel Trivia Night, or whatever you guys do when you get together for games." He stopped. "Okay, so rather than beat around the bush for six hours, I should probably just say something."

Tabris stopped, his stomach tight and his hands trembling. Sebastian stepped closer and looked into his eyes.

"So I'm not that subtle and you can probably see right through me because you've known me since I was a blastocyst, but I've been praying lately, and working really hard at it. Casifer said I'm doing pretty good, whatever that means. I see God a bit clearer now, and it doesn't leave me feeling like I want to run and hide all the time."

That was terrific: at least one of them should feel that way. Tabris said, "That's a big step toward entering Heaven."

"That's what Casifer says too."

Tabris felt Sebastian teeter on the cusp of changing the conversation to an academic discussion of the steps one goes through prior to entering Heaven. Not that it was totally obvious. Not that Tabris had ever deflected a conversation the same way.

The urge passed. Sebastian took Tabris's hands, and Tabris squeezed. The boy said, "But anyway, I've learned a lot about God and looked back at the stuff I remember and saw a lot of the things He's done for me, and— Well, God's always forgiven me for everything, and I've done some pretty bad things, you know, but He took me back when I asked, and I want to be like Him."

Tabris's hands tightened. Sebastian looked at the ground. "And the thing is, I can't be called a Son of God if I'm not acting like Him, and—"

Tabris could feel him in a bit of a panic because he'd gone too far to back out. "I prayed about it, and I need you to help me out here. Because I get totally pissed off when I think about what you did to me. I don't get why you did it, and I wish you hadn't. I'm supposed to forgive you, and I don't want to. But I've been trying."

Tabris said, "What can I do to help?"

Sebastian said, "Well, so far I've tried what Voriah said. He told me to pray to want to forgive, and if I couldn't do that, to pray to *want* to want to forgive—"

Oh, that trick. "How many levels back did you get before you could do it?"

"Four," said Sebastian. "God worked it down to two. I want to want it."

Tabris raised his eyebrows. "You're doing better than I would have."

Sebastian looked up. "Really?"

Tabris shook his head. "I'm not at that point myself."

"Well, I'm stalled. And then I had a great idea. I thought, maybe if you and I prayed together, I could understand what happened and I'd be able to see your heart and then I'd be able to forgive you."

Tabris went numb, just numb all the way to his core. And then the anger built, and he yanked his hands back from Sebastian, clenching his fists.

Sebastian said, "What...?"

"I... This is blackmail!" he shouted at God. "I thought you wanted me on my own terms! You said I could wait it out!"

Sebastian took a huge step backward. "But—"

The Holy Spirit coalesced before them and with a touch calmed Sebastian. At the same time, Tabris felt the presence of God urging him to stand down: God was in no way forcing this. Praying together had been Sebastian's idea, and Sebastian on his own had decided to ask.

Sebastian was saying, "They always said the family that prayed together, stayed together, and you're supposed to be something like my family, right? Voriah thought it would help for him to pray with me, and he's not even part of this."

Tabris stopped glaring at God and looked Sebastian in the eye. "I don't expect you to understand, and you didn't know what's going on. I haven't prayed—really prayed, not human prayer—since you died. All along, there's been coercion from Rachmiel and Voriah and your mentor, and God's been asking me to do it, and I keep saying no. I'm not ready. That's not something anyone can force."

Sebastian's eyes were wide. "And—how do you know when you're ready? When will that be?"

"I don't know. It takes time." Tabris glared back at God, his eyes darkening. "And you approved this? It's blackmail."

The Spirit made Himself more fully present to Tabris: Sebastian would forgive him in time whether he helped or not. The grace would be his, and the gift of forgiveness would be given to him. Tabris was free to refuse. God loved him and would continue to love him even if he never opened his heart again.

Sebastian turned away. "I shouldn't have said anything. It was a dumb idea. I was tired of being angry and I thought this would be easier. I understand if you don't want me. I should have tried to work it out on my own."

Tabris grabbed Sebastian before he could call Casifer to take him back. "This isn't between us. The prayer issue is between me and God. It always has been."

The Holy Spirit put a picture into Tabris's head: two hands together. *You won't trust me?*

Tabris thought back, *Apparently not.*

Sebastian pulled away. "I don't actually care what you do with God." He clenched his fists. "I thought you'd want to help me."

Tabris looked away from Sebastian, his feathers standing apart. Calm from the Holy Spirit; shock from Sebastian. And from himself—Tabris couldn't begin to catalog it. *This isn't between us.* But it was between them. Or rather, Sebastian had gotten caught in the crossfire, and whose job was it to fix that?

That fire churned inside, the one that led him to risk damnation for the sake of his charge.

"I do want to help." He spit out the words without thinking about the consequences. "I'll do it." Just do it. Clench your teeth and go through with it. He couldn't do it for himself. He'd have to do it for the kid.

Sebastian folded his arms. "Maybe I don't want you to anymore."

Tabris said, "Please don't give me the chance to change my mind."

Sebastian looked at him, and his mouth set. Tabris could tell the Holy Spirit was talking to him, and the kid glared off sidelong. "Fine." He sat on the ground. "I know you guys pray best standing, but I need to be sitting." Tabris sat facing him. Sebastian made himself quiet, and Tabris did the same.

Sebastian began by whispering a formula prayer, and Tabris joined him: *Holy One, Mighty One, Immortal One, hear your creatures and*

202

look on us... Words were easy. From the start he'd been able to do the words. What came next...well, best not to dwell on that yet. *You are holy, you are holy, you are most holy...* Praise. Thanksgiving. Petition. Unification.

Unification. Or, the time when God refused him.

When they reached that point, Sebastian took a deep breath like a skin diver and opened his heart. He'd been practicing since that night on the cliff and didn't need any help to get started. Tabris felt God pour into the young soul, filling him to capacity.

With teeth clenched, Tabris thought of Sebastian, and steeling himself for rejection, he reached forward with his heart to meet God on holy ground.

God rushed him like sea water, sweeping back Tabris's anticipation of aridity. Tabris cried out, his spirit blown back by the contact, the coolness, the soothing of an ache he'd thought never would ease.

Rain over the desert. The withered parts of his heart crinkled out, drinking in the water and the spirit, releasing the tightness necessary to preserve life during a rainless season. Eyes closed, Tabris let out a long sigh that turned into a shiver.

He visualized an old woman revisiting her childhood home, racing from room to room accompanied by the past, hungering to see every space, seeing the bed where she was born, recalling the old positions of the furniture, noting all the changes but still loving the house as her own.

His vision of God in the world heightened until once again he registered all the motes of God's presence in every created thing. Like a string of Christmas lights illuminating one bulb at a time, the world went from dark to light: the air, the ground, the palm-sized puddles between the rows of newly-planted crops. It ached: he'd been so hungry for this, craving any glimpse he could find, and now after so long here it was, only he didn't want to stop focusing on God to look at the world.

It's okay, said the Spirit. *The world will still be here afterward. Although to be fair, so will I.*

I'd rather be with you, thought Tabris.

Likewise, replied the Spirit. *But Sebastian needs you right now, and we have to do some housekeeping.*

Tabris became conscious of Sebastian squeezing his hand, and he was too caught up to squeeze back, like a tourist in New York highway traffic afraid to take his hands off the wheel.

Tabris began forcing open his interior guards as he'd done for Rachmiel, and God entered all those shadowed parts to shine light on the shameful things. When God started touching them, Tabris clutched Sebastian's hand.

God came to the dark part where Tabris had refused to allow Rachmiel...and waited. The place in his soul where Tabris had killed Sebastian once and continued killing him every moment since, the moment he'd abandoned God and would do so forever.

Sebastian asked to link his heart to Tabris's, and Tabris looked to God.

It's up to you, said the Spirit. *He won't be harmed by anything he finds.*

Tabris thought, *He's the reason I'm doing this. I'd be stupid to tell him no.*

Sebastian's soul within his own felt comfortable, a perfect fit. With Rachmiel there had been friction because of the ways they differed and their varied perspectives. But with Sebastian, they'd been designed to suit one another, and the warmth spread through Tabris.

Sebastian blinked. "Oh! This is different than Casifer."

Tabris looked through Sebastian's soul, and everything he found, he loved. They were meant to be braided: Sebastian and Tabris and God. He remembered every part of this soul. Everything. He'd have given anything to save him.

Sebastian looked up, confused and angry. Tabris tried to pull back from God, then, as the thought went right through both of them: Tabris had no right to enjoy the presence of God when Sebastian couldn't have it yet, and how could God forgive him for what he'd done to Sebastian when Sebastian was still suffering it? How was that fair?

God refused to let him go. Tabris shivered. Sebastian's eyes glinted. He couldn't tell which of them had thought it first.

The next thought was definitely Sebastian's. A desperation, a question, a question he might have asked Casifer and Rachmiel but which they couldn't have answered. *Why did you kill me?*

And then, unsure if Tabris would hear his thought, Sebastian said it aloud. "Why did you do it?"

Tabris said, "I screwed up." He looked at his lap as Sebastian slipped his hands away. "It shouldn't matter. I wouldn't do it again."

Sebastian said, "But why?"

Tabris said, "Knowing why can't change things. It's not as if I can put you back together if I say the magic words."

"But you can," Sebastian said. "The magic words would be your reason. How can I forgive you if I don't know why you did it?"

The anger in the boy's voice clashed with the smoothness of his spirit. He and Tabris matched: they were both furious at the same person.

"How could you forgive me if you did know?" Tabris shook his head. "If I tell you, you're not going to want to want to forgive me anymore, or however many levels back I've already pushed you. You'd be working another ten years in Limbo to undo the damage I'll cause trying to undo the damage I already did. I'm not good for you! That's why we were separated!"

Sebastian looked aside.

The Holy Spirit said, *I don't make mistakes.*

No, Tabris thought. *I do.*

Sebastian said, "So is this a no?"

"It's not a no. It's—" Tabris steeled himself. "I failed you."

Sebastian said, "I know that."

"Before then." Tabris reached for Sebastian's hands, and when they touched, he wished he could still feel them warm with life. This was awful. Awful. This would be the last time he ever saw Sebastian, even if the child forgave him. But he owed Sebastian anything he wanted, even if that ended everything. "I failed you as your guardian, and I kept failing you. Guarding a human soul—I didn't expect how little there would be by way of benchmarks. Everything started so well, but then you were getting older, and you started facing choices, and I could only guess at the way things should be, and you weren't doing them that way."

Sebastian frowned. "Like how?"

He closed his eyes so he didn't have to see Sebastian going indifferent to him. "Everything I tried, it didn't seem to work. You'd face a decision and I couldn't figure out which was the best way to go, and God wouldn't tell me, so I'd get you on the path I thought you should take. But the roads kept branching in directions I hadn't anticipated. It shouldn't have been that hard, but I kept failing you, over and over. And then one day I realized, I just wasn't good enough to keep you pure."

Sebastian said, "But—what are we talking about?"

"Let me finish." And then Sebastian would leave. "Don't ever blame yourself for what I did to you. It was my fault, only mine. Because when you finally did something serious enough to cut off the life of God in your heart, I realized my help wasn't sufficient to get you into Heaven. I had never committed a sin, but after you did that, I felt as if I had. It was the worst feeling because after failing you, I didn't even want to look God in the face anymore. And—" Tabris swallowed hard. "When the time came...I saw a way I could force you into Heaven."

Sebastian sounded small. "What bad things was I choosing? Like sins?"

"Sometimes sins. But always decisions." Tabris wouldn't look Sebastian in the face to see the moment the boy gave up on him. He'd remember a moment like that forever, but he didn't want to be able to nail it down to the exact second: *this was the point where he saw the truth about me.* "There are seven vows guardian angels take. It's a big job. But my job *isn't* to get you into Heaven. Rachmiel showed me that. My job *isn't* to save your soul. That's God's job. My job was to keep you free to choose the right thing, or decide between good things, over and over. To ensure you could develop your own relationship with God."

Sebastian nodded. "That's free will."

"I kept trying to force you to select one good over another, or the good I thought would be best for you. I knew what had worked for me, and I wanted it to work for you too."

Sebastian said, "So, not bad stuff?"

"Not bad stuff. Your stuff. You were developing your own identity." Tabris went sick inside. "I kept getting between you and God because I didn't think God was doing enough to push you into the right paths." Tabris closed his eyes. "I understand if you can't forgive me. I can't forgive myself. I spent years thinking I was failing you, and in reality, I failed you in a different way. I took away your free will because I loved you too much to risk losing you. And then I lost you anyhow."

A car passed on the distant highway. A dead leaf blew through his form as the wind ruffled his feathers.

Sebastian leaned forward. "You loved me?"

Tabris said, "Of course I did."

His hands were still wrapped in Tabris's. "And do you still love me now? Even after all this?"

The question called for a sonnet written in gold in the annals of Heaven. Tabris managed to nod.

Sebastian scrambled toward Tabris and hugged him.

The link between them opened wider, and Tabris thrilled with surprise even as Sebastian clutched him tight, working his fingers up through the tertiary feathers. Tabris wrapped his wings around them both, and he rocked Sebastian while the boy made himself small.

"I still love you," Tabris said. "I would choose to love you all over again even knowing you can't forgive me. I'm sorry. I wanted to give you my best."

The boy's spirit felt razor sharp, and Tabris gave him the only thing left: he opened that last dark part of his soul. *I failed you.* The moments stacked on moments, every time he felt defeated by a child's decision or a child's impulses. An angel wrestling a human soul: which one should win? And every time the child won, Tabris had felt he'd lost even though Sebastian's decisions only meant he was doing the job correctly.

You were weaving your own relationship with God, Tabris thought. *I had no right to stop that. God would have reached you. I didn't step back enough to give Him a chance. I got angry at God and then at you. I didn't trust that He'd give you all the grace you needed.*

Tabris couldn't tell any longer if the tension were Sebastian's or his own. Sebastian stayed at the cusp of that God-forsaken part, and Tabris braced himself.

With God still surrounding that area, but not entering it, Tabris bowed his head and asked to be forgiven, for God to descend that spiral staircase and enter that dungeon to purge it with light. There would be dust, grime, sin—but it had to be done. He wanted to be forgiven.

I forgive you, said God.

With the light came a sense of sea water, powerful and clean, sharp with salt and relentless as the Earth itself. The past was still there; the corruption was gone. Tabris shuddered in relief, sensing the balance righted between him and his Father.

Sebastian gasped, and Tabris caught a glimpse of himself through Sebastian's eyes, his own soul changing from the periodic flashes of a lighthouse to the constancy of a spotlight. The darkness had vanished, replaced by clarity and internal refraction.

Tabris held him tighter. Only one more thing mattered.

Sebastian whispered, "Can I forgive you now?"

"Can I forgive myself?"

Tabris realized he was crying. Sebastian clung to him, saying, "Yes. Yes to both."

Thank you, Tabris prayed. *Thank you. Thank you. Thank you.*

By the pond near the Hayes house, Tabris made pictures in the air to show Sebastian funny scenes from when he was a baby, and Sebastian kept asking for more. They'd been there for three hours when Jesus arrived.

Tabris and Sebastian both knelt, heads bowed. Jesus asked them to stand, and Sebastian jumped up to hug him. Jesus extended a hand to Tabris, and as Sebastian stepped back, Jesus drew him close enough to hug. "Welcome home."

Until Raguel spoke, Tabris didn't realize he'd arrived too. "Congratulations!"

Flustered, Tabris glanced at Sebastian. "Thank you. We're trying to make up for lost time."

Raguel said, "Not just for making amends. Congratulations on ending probation! You're fully restored."

Sebastian jumped in place. "That's great! You're safe now!"

Tabris shook his head. "But what about Elizabeth? What if—?"

Jesus touched his arm. "You've changed your own soul enough that you won't fall prey to that way of thinking again." He smiled at Sebastian. "Besides, you have someone to help you out if you need a reminder."

Sebastian said, "Oh, cool! So I get to be a guardian to my guardian!"

"You've still got a whole lot of growing up to do!" Tabris said, giving Sebastian a mock push, and Sebastian grabbed him in a wrestling hold and pretended to fight.

When they looked up from playing, Raguel had departed, but God had not—and never would.

Twenty-Six

When Tabris and Sebastian returned, Rachmiel rushed them both with a hug. "You guys talked everything out! I can tell!"

Tabris grinned compulsively. That and his honey-gold eyes made Rachmiel want to cheer like a fan watching a grand slam at the bottom of the ninth.

Sebastian said, "How did you know?"

"How could I not know? You look different—you both do. You're projecting everything. Tell me!"

Tabris laughed, and Rachmiel held him at arm's length, looking him over. It was good. It was so good.

Sebastian started pouring out the story in bursts while Tabris stood back. The interplay of their souls brought a smile to Rachmiel even more than the way Sebastian related it.

When Sebastian said, "And Jesus said he's off probation now!" Rachmiel cheered and gave Tabris another hug.

The other six household angels crowded into the room, and Rachmiel didn't need to explain: the combination of his own agitation and the changes in Tabris, not to mention the presence of Sebastian, worked like a news broadcast. They'd been praying for this, and now they celebrated. Voriah called Casifer, and for an hour the angels had a spiritual party while the human family dreamed, a festive atmosphere that swept through them like a wind, the spiritual equivalent of balloons and streamers. Wearing *That Look,* Tabris didn't leave Sebastian's side.

In the middle of it all, Sebastian turned to him. "You're staying here, right?"

Rachmiel looked up when he felt Tabris's heart vibrate. "I'm sorry."

Sebastian shook his head. "You have a job to do. I'd rather you were with me, but you're only a word away. I'll see you at night. I can pray for Elizabeth, and we can be together afterward."

Tabris said, "In eighty years?"

Sebastian looked so brave to Rachmiel, less a child than he'd been the last time they'd visited. "I love you, and time doesn't mean anything to love. Eternity is a long time, and we've got God to hold us together. That's everything."

Tabris pressed his face into Sebastian's hair.

"I've got a lot of things I want to do with you," said Sebastian, grinning with Tabris's asymmetric smile. "Later on, when we're together."

Before dawn, the angels dispersed, and Casifer escorted Sebastian back to Limbo. Rachmiel and Tabris sat against the foot of Elizabeth's bed, bright-eyed but spent.

Rachmiel had been emitting bursts of joy all night, and Tabris looked at Elizabeth to find that as he'd suspected, she was smiling in her sleep. He settled back on the floor and projected his amusement.

Rachmiel squinted at him.

"You look like you've thrown a party and now dread cleaning up the mess." Tabris put a picture to the words so Rachmiel would have the benefit of seeing himself as a man with his shirt collar unbuttoned, his tie unknotted, sprawled on a chair amidst stained paper plates and empty pizza boxes.

Rachmiel laughed out loud.

A shaft of morning light broke free of the horizon. Tabris glanced at Rachmiel and raised an eyebrow.

Rachmiel shook his head.

Tabris frowned at him.

Rachmiel shrugged. "I figured, since you're going to be here for the next eighty years or so, maybe you should give it a try."

Tabris glimpsed the future in an instant, a trail lined with joy and heartbreak, drudgery and excitement, frustration and relief. He saw a red-headed woman leaving home, having her own family, running for public office, changing the world in the hundreds of small and important ways that every life must change it. And all through that future, he had a part.

Tabris sprang onto the bedside and put his head beside Elizabeth's.

"Hey, Kiddo, wake up," he said. "Morning's here, and you should see what God has for you today."

She opened her eyes, and Tabris rushed with the warmth of God until it overflowed into the girl by his side. With relief, he raised his eyes and told his Father again how good it felt to be home.

Author's note and acknowledgments

The idea for "Tabris" came to me when I was nineteen. I wrote it with all my heart, used every fiction technique I'd learned so far, and I edited it, and a year later Thomas Nelson published it.

I requested and received back my rights in 2011, and when I read the book again with a critical eye, I saw so many places I could do so much better now, not just in terms of writing technique but also in terms of human nature and how the world works. This makes sense: if I hadn't learned anything in twenty years, I'd probably deserve to be shot.

Hence we have a ground-up rewrite of the novel. I started with a blank document, and this is the result: all new text, a new title, an awesome new cover (thanks to Charlotte Volnek) and now it's even published under my legal name.

The first edition acknowledged many who influenced that version of the book, including fellow writer (and fellow MIU author) Pauline Griffin, my college housemates and my friend Toni who put up with me living in two worlds at once, my boyfriend James who looked at the first chapter and said, "Yeah, keep going," my parish priest Father Murphy, and poet EA Miller who was one of the sharpest critique-givers I ever had the pleasure of learning with.

For the second edition, I would like to mention that my boyfriend is still a terrific support and is now my husband. Thanks also to Normandie Fischer (fellow author) who pushed me to do the rewrite, Sarah who keeps reading everything I write, my agent Roseanne Wells, editor and publisher Lea Schizas, and Madeline and Evan, who help more than they can ever possibly know.

Thank you so much for reading *Annihilation*! Please consider leaving a review at Amazon or Goodreads (or both.)

If you'd like to read more of my angels, please check out the Seven Archangels series.

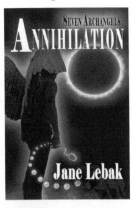

Seven Archangels: Annihilation
Angels have always known they'll live forever, but now Satan's figured out how to destroy one. He starts with Gabriel.

Also check out *Seven Archangels: An Arrow In Flight* and *Seven Archangels: Sacred Cups*, both coming soon. (One sooner than the other, of course. I may write about angels, but I myself am quite human.)

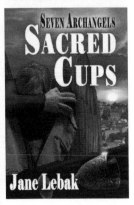

If you'd like to hear from me when new books appear, you can check the box at my amazon central page or feel free to contact me at JaneLebak@gmail.com or my Facebook page at http://www.facebook.com/JaneLebakAuthor.

Thanks again for reading about Tabris and Rachmiel, and I hope to hear from you!

Made in the USA
Columbia, SC
06 April 2021